PRAISE FOR TANYA LANDMAN'S NOVELS

Hell and High Water

"Strong characters, important themes, terrific writing"
Guardian

"Gripping ... Landman's research is impeccable"
The Times

"An amazing novel which left me lost for words – everyone should read it. Can I give it eleven out of ten?"
Guardian Children's Books Website

Buffalo Soldier

"Gripping, vivid, superb" *Independent*

"Deeply thrilling ... a must-read" *Amnesty International*

"Hard-hitting, bleak and full of heart" *Metro*

Apache

"Magnificent ... a disturbing but exhilarating experience" *Independent*

"Beautifully written and unforgettable" *Time Out*

"This ... has a ... become a
... *ps*

Hell and High Water

TANYA LANDMAN

WALKER
BOOKS

Northamptonshire
Libraries & Information
Services
NC

Askews & Holts

This is a work of fiction. Names, characters, places and incidents are either the product of the author's imagination or, if real, used fictitiously. All statements, activities, stunts, descriptions, information and material of any other kind contained herein are included for entertainment purposes only and should not be relied on for accuracy or replicated as they may result in injury.

First published in Great Britain 2015 by Walker Books Ltd
87 Vauxhall Walk, London SE11 5HJ

This edition published 2016

2 4 6 8 10 9 7 5 3 1

Text © 2015 Tanya Landman
Jacket photograph compass © 2015 DEA / G. DAGLI ORTI / Getty Images; Boy looking away © 2015 Comstock / Getty Images; Map © 2015 DEA / M. SEEMULLER / Getty Images; Border © 2015 WLADIMIR BULGAR / Getty Images; Ship sailing on stormy seas © 2015 John Lund / Getty Images

The right of Tanya Landman to be identified as author of this work has been asserted by her in accordance with the Copyright, Designs and Patents Act 1988

This book has been typeset in Bembo Educational

Printed and bound in Great Britain by Clays Ltd, St Ives plc

All rights reserved. No part of this book may be reproduced, transmitted or stored in an information retrieval system in any form or by any means, graphic, electronic or mechanical, including photocopying, taping and recording, without prior written permission from the publisher.

British Library Cataloguing in Publication Data:
a catalogue record for this book is available from the British Library

ISBN 978-1-4063-6691-4

www.walker.co.uk

To Rod Burnett, for endless creative inspiration

PART 1

1.

The city of Torcester.

High summer.

Market day.

Thronging streets: honest men mingling with thieves, clergymen with vagabonds, gentry with peasants, housewives with whores. The noise, the jostling of so many people in the narrow lanes! Sweat and shit, pies and ale, unwashed bodies, horses – the combined stench worked like a draught of the finest spirits on Joseph Chappell. His eyes shone, his breath came faster, the blood raced through his veins.

Caleb watched his father pushing the handbarrow through the crush with bemused envy. He shared neither Pa's fair skin, nor his tastes or temperament: he loathed the city. Only when they were far away from people and their constant, invasive curiosity was he truly comfortable. A quiet valley with rolling hills, an open stretch of moorland – these were his favourite haunts. But no money was to be made in such places. A winding river, an expanse of purple heath might please the eye but pleasant views, Pa said, did not pay for meat or ale. It was true enough, and yet Caleb knew there was something else that drew them to Torcester so often. The fact was inescapable – Joseph may have been born the son of an earl, bred to a life of idleness and luxury, but at heart he was a showman, and a showman cannot live without a crowd.

Pa took his favourite spot on the cobbles beside the cathedral's green. As soon as he saw them the bishop of Torcester crossed the grass, a welcoming smile on his face. He might be a man of God, but he liked a good belly laugh as much as any common sinner. First nodding to Caleb, the bishop then took Pa's right hand in both of his, shaking it with such enthusiasm that Pa's fingers were in danger of being crushed.

"Well met, Mr Chappell," the bishop said. "Well met indeed!" He lowered his voice to a theatrical whisper. "And what antics shall we have today?"

"Many and various, as always."

"And shall the Devil finally carry Mr Punch to hell as the old sinner deserves?" the churchman asked, winking.

"I fear not," replied Joseph with mock regret. "He must sin, and sin again, or what should I have to live on?"

"What indeed?" The bishop threw back his head and laughed. "We both depend on sinners to earn an honest living, do we not?" Clapping Pa on the shoulder, the bishop went on his way, but Caleb knew he would be back when the entertainment began, for the churchman was a great admirer of Pa's skill. This last winter Joseph had carved new puppets and built a new stage for them and each time the bishop watched he was in raptures about Pa's ingenuity, questioning him long and hard about the theatre's frame, wanting to know how Pa had got the idea, how he'd managed to build it, whether he'd done it all himself or employed a craftsman – the man's curiosity was boundless!

Caleb helped Pa set up the show. When Joseph judged there were sufficient people milling about by the green he rang a handbell to gain their attention and announced that the first performance would commence very shortly. Sure enough, the bishop took his place before Pa had even finished speaking.

The first performance went smoothly, as did the second that followed an hour or so after. A short break for Pa to get his breath back and quench his thirst and then on to the third and fourth of the day. Each time the crowds grew larger.

At last they came to the fifth and final show. Joseph was more than halfway through, Caleb standing at the side watching the hangman, Jack Ketch, slowly explaining the process of death-by-hanging to Mr Punch. Once, twice, he'd told the grinning hunchback what to do and once, twice, Punch had got it wrong. Jack was now giving the instruction for the third time.

"You put your head in here. Look, see?" Jack opened the noose wide. "And then you have to say 'I've been a very wicked man. I'm sorry I done it!' And then I pull that knob there."

Once more Punch slowly approached the noose. Last time he'd ducked to the right, missing it by an inch and giving the playboard a loud whack with his hooked red nose. This time he ducked to the left. There were shrieks of delight from the crowd, the bishop laughing loudest of all.

"No!" screamed Jack Ketch. "You dolt! You simpleton! You're a very foolish man! And because you're so foolish I'm going to have to show you. You do it like this. You put your head in here, see?" Jack Ketch, the hangman, slid his head through his own open noose.

"You put your head in here," repeated Punch.

"That's right. You say, 'I've been a very wicked man.'"

"I've been a very wicked man," Punch repeated obediently.

"I'm sorry I done it!"

"I'm sorry I done it!" wailed Punch.

"That's right," said Jack. "But don't over-act. And then I pull that knob there."

"And then I pull that knob there." Punch darted from one side of the stage to the other. The outcome was totally predictable, but that was the joy of it. Pa always said that anticipation was the greatest part of comedy.

"No! Don't pull the knob!" screeched Ketch.

Alas! Too late…

Punch pulled it, tightening the noose, and the hangman began making ghastly choking noises. When he eventually fell silent Punch said, "Are you dead yet?"

"No. I'm not." More ghastly choking followed. Joseph always knew precisely how long he could draw out the thread of a joke before it snapped and today the crowd was in a mood to see the hangman suffer. By the time the puppet finally fell down dead they were convulsed. Snot flowed down the face of a lad in the front who didn't have so much as a sleeve to wipe it on. A fine gentleman at the back pressed a silk handkerchief to his face to smother the stink of the common folk who were now stamping their feet, yelling and roaring for more, more! They were hungry – ravenous – for Punch's outrageous antics and, ever the showman, Pa was delighted to satisfy them.

Punch picked the hangman up and threw him over the playboard where he dangled, wooden and lifeless, just over the heads of the children who had gathered by the front of the show. They reached out, trying to seize the puppet, but before they could Punch took up the gallows and whirled Jack Ketch at the end of his rope full circle once, twice, thrice before throwing gallows, hangman and all down into the theatre and out of sight. Then he bobbed back up to the stage grinning, clapping his hands, shrieking, "That's the way to do it!"

Caleb scanned the crowd. Timing is everything: Pa had told him often enough. He was talking about his own performance but it applied equally well to Caleb's part in things. He picked up the bottle. Pa had discovered long ago that a hat was too easy for a light-fingered thief to remove coins from. "They'll put in a farthing, take out a shilling." But once a penny was dropped down the neck of a leather bottle no one but Pa could remove it.

Caleb watched the watchers with a knot tightening in his belly, fearing that he'd pick the wrong moment, that he'd walk past the open-handed and approach only the tight-fisted. People were so hard to judge! Now, he hoped, was a good moment. He'd go round again later once Punch had beaten the Devil, but right now the pieman on the left was about to move off. He had to be good for a farthing or two, didn't he? As did the big-bosomed flower seller next to him who was rocking with laughter. And the ginger-haired youth close by? He was barefoot and clad in tatters. Though he was watching the puppets intently Caleb didn't feel he could ask someone so obviously destitute for money. No … he'd give the lad a wide berth.

The fine gent was a different matter, though – he could afford to give, and give generously. Caleb would save him for last. Once the show was over and Punch had beaten the Devil – that would be the time. Gentry kept the strings of their purses tightly tied. It was how the rich stayed rich, Pa said: by never giving anything away. But after Punch's grand finale maybe this one would contribute a little something? As for the bishop, it was best to let him watch the Devil being sent back down to hell before asking him. He never liked to have his entertainment interrupted.

Clearing his throat, Caleb yelled, "Any money for Mr Punch?"

The pieman had been about to go on his way but when Caleb rattled the bottle he stopped, reaching into his pouch and pulling out a couple of pennies to drop down its neck. The flower seller was next. She ruffled Caleb's hair so violently it sent ripples across her gigantic bosom.

"Woolly as a sheep," she giggled. "Does your master shear you in the spring?"

Caleb winced. Her teasing was nothing he hadn't heard before and yet the words cut deep. He smiled as best he could and gave the answer he was used to trotting out in such situations. "Why yes he does. A quality fleece, is it not? He has to make a penny where he can." Pa had always advised him to turn aside foolish remarks with a joke of his own. It was a decent enough quip and one he'd used several times before, but he still felt the colour rising in his cheeks. It was fury, not embarrassment, but the flower seller misunderstood the cause.

"Lord love him, look at that! I never knew darkies could blush. He's gone purple as a plum!"

Had Caleb been generously rewarded it might have been more bearable, but she dropped only a single farthing into the bottle before sending him on his way with a bruising pinch on the arse. He was too angry to approach anyone else and strode back to the side of the theatre just as the Devil rose from its bowels, appearing on the stage and bellowing, "I'm coming to get you!"

Punch was trembling behind the curtain, but his hiding place was betrayed by the children, pointing, shouting out, some now so excited that they were in danger of pissing themselves.

"I am Satan," boomed Pa. He sounded barely human. "I am Beelzebub! I am the Devil."

Eternal damnation loomed but was Punch afraid?

"The Devil? Oooooh! I married your sister," he said saucily.

Caleb laughed. That was a new one, made up on the spur of the moment. He must tell Pa to keep it in the show. The joke made the bishop chuckle so much his broad belly quivered.

"I have come to take you down to hell," roared the Devil.

"I don't want to go."

"Then we'll have to fight. And the winner takes all…"

Cheering Punch, jeering the Devil, the crowd's heads snapped from side to side in unison as the fight went back and forth.

It was nearly time. Caleb knelt on the cobbles behind the theatre, striking Pa's tinderbox and lighting the hellfire flame's candle.

It was a simple device: a pewter pot, small enough to cup in the palm of one hand, with a lid, punctured with holes, on top of which stood the candle. A tube fed into the side like the stem of a pipe.

Caleb listened, poised and ready. When Punch's slapstick finally cracked once, twice, thrice over the Devil's head both his horns would come flying off into the crowd, making them shriek with wild excitement. Now! Shielding the flame with his hand, Caleb carefully passed the pipe through the folds in the theatre's cloth cover, hoping and praying that the candle wouldn't snuff out.

As Mr Punch threw the Devil through the gates of hell, Pa blew down the pipe's tube. A cloud of the powdered resin contained in the pewter pot now billowed into the air, igniting as it passed through the candle's flame. The crowd saw a great ball of hellfire burst through the open top of the theatre, followed by coiling black plumes of smoke, and cried aloud with wonder. Caleb grinned at their noise: it was always a delight. Such a simple piece of trickery, but so very dramatic!

His task backstage completed, he darted round to the front. When Punch came up to take his final, triumphant bow, Caleb took off again with the bottle, weaving between the watchers, "Any money for Mr Punch?"

The fine gent had watched the show, beginning to end. Admittedly, he had not laughed much: his expression had remained sour, his mouth pinched. But a man's face does not always show what is in his mind. Caleb headed first for him, calling out, shaking the bottle. He came to a halt in front of the gentleman but it was as though Caleb was a creature made of light and air, for the man looked right through him. *How very skilled the aristocracy are when it comes to ignoring lesser mortals,* Caleb thought. *Where do they learn such tricks?*

No matter. He turned away. The bishop's generosity made up for the gentleman's lack of it and others in the crowd gave as freely as they could. By the time everybody had dispersed, the bottle was full of money – plenty enough to keep Caleb and Pa fed until next market day.

Emerging hot and sweating from the theatre, Pa took the bottle and shook some coins out into Caleb's hands.

"A good day, but a long one!" he said with a smile. "I feel half-starved, and no doubt you're the same. If I don't eat soon I'll be swooning like a lady. Go get us a pie from Porlock's. Tell Mrs P we'll be along later, when we've packed the show down. Ask her to put on a fresh pot."

Caleb sighed but did as he was told, weaving through the streets to Porlock's Coffee House. Here was another topic on which his opinion differed from Pa's.

Porlock's was a meeting place where businessmen discussed commerce and learned men from the city's university sat and debated. Joseph had no interest in the former, but he loved to join the latter in talking of philosophy and politics. Such things bored Caleb almost to tears and, in addition to the tedium, he often had to endure remarks from men who took to him to be Pa's slave, not his son. Engrossed in conversation, Pa – usually so quick to shield him – rarely noticed these slights. Caleb associated Porlock's with discomfort, although even he had to admit that their mutton pies were the best to be had in Torcester.

He was returning to the green with two of them. From ten yards away he could see that Pa had already packed his puppets and was starting to dismantle the theatre when there was the cry, "Stop thief!"

Both Pa and Caleb swung round.

A slap of running feet. Yells. Noises of pursuit.

Then the ginger-haired youth, clad in tatters, darted over the cobbles towards the cathedral. As he passed, he hit Pa in the belly. Thumped him so hard that Pa doubled over, clutching his gut, groaning with shock and pain.

Dropping the pies, Caleb ran to him, so concerned for Pa that he did not even notice the fine silk purse that had fallen at his father's feet.

2.

Joseph was bent over, winded, his eyes fixed on the ground. When he had recovered his breath a little he stood, but not before he'd reached out a hand for what lay at his feet.

The moment Pa picked up the purse their lives began to unravel. Two constables rounded the corner and saw him holding it. Joseph Chappell was caught red-handed, so they said.

Congratulating themselves on the remarkable speed with which they'd solved the crime, they seized him, grabbing him by the arms, forcing his hands behind his back, pushing his wrists up so hard that he cried out. Pa was unable to resist. When Caleb tried to pull the constables off, he was struck. A savage blow under his chin threw him back onto the ground, smashing his head against the cobbles.

The owner of the purse – the very same fine gentleman who had watched the show and put nothing in the bottle – was called forward. He confirmed the thing was his and that was that. The constables started to pull Pa away and when he tried to protest he was knocked almost senseless. They dragged him between them, his blood dripping onto the street.

Caleb, struggling to his feet, made a move to follow but Pa managed to say, "Stay... The show..."

To abandon the newly made theatre and the puppets that his father had carved with such care was unthinkable. Caleb was left, head and jaw aching, standing alone looking about stupidly for the culprit, but the ginger-haired thief had disappeared. It had happened so quickly! There must be someone – a friendly face, a kindly soul who might intervene on Pa's behalf. The bishop? No ... he was gone, along with the rest of the crowd. There was nothing but a motley collection of indifferent passers-by.

Cold, blind panic made Caleb's limbs so heavy he couldn't move and his throat so tight that he struggled to breathe. But he couldn't just stand here like a statue! There was work to be done. As swiftly as he could he finished the job Pa had barely started. Removed the cloth cover. Dismantled the theatre. Collapsed the frame. Pa's new system made it a work of minutes. He rolled it up in its cover, then wrapped the whole in a length of sacking, tying the bundle tight before loading it and the puppets onto the handbarrow. Once the task was complete he sat and waited for Pa's return.

He would be back. Of course he would. This was a mistake. The constables would find they were wrong and set Pa free. He would come striding across the green, cursing their idiocy, laughing at Caleb's distress. He would take the handles of the barrow and push it ahead of him effortlessly over the cobbles as he always did. They would leave Torcester. Soon. Soon.

The night, if slept through in a fine feather bed, lasts no time at all. There had been occasions when Caleb had lain down, shut his eyes and, seemingly in one breath, the dawn had come. Yet now, sitting awake, riddled with fear, that single night lasted for years.

Oh, he had gone through some difficult ones in his life: when he had been cold and hunger had gnawed his insides. But there had always been Pa. Pa, holding Caleb in his arms when he was small, whispering stories in his ear to distract him. And when he had grown too big for Pa's lap – sitting beside him, Pa's arm thrown around his shoulders, talking, laughing. Always Pa, minding him when he slept, watching over him, keeping him safe. With Pa gone, Caleb felt shrunken, exposed. Alone in the street through those long hours of darkness he waited and prayed. Prayed and waited. He had stumbled into a nightmare from which he would surely wake.

It was only at dawn, when black ebbed to grey and red lines threaded the sky that he realized Pa was not coming back. Only then did he think to move from the place he'd waited. If Pa wasn't returning, why then ... he needed to go and find him.

Getting to his feet, moving slowly, stiffly, as though he'd aged a century in that one night, Caleb began to look for the gaol. He pushed the handbarrow ahead of him. Pa had moved it as though it was no weight at all, with the same unthinking ease with which he powered his own limbs. But for Caleb, in his pitifully anxious state, it was awkward and cumbersome. It tipped on cobbles, twice spilling its load. He righted it. Reloaded. And then the wheels became stuck in a rut. Passers-by cursed his clumsiness. They jeered, they called him foul names and there was no Pa to intercede on his behalf or tell Caleb that they were ignorant fools with no more sense than a gaggle of geese.

By the time Caleb found the gaol, hands blistered, sweat running in rivulets down his back, Joseph Chappell had been taken to court.

The wheels of justice turned swiftly that day. It didn't matter how loudly Joseph Chappell protested his innocence. He was brought before the judge and identified as the culprit by the fine gentleman and several passers-by who had seen him holding the purse. That was all the evidence the judge required. In a matter of minutes he was condemned.

And the sentence for the theft of a fine silk purse, heavy with coins?

Death.

By the time Caleb found the court building the trial was over and done with. It was the clerk who told him, "Judge said he was to be hanged by the neck until he's dead."

Hearing those words, Caleb had to lean against the wall, for suddenly his legs would not bear him. A pain squeezed his chest, as though iron bands had been fastened around his ribs and were being slowly tightened.

The clerk was utterly unmoved. He yawned deeply, regarding Caleb as though he was of no more interest than a chipped stone on a cobbled street.

Finally Caleb found his voice. "Hanging? He is to be *hanged*?" He could not take it in. The words were monstrous! Surely there could be no truth in them?

"Your master, is he?" asked the clerk, his curiosity stirring.

Caleb understood the implications of the question. The clerk thought him a slave, and a slave must belong to someone. With Joseph convicted, his worldly goods would be disposed of as the judge saw fit, human chattel included.

With as much dignity as he could muster Caleb told the clerk, "I am a free man. Joseph Chappell is my father."

"Is he now?" A knowing smirk crossed the clerk's features. "This has been a lucky day for him."

"Lucky? How?"

The clerk tipped his head to one side as if considering whether to answer. At last he said, "The Bishop of Torcester got to hear of it. He came along and spoke up for him. Said Joseph Chappell was a man of good character. That the whole thing was a mistake. I suppose he thought that purse just flew into your father's hands of its own accord!" The clerk found his own joke so hilarious that he slapped his thigh and roared with laughter.

The man was vile but Caleb felt a sudden surge of hope. Had the clerk been merely playing a prank this whole time? "A mistake?" he said eagerly. "Yes, indeed it was. Pa is no thief. And so he has been freed?"

"Lord love you, no! One bishop's word against a dozen witnesses? And with the victim himself swearing the thief had been caught red-handed? Oh no, no, no... The judge found Joseph Chappell guilty as charged. Couldn't do nothing else, could he?"

"And yet you say my father was lucky?"

"Well, the bishop speaking up came in useful, see? He saved his life, in a manner of speaking." The clerk yawned again and stretched, taking malicious delight in the fact that he had knowledge Caleb was desperate for. Only when he'd had his fill of amusement did he reveal that the judge had commuted Pa's sentence from death to transportation. "They'll take him off to the colonies. America. Maryland or Virginia, I'd say."

That was halfway round the world! People who made that voyage never came back. This was scarcely better than a sentence of death. Caleb was on the verge of tears. "Must they take him so far away?"

"They must. That's the law, right enough. If I was him I'd be on my knees thanking the Lord. You too. Be grateful for small mercies."

Too stunned to reply, Caleb turned his back on the odious clerk. He pushed the barrow back to the prison but he was not permitted to see Pa, the gaoler said, unless, of course, he could make it worth his while. The man held a filthy, outstretched hand under Caleb's nose so his meaning couldn't be mistaken.

Bribery. Pa despised it. And yet how else was Caleb to get in?

How much should he give? He dropped one coin then two into the gaoler's palm. The money was quickly pocketed but then the hand was held out once more. Half the previous day's takings was gone before Caleb was allowed over the threshold.

The inside of the gaol was no more than a stone barn. Men and women and a few ragged, bony children were herded together in a place where there was not even a pot to piss in. It stank worse than a byre.

And Pa was not here. Caleb's eyes ran over the mess of humanity once, twice. He was turning to protest that the gaoler had tricked him when he heard his father's voice.

"Oh my boy, I am so glad to see you."

Pa was sitting on the floor by the wall. His clothes were torn, smeared with human waste, his powdered wig was gone. Blood had dried on his forehead and cheeks, a dark bruise coloured one eye. He was filthy, with straw in his hair, and grime under his nails. Dear God, Caleb had taken him for a vagrant! To see Pa so degraded was like a blow to the stomach. He couldn't draw breath.

Seeing the horror on his son's face, Pa struggled to his feet and reached out his arms but before they could embrace he folded them over his soiled clothing, hanging his head and saying sorrowfully, "I dare not touch you! I will only make you stink as much as I do. "

But he was Pa. His Pa. His only family. Caleb stretched his arms around his father's hunched frame.

"I don't know what to do. I am ruined!" Pa whispered. "How could such a thing happen, Caleb? I don't understand."

The ground under Caleb's feet seemed suddenly to lurch. He'd believed that if he could only see Pa, he would tell him what to do. Pa would have a plan – he always did. There would be an answer. A solution. But there was no sign of that in this bruised, shattered man. Pa was at a loss. As was Caleb. In a small, unsteady voice he asked, "Can nothing be done?"

"Nothing, nothing, nothing."

"But the bishop... Could I not go to him?"

"Bless the man! He has done all he could. He saved my life, Caleb, he can do no more. It is the law. It is an ass, but it is the law. We must try to accept what Fate has dealt us." Tears had carved clear furrows through the filth on Pa's cheeks. "Seven years I will be gone."

"Seven years?" Caleb had turned fifteen last winter. He was old enough to be called a man, and yet now – to his shame – he found himself whimpering like an abandoned child. "Where am I to go? How am I to live?"

"Time's up." The gaoler stepped between them. "You got to leave now. Unless you got more." Out came the grubby palm. Caleb reached for his coins but Pa slapped the gaoler's hand away.

"Keep the money, my boy. You will need all you have."

The gaoler went to the door, fingers fumbling to fit key to lock.

The moment of separation had come. Pa's hands gripped his son so tightly that the ring on his third finger dug in, bruising Caleb's arm. For a moment he was himself again. "Follow the river," he said urgently. "It flows north to the coast. It will take you to Norton Manor, the home of Sir Robert Fairbrother. Can you remember that?"

"Sir Robert Fairbrother. Yes. But who is he?"

Pa said only, "I believe his home is close by to Tawpuddle. It will be a grand house, I'm sure. There you'll find my sister, Anne."

"Sister?" Caleb frowned. Pa had always said the two of them were alone in the world. "Is your sister married to Sir Robert?"

"No! Anne is a maid there."

"But…"

"She will help you. Tell her she must." A last, desperate look. A promise. "I'll come back, Caleb. The ocean is wide, but it won't keep me from you. Be certain of that. I will find you again, my boy, come hell or high water."

3.

Time was out of joint. The world had been tipped sideways. Everything was off balance, gone awry. Two lives had been dissolved in the blinking of an eye. There should have been something to mark the occasion, Caleb thought later. A clap of thunder. A bolt of lightning. Even the mournful tolling of a bell would have sufficed. Instead there was nothing but the sounds of a city going about its business as day turned to evening, careless and unheeding of the tragedy that had unfolded in its streets.

Questions tumbled together inside his head. This sister. His aunt. Pa had never spoken of her. Not once in all Caleb's years of life. Why? Had she done something terrible? Had they quarrelled? It was impossible! Pa was the most forgiving of men.

So what could have caused this utter silence? Was it something Pa had done?

He felt suddenly sick to the stomach. Oh dear God, was Caleb the reason for the rift? Was she ashamed to have a relative his complexion? Had she turned her back on Pa because of him?

But if that was so why had Pa told him to go to her now? He must have believed she'd take him in, give him a home. Yet how could he throw himself on the mercy of a complete stranger?

The sun was already low when Caleb left Torcester. There were two, perhaps three, hours of light before darkness came. He had no home to return to, no possessions to collect. They had carried their worldly goods loaded on the barrow. There was nothing to keep him but the thought of Pa, trapped in that miserable, stinking hellhole of a gaol. And Pa had told Caleb to leave. What could he do but obey? Wheeling the barrow over the cobbled streets, skirting the edge of Gallows Hill, he followed the river out of the city and kept on walking until nightfall. The going was hard. Though mercifully dry, the road was deeply rutted. He had travelled only two or three miles before darkness made going any further impossible. The weather being fine, he lay down – as he and Pa often had – under the stars. Sleep was slow to come. Caleb, who had always longed to be away from the crowds, now found no peace in solitude. A deep, gnawing dread, a weight of guilt clawed at him. He had let Pa down. Why hadn't he chased the thief? He'd just stood there and let it happen. Why hadn't he done anything? If he'd thought quicker, acted faster, *done* something, things would be different.

Caleb was awake long before dawn. As soon as the sky began to lighten he went on, his limbs sluggish, his muscles aching. After about a mile the river and road went their separate ways, one twisting and winding to the right, the other running over a bridge to the left and then heading in a straight line over the hill.

"Follow the river," Pa had said.

Caleb could see that it wound and looped and curled back on itself like an eel. The road would no doubt be easier. But obeying Pa's instruction was all he could do for his father now. In his grief Caleb reverted to childish superstition: Pa's command must be followed to the letter or some further, yet more terrible catastrophe would occur. And so he crossed heaths, wormed his way through hedges, waded through mud and mire. When he could not push, he dragged the barrow. By noon his hands had blistered and bled and soon his feet were in the same pitiable state. He struggled through woods, tugging the barrow through snagging brambles, cursing, constantly on the brink of tears of sorrow and frustration.

Exhaustion had begun to overwhelm him when there was a loud snap and he was thrown onto his back with the force of something that burst from the undergrowth. For a moment he thought a huge animal had attacked him. But no … this was a man-trap, set by some gamekeeper to catch poachers. Most luckily those iron teeth had closed not on his leg, but on the barrow's wheel, shattering the spokes completely.

Caleb had Pa's tools but not his skill with them. He knew he couldn't repair the wheel, couldn't even prise it from the trap. He had no choice but to abandon the barrow. As for the theatre, the puppets? For a moment Caleb wavered. He was no showman. It was Pa who had given those wooden dolls life and soul. To him they were nothing but a burden!

And yet Pa had promised he would come back, and he was a man of his word. When he returned – how could Caleb tell him he'd left the show to rot in the woods?

Joseph had often carried the theatre on his shoulder, lightly, as though it weighed nothing. Caleb tried to do the same, but his frame was not broad enough. In desperation he tied the puppet sack to his back and dragged the theatre behind him. Snapping a branch from a dead tree, he picked his way slowly through the undergrowth, poking the ground ahead in case other traps were concealed there.

On he went, following every bend and curve of the river. He lost all sense of time. Day followed day. Night followed night. He picked leaves and dug roots when he came across them. Poached trout from the river. Used Pa's money to buy an occasional loaf from a house if he passed one. As he trudged onwards he felt a darkness seeping into his mind: it was as though an inkpot had been upset, and the blackness now oozed into every corner.

The river gradually became wider. Murkier. He could no longer see its stony bed to judge its depth. Its taste began to change. And then one morning Caleb woke to find the water had almost entirely gone. All that remained was a thin trickle gouged deep through the mudflats either side. He leapt to his feet. His first thought was that a monster – an ogre or a giant – had drunk it. But as he watched, little by little the river filled again. He sighed wearily. He was a damned fool! Had his wits entirely deserted him? Hadn't Pa once bored him half to death in Porlock's trying to explain Sir Isaac Newton's scientific theories on the moon and tides? He must have reached the point at which the river became tidal – he was surely nearing the coast? How amused Pa would have been by his thoughts of monsters! He'd have laughed long and loud and Caleb would have joined in until they were both weak with it. The pain of missing Pa hit Caleb like a punch to the head. For a while he was so dizzied with it that he was quite unable to move. But move he must because Pa had told him to. Gathering his belongings, once more he went on.

As the river changed, so did the trees. The tall, graceful beeches that crowded together near the city were a thing of the past. Now those few that grew looked withered and hunched, as though the land did not give them sufficient nourishment. Oaks at the tops of hills leaned away from the prevailing wind as though they yearned to flee inland and would do so if only their roots did not hold them back.

The birds too altered with each passing day. There was still the sweet sound of robin and thrush from the woods but now their calls were joined by those of the birds that pecked in the mud at low tide. Some piped shrilly, as though stabbed by sudden, dreadful pain. Others made strange, keening cries that seemed to speak of loss and sorrow. And the gulls! Their cackles sounded like malicious jeers. They mocked Caleb's struggling footsteps, his laboured breathing, his calloused hands and feet, his sweating brow.

The journey was hellish, but at last he saw – some distance ahead – a bridge, spanning the river's broad girth. Beyond it lay a town – a port so bustling with life and vigour that the shouts and chatter reached him from half a mile distant.

Caleb had been entirely alone for more days than he cared to count. Suddenly to find himself amongst so many people was enough to make him panic. His guts tied into a knot, his heart lodged in his throat, his teeth were clamped so tight together his jaw began to ache.

He expected stares. Jeers. To be challenged, perhaps, as a runaway slave. It had happened before and would no doubt happen again. But no one gave him a second glance as he wandered through the teeming crowds on the quay.

Pa would have loved this place! It was more frantic than Torcester on a market day. Unfamiliar sounds and smells and sights overwhelmed his every sense. There were ships – so many of them! Masts swaying, the creak of timber and rigging, the slap of water against their hulls, and the stink – of salt, of fish, of oakum and tar, of sweat and brandy, ale and tobacco, of midden heaps piled with shit and rotten food. All around him men yelled oaths and curses. Painted whores sat with skirts hitched up, swinging their legs, shrieking and gossiping. They started to call to him.

"There's a handsome lad!"

"Looking for some sport, lover?"

"You go with darkies, don't you, Betty?"

"I'll go with anyone, me!"

Caleb squirmed with embarrassment. He had seen women like that before but Pa had been with him. Pa, with a steadying hand on his shoulder, with an easy manner and ready laugh, sharing a joke with such creatures even as he rejected their offers. All Caleb could do was walk past with his face turned away, their calls ringing in his ears.

He had no idea of the town's name and it was a while before he found the courage to ask. At the far end of the quay was a building whose door stood wide open. Inside a line of gentlemen sat at desks writing busily in ledgers. He stepped over the threshold but before he could speak one of the gentlemen asked, "Are you off the *Mary-Louise*? Do you bring the bill of lading?"

The words made no sense but Caleb answered that no, he was not off the *Mary-Louise*. And then he asked, "Sir, is this Tawpuddle?"

The man looked at Caleb as though he was a simpleton. A terse "yes" was his only answer before he went back to his work. And so it was a passing fisherman – judging from the look and smell of him – whom he asked for directions to Norton Manor.

The fisherman gave them in a straightforward manner with no sideways look, or sneer, for which Caleb was grateful, but his route now took him along the road and not the river as Pa had instructed. He felt immediately ill at ease and perhaps his childish superstitions were not so foolish after all, for, without the river to guide him, he managed to lose himself entirely.

A spider's web of lanes and paths was edged on either side by hedges so high and thick he could see nothing past them. After an hour of wandering he had lost all sense of direction. He didn't know where the river was or the town, or how he was to find Norton Manor. He might as well have been walking in circles. His shoulders were rubbed raw, every muscle in his body screamed for rest. He must be so near now, and yet how was he ever to find the place?

Despair was beginning to seep through him, but then he turned a corner and before him was an elaborate pair of wrought-iron gates. This must be the entrance to Norton Manor. Lifting the latch, passing through, he walked along a wide carriageway that led down into a valley. The trees on the hills had been whipped into strange contortions by the wind, yet as he went further he found that the valley was sheltered, the wind passing straight over from one side to the other. It was the perfect spot to build a house.

And what a house it was!

Vast. Opulent. A four-storey brick-built structure with two wings either side that stood with its back to him. It did not look up the valley, inland, towards the road to welcome guests, but faced down towards the river. Its full splendour could only be seen from the water.

Caleb had stopped for a moment to admire the place when there was a sudden clatter of hooves. He swung around and saw, cantering towards him, a cobby bay gelding.

Its rider was smartly dressed wearing a powdered wig beneath his hat, a finely tailored coat and polished leather boots. Though he had an air of authority Caleb decided he lacked the aristocratic bearing of a gentleman. And his horse was not showy enough. He must be a servant. An important one, certainly, but this was not the master of the house.

"What's your business here, boy?" the man demanded. A working man's accent, thicker than those in Torcester, harder to understand. Contempt showed in every inch of his face. His whip was raised, ready to use if Caleb's answer didn't satisfy him. He kicked his horse on suddenly, and then swung it hard round so it stood dancing in front of Caleb, held in on a tight rein, but being spurred at the same time, jittery and ready to leap in any direction. If Caleb moved to one side or the other, the horse would knock him down.

Reluctantly he said, "My name is Caleb Chappell."

"I didn't ask your name. I asked your business."

"I'm looking for Anne Chappell. I believe she's a maid here."

"What do you want with her?"

"She's my aunt."

"Aunt?" The man exploded in a loud guffaw. He looked Caleb slowly up and down. "Do you jest with me, boy?"

"I do not. My father is her brother."

"And what happened to him? Die on you, did he? The pox, no doubt! Caught from the whore he got you on!"

Caleb's free hand balled into a fist. "My father lives still, sir."

"And has he cast you out? Disowned you?"

"He has been transported."

"Transported?" That brought the man up short. His eyes narrowed. There was a sudden, intense interest that Caleb found unnerving. "His name?"

"Joseph Chappell."

"Transported for what?"

"Theft. He was wrongly accused."

Something strange happened then. For a second the man looked away, his brow furrowed as if making a shrewd calculation. Yet when he looked back at Caleb it was as if his face had been wiped clean. There was nothing but the sneer that curled his lips. "There is not a villain incarcerated or a thief transported but swears he is a wronged man. If that were so His Majesty would not be building so many gaols, would he, boy?"

"My father is an innocent man."

The man threw back his head and laughed. "Keep saying it, boy. There isn't anyone but you who'll ever believe it."

"Let me pass, sir."

"I will not. Anne Chappell isn't at the manor. She married a sailor by the name of Edward Avery. You'll find her in Fishpool."

"Fishpool? Where is that?"

"Back to the gates. Turn right. Follow the road until the land runs out." He waved a hand as if shooing away a fly. "Get you gone. And don't let me see you setting foot on Sir Robert's land again."

"Road" was too grand a word, thought Caleb as he walked down a track so thickly hedged with stunted oaks that he could have touched the leaves either side if he'd stretched his arms out. But still, he was glad to be away from the horseman whose sudden helpfulness in giving directions had been even more disturbing than his contempt. And that look when Caleb had mentioned Pa's transportation – did it mean something or was he imagining things? Seeing ogres and monsters again where there was only the river's ebb and flow?

Cresting the brow of the hill, Caleb stopped dead. The village of Fishpool lay below him but he did not even see it at first, for here the river met the sea. There were swathes of mud and marsh, a line of dunes, a beach and after that – dear God, so much water! A great stretch of blue and grey. A rocky island – a tiny dot in the centre of the bay. Beyond that water, water. More water. An endless expanse of it.

Caleb and Pa had travelled far and wide but they'd always kept away from the coast. There was no telling when the damned fool king might start another war, Pa said, and able-bodied men would run the risk of being pressed into his navy. It was best to keep away from places where the press gangs might be working.

The sheer vastness of the sea now reduced Caleb to the size of an ant. Less than an ant. He was nothing. Nothing! He knew the world to be round, but in that moment he could better believe the old tales: that the Earth was flat and if a man walked too far he would fall over the edge. He'd reached the world's end and now teetered on the brink. One step more and he would fall into oblivion.

For a minute or so all he could do was stand and look. But at last he tugged his eyes from the horizon and surveyed the land. There was Fishpool two hundred yards away. It was no more than a single street with a line of squat, ramshackle houses either side. There was a starkness to the scene that chilled him: no flowers tumbled together with vegetables in lush cottage gardens, there were no soft curves of thatch. Instead the roofs were of grey slate, and where there should have been roses and cabbages there were rickety wooden jetties, jutting into the river's mouth. Boats were moored beside each one – not the stately, elegant vessels he had seen in Tawpuddle but small shabby things that seemed to struggle to stay afloat. The cargo of a tiny fishing boat had just now been unloaded onto a cart which started up the lane towards him. The horses came at a brisk trot, the driver unaware or unheeding of Caleb's presence. There was not room for them to pass safely but the cart did not slow. Caleb clambered into the hedge to avoid being run down and as the cart bowled by him he noticed it was loaded not with fish, as he'd expected, but with bales of fine white linen. He registered its strangeness but only for a moment. He was almost at journey's end. Climbing down from the hedge and brushing leaves and twigs from his coat, mouth dry, heart pounding, Caleb continued on his way.

He had moved through Tawpuddle as though he was invisible. In Fishpool the opposite was true. The moment he set foot in the street folk stared at him, their looks harsh and hostile.

Outside the tavern a line of men with sunburned faces and salt-crusted hair leaned against the wall. They fell silent as they took in the sight of this dark-skinned stranger. Close by a group of women were clustered around the well, drawing water. They too ceased their chattering. Then the oldest of them demanded, "Who are you, boy?"

"I am looking for Anne Avery."

"What's she to you?"

"She is my aunt."

A chorus of whoops and shrieks.

"Lord above!"

"Who'd have thought it?"

"She got a darkie for a nephew?"

"She never said!"

"That's the kind of thing you want to keep quiet!"

And then one stepped in front of him and asked, "She know you're coming?"

Caleb shook his head. "No."

"That'll be a fine surprise for her then!" They were cackling like gulls and Caleb's skin crawled with discomfort. The temptation to turn and run was overwhelming. But he was so very tired! He could do nothing but stand there.

The woman regarded him steadily. After a while she pointed down the street. "'Tis along there. You can tell her house from the air of gentility that wafts from its door."

She stepped aside as the villagers burst into yet more laughter. Caleb went on his way. Tears of exhaustion had begun to fill his eyes when he came to a group of children playing on the cobbles halfway down the street. Their games halted. They watched him, eyes wide, nudging each other.

He was used to defending himself: there were times when no amount of wit could deflect a gibe and his fists had been the only solution. He stood a good head and shoulders above the tallest of these children, yet they were a dozen or more, and he was alone. A prickle of fear ran down his spine. He walked a little faster.

Sure enough, as he passed them a stone stung his ear. Then another. Had the thrower been more skilled he might have been knocked out cold. He turned to face his attackers. A boy of maybe three or four years old poked his tongue out before bending down and picking up another stone. Caleb backed away. They advanced.

Whether they would have hurt him he never knew because at that moment a woman looked out from her front door. He hoped she'd tell the children to be off, but she made no move to intervene.

"Anne?" Caleb asked, hurrying towards her. "Anne Avery. Can you tell me where she lives?"

The woman waved a dismissive hand at the pack of urchins. There was a collective sigh, and various cries of protest, but they returned to their games.

"That house – there." She pointed further along the road. "Right at the end."

She disappeared back inside before he even had a chance to thank her.

A few more footsteps, that was all. Caleb took them slowly. Since he'd left Torcester the thought of a destination had been his only comfort. Now he'd nearly reached it he was filled with terror. If his aunt turned him away – where could he go then? The workhouse? With each step he prayed that Anne Avery would not close the door in his face.

The last house in the village leaned a little as if straining towards the sea. It looked as if he'd only have to loosen a rope for it to set sail. The door stood open. He raised a hand to knock. Peering into the gloom, he saw a woman standing by the fire, stirring the pot that bubbled over it. She was small, fine-boned, porcelain-pale – dainty and delicate as a lark or a wren. And yet there was a likeness to Pa that made Caleb feel sure this was his aunt. He knocked, opened his mouth to speak, but said nothing.

For she turned and saw him.

As her eyes met his they glazed, and she fell to the floor in a dead faint.

4.

The pot the woman had been stirring fell with her. Stew splashed into the flames and then spilled across slate slabs in a steaming, scalding flood. A drop or two must have hit the face of a baby girl sitting on the floor and she began to wail. Setting down Pa's theatre, shrugging the sack of puppets from his back, Caleb hurried into the room and picked up the infant to comfort her but she screamed all the louder. Soon her shrieks brought the village children to the door and they crowded into the cottage, yelling accusations of murder and mischief, treading in the stew, slipping, falling, and knocking Caleb and the struggling baby sideways. For several moments all was noise and chaos.

Then a voice sliced through the uproar. The accent was strong and it took Caleb a second to understand the words.

"Out! Out – all of you. Get on. Now!"

The whimpering baby wriggled so hard that Caleb set her back down on the floor and she crawled towards the woman standing framed in the doorway. Caleb saw only an outline at first, the light at her back making a flaming halo of her red hair. A shapely figure, full-bosomed, wide-hipped, narrow waisted, standing almost as tall as himself. She was a force to be reckoned with – as strong and sturdy as Anne Avery was dainty and delicate. If he was to be turned away, Caleb thought, she would be the one to do it.

"I said get out!" On her command the village children left without another word. She stepped aside to let them through the door and it was only then that Caleb saw she must be his age or thereabouts. Her features were not so much pretty as striking: a square jaw, high cheekbones, a broad forehead. The baby was at her feet, arms up, wailing. Picking her from the floor, the young woman soothed, "Hush, Dorcas" and the little girl's cries ceased.

Turning her green eyes on Caleb she stared at him with an intensity that he found disturbing. "Who the Devil are you?"

"My name is Caleb Chappell…"

"Caleb Chappell?" she repeated. She seemed so shocked she almost dropped the baby. "Oh my Lord! Are you…?"

Before she could finish her question the woman on the floor – ivory-faced, her hair dripping with stew – spoke for the first time.

"Letty, Caleb is my nephew." Her voice was soft but clear – well bred, not unlike Pa's, at odds with the squalid setting. There was a note of panic in it, Caleb thought. But she knew his name. She didn't deny he was her relation.

That alone was a huge relief.

She pulled herself into a sitting position but remained on the floor. "You are Joseph's son, are you not?"

"I am. And you are my aunt, I believe. Anne. Anne Avery?"

"Yes." Her eyes darted towards the young woman, who gave the smallest of nods. Some unspoken message had passed between them. But there were no questions. No doubts. They both accepted him without a murmur. Yet why did the redhead stare at him so? It was almost like a challenge.

Caleb regarded her for a moment. And then he threw her words back at her. "And who the Devil are you?"

He thought he caught a flicker of amusement pass across her face but before she could reply his aunt intervened, "Letty is Edward's – my husband's – daughter. My stepdaughter. He is away at sea just now. Letty's mother died when she was just a baby." She looked towards the door. "Where is Joseph? Is he with you?"

"No... I am alone."

Anne Avery struggled to her feet, giving a small cry of pain as she did so.

"Are you hurt?" Caleb asked. "Have you been scalded? Should I fetch water?"

She hadn't noticed the fallen pot and when she did so she let out another cry. "It is spoiled! What are we to do?" She set it to rights and began to scrape what she could from

47

the floor but Letty made no move to help. Indeed, Letty had not yet taken her eyes from Caleb's face. She stood transfixed.

What was this? Had she never seen a man who looked like him before? Here – at the world's end – maybe not. He knew too well where that kind of curiosity led. Any moment now she'd grab him by the hand and rub his skin to see if his colour would come off. She'd ruffle his hair and pinch his arse and make some poor joke about shearing sheep. But no … she stayed silent. Was that contempt in her eyes or not? And why did she thrust her jaw out like that? She looked angry. Dear God, did she think this mess was his doing? Did she imagine he'd walked in and deliberately poured good food upon the floor? That he'd invited the children to tread their filthy, muddy feet through it? He bridled but said nothing. If she didn't speak, then neither would he. Better to help his aunt salvage what food she could than ask Letty why the hell she was staring at him like that. He knelt down and began to clear up the mess.

When what was left of the spoiled stew was set in bowls upon the table Anne invited Caleb to sit and eat. She was awkward. Embarrassed. There was a mild gentleness to her that he found both appealing and discomfiting. Perched beside her on a small stool at a small table in a tiny room his hands felt clumsy as butter paddles at the end of arms that had grown suddenly overlong. He seemed too large, too

rough, too ill-bred, too masculine for this household. He was
unused to the company of women – his manners were those
of the road. The inn. The tavern. He felt uncouth. Vulgar.
But oh God, he was hungry. He started to shovel spoonfuls
of stew into his mouth. But then Anne asked again about
Joseph.

"Where is he? Why is he not with you?"

Laying down his spoon, Caleb chose his words with
care. When he finished, Letty's mouth opened as if she was
about to speak, but then she looked at Anne and appeared
to think better of it.

Anne didn't notice. She was so distressed by the disaster
that had befallen her brother that Caleb feared she might
faint once more, but instead she started weeping. "Truly, the
Lord works in mysterious ways. How could he allow this to
happen to such a good man?"

There was no answer that Caleb could give and so he
said nothing, but her question had answered an unspoken
one of his: Pa and Anne had not quarrelled. She did not
hate Pa. And here was Caleb eating at her table. What on
earth had caused their long estrangement?

His aunt asked, "He told you to come to me?"

"He said you would help me. He said you must."

Anne stared into her bowl. She gave a slight nod of
the head but her shoulders sagged as if a great burden had
been placed upon them. She looked ill-equipped to carry it,
Caleb thought, and his heart sank.

Letty spoke. "What did he do then, your Pa? I mean, how'd he pay his way? Make a living?"

"He was a showman. A puppeteer."

"Is that what's in the sack? Let's have a look."

If she'd asked him to remove his clothes and stand naked in the room Caleb couldn't have felt more exposed. The idea of anyone but Pa touching the puppets appalled him. "No!" he snapped.

"Suit yourself."

There was an awkward silence. Anne broke it, saying softly, "Perhaps it's best if we don't speak of Joseph again. The people here don't know my brother's history and I'd rather they remained in ignorance. The past should be left where it belongs." Her voice cracked a little as though she was struggling to contain her feelings.

For the remainder of the meal they ate without speaking. The stew was of vegetables with only a lump or two of meat so gristly it might as well have been leather and yet Caleb worked away at it relentlessly. He had barely eaten for days. When the last morsel was swallowed he looked up to find that Letty's steady gaze was still fixed on him.

He could control himself no longer. "Stop it."

"What?"

"Why do you stare like that? Do you think me something from a freak show?"

She blushed, bright scarlet to the roots of her red hair.

Anne came quickly to her defence. "Letty has never

seen a person of your complexion, that is all. You cannot blame her for her curiosity, Caleb."

"It's not that!" Letty protested. "I've seen plenty. Men like him sail into Tawpuddle from time to time."

"Well?" demanded Caleb. He was being rude. Boorish. He knew that Pa would have told him to calm himself, to count to twenty before speaking again. But Pa – blast him! – was not here. The damned fool had picked up that wretched purse and abandoned him to this! "What is it then? What so troubles you about my looks?"

"I…"

Caleb waited for more, but it didn't come. Flushing, Letty looked to Anne. Anne looked at the table. Dorcas whimpered a little, leaning away as if afraid of him. Sweet Jesus, he was scaring a baby!

His temper evaporated. He was a simpleton! What was he thinking? He was on eggshells here. His aunt could ask him to leave at any second – he had no right to stay. The thought of being turned out onto the street was too much to bear and a great weariness overwhelmed him. Elbows resting on the table, he took his head in his palms. He would have apologized, but before he could arrange the words in his mouth he found that Anne's small hands were cupped about his and she was saying, "You have suffered so much, but now you are home. You must rest, now. I think perhaps we all should. It is late. We will talk more in the morning."

* * *

The house consisted of two rooms, one piled on top of the other, linked by a roughly hewn ladder. When Anne, Letty and Dorcas retired for the night Caleb was left to curl by the hearth like a dog, clutching the bundle of puppets to his chest for comfort. If he could have wrapped his heart in sacking to protect it, he'd have done so. Lying awake, listening to the strange sounds of wind and water, his thoughts turned to Pa.

Joseph had rarely spoken of his past. What little Caleb had learned of it had come in fragments that he now attempted to piece together. He knew that Pa had been born a gentleman – the son and heir of Charles Chappell, the Earl of Gravesham – but the earl had been a drinker and a gambler who had frittered away his fortune. In a lunatic attempt to recoup it he had invested heavily in a ship that plied the golden triangle. The one time Pa had mentioned this it had been with utter revulsion. Cheap trinkets shipped from England to Africa. Slaves seized from there and sold in the Indies. Sugar and rum from Jamaica carried home to England. Vast profits to be made on each leg of the journey. That, at least, had been the plan. But the vessel had sunk in a storm and, ashamed to be reduced to beggary, the Right Honourable Earl of Gravesham had first shot his wife and then taken his own life. Pa had been left to fend for himself. All that was left of his father's fortune had been the signet ring Pa wore on his third finger. The loss of a ship, the loss of a fortune, the loss of both parents – that was the sum of Caleb's knowledge.

And it seemed that Anne – the sister who presumably shared the selfsame history – had no intention whatsoever of adding to it.

5.

At first light, Caleb heard voices from the room above – Anne's soft murmur, Letty's deeper tones. Though unable to catch every word he heard his name often enough to know they were discussing him.

Letty came down the ladder first. He felt the urge to apologize for his outburst the night before, but she didn't look at him. Indeed, she seemed determined to pretend that he simply wasn't there. Silently, she stirred up the fire's embers and gave a little driftwood to feed the flames. Then she crossed to the window and threw open the shutter.

For a moment sunlight filled the room. It brought no cheer, only highlighting the house's shabbiness. A gust of wind carried the tang of salt on the air.

"Over the bar, come on now, let's be having you," Letty muttered, looking out through the window, her back to him.

Caleb stood, awkward, not knowing what to say or do. He had no idea what her cryptic utterance meant. Was she talking to him or only to herself? He caught the merest glimpse of a dozen or more ships in full sail coming in from the sea and heading upriver before she thrust her head and shoulders through the window and plunged the room into murky gloom.

What Letty was looking for, why she scanned the vessels with such eagerness, Caleb didn't know but evidently she found what she sought for after a few minutes she pulled her head and shoulders back in and yelled up the ladder, "*Mayfly*'s crossing the bar. And the *Bethany* is following close on."

How she could tell one ship from another and why it should matter so much to her was mystifying.

There was the noise of activity from the room above and Anne was calling her, "Letty! Letty! Not in the boat!"

But Letty did not – or chose not to – hear. Without even stopping to pick up a shawl she was gone out through the door and around the side of the house. Through the window Caleb watched her stride along the creaking jetty, hitching her skirts up to her knees, revealing a glimpse of shapely, muscled calves, before she jumped into a tiny rowboat, cast away the rope that held it fast and hauled on the oars, heading in the same direction as the sailing vessels.

And now Anne came down the ladder carrying Dorcas in her arms. With a rueful smile she sighed, "Time and again I have begged her to walk there! Rowing is hardly fitting for a young woman. I try to teach her to behave in a more decorous fashion but I waste my breath, I fear. She was too long without a mother's care, poor thing."

"As was I," said Caleb quietly.

He had meant to follow the comment with an apology for his uncouthness yet before he could Anne asked him haltingly, "She died, did she not?"

"Yes." Pa had told him his own mother had died in childbirth but that was all he'd ever said on the subject.

"Did you miss her? I mean, did you feel her absence?"

Caleb shrugged. "I couldn't miss what I never had. Pa was everything to me." He felt tears were dangerously close and so he changed the subject. "Where's Letty gone?"

"To Tawpuddle."

"For what purpose?"

"In pursuit of ships coming over the sandbar. Some will be returning from long voyages and their captains will be in need of new garments. She catches them on the quayside before they can make their way to the tailor. We are seamstresses, Letty and I. She will bring back work when the tide turns, I do not doubt. She is a good, hard-working girl, for all her manners are so rough."

After this brief exchange, silence descended.

Anne Avery might have the voice of a lady, but she didn't have the income of one. Caleb knew he couldn't expect to be fed and housed without paying his way and yet in this bleak, alien landscape and without Pa how was he to earn his keep?

He said, "Aunt, I don't wish my presence to be a burden. I'll work for whoever will have me."

She smiled once more, nodding, although her mouth was tense and tight as though she was nervous. "Well, then. Let us see what can be done."

Together they stepped into the village street, Anne carrying Dorcas on her hip. The smells, the sounds, the very taste of Fishpool's air − all were strange and foreign to Caleb. He was used to a countryside where the sky was suspended between hills and tall trees like a sheet hung out to dry. Here it arched before and after and to either side in a great dome that dwarfed even the jagged cliffs that hemmed in the bay. If the sky was overwhelming, the sea was even more so: too vast, too deep, too large to comprehend. The island in the distance was a dot, a full stop on a blank page, nothing more. And on land there was no softness of vegetation, no gentle curve of hill or river, nothing but harsh starkness and a sense of nature's brutal force.

Caleb looked to the left along the jetty where Letty had gone. The water bubbled and popped as though the river itself had begun to boil. Noting his alarm, Anne explained that there were creatures − cockles, lugworms − that buried themselves deep in the sand and mud when the tide ebbed. The tunnels they made left pockets of air so that now, as the tide came flooding in, this unearthly effect occurred.

"There was a time when it troubled me," Anne said gently. "But it is astounding what a person can get used to if their circumstances change."

They walked along the street. Fishpool, Caleb discovered, was a village where folk turned their back on grassland and meadow, looking instead to that expanse of salt water to make their living.

And a meagre living it was. As they went from sail-maker to chandler to fisherman, he saw hardened faces, wearied with daily struggle and pinched with want. These people had barely sufficient to cover their own family's need. Despite his aunt's entreaties no one could offer him a scrap of work.

They didn't say as much at first but it was the same everywhere they stopped. Anne would introduce her nephew, explaining that Caleb had fallen on hard times and that she'd taken him in. And then the questions began: always addressed to her, as though Caleb was both deaf and dumb.

"Where'd he come from, then?"

"What happened to his father?"

"Who's his mother?"

"How old is he?"

"Can he speak English?"

The bolder amongst them asked, "Do it wash off in the rain?"

And even, "Filthy thing! How can you bear to have him in the house?"

Caleb passed an uncomfortable morning being subjected to looks ranging from the curious to the antagonistic. Some of them seemed to regard him as not quite human:

a creature located somewhere in God's creation halfway between mankind and the brute beasts.

And yet he observed that Anne – who had lived amongst these people for many years – was no more at her ease with them than he was. Indeed, as the morning wore on he began to think she suffered more than he did. He was used to such barbs. He felt their sting but there was nothing novel or original in them. Yet Anne flinched at each foolish question and winced at each malicious one as if they gave her physical pain. As they neared the end of the village she suddenly put her hand on his arm and whispered, "Has it always been like this? Are people everywhere so thoughtless? So cruel?"

Caleb shrugged. "I have heard nothing here that I have not heard ten score times before."

"I could weep at it!" she said, turning to face him, her eyes filling even as she spoke. "Joseph … how did he respond to such insults?"

"He would turn them aside with a joke. Or sometimes he got angry and used his fists."

"And I can do neither." She was struggling to control her tears.

Caleb found himself apologizing to her. It was wrong to expose someone so gentle and mild-mannered to the crude roughness of these folk – he would have managed better looking for work on his own. He urged her to go back to the house but she refused to leave him.

They walked on until they came to the last creaking jetty that jutted out over the water. In the town of Tawpuddle, a mile or so upriver from Fishpool, a bridge spanned its width allowing people and horses from one side to the other. Caleb had crossed it himself only the day before. But at the river's mouth there was but one way over the water. Anne introduced Caleb to Harry, the ferryman, and a long exchange followed in which Harry asked the same questions that had been asked by every other person in the village. Only when it came to the matter of work did their conversation take a different turn.

His back troubled him these days, Harry said. He could use a pair of strong arms and was willing to give the lad a try.

Anne thanked him, her lip trembling. "And when should he begin?"

"Right now. Come on, boy, let's see what you can do."

Caleb followed Harry to the jetty's end. He had never been on the water in his life but had that morning watched Letty step lightly down into her rowing boat. Old and aching Harry might be, but he too made the transfer from jetty to boat look simple. When Caleb attempted the same thing the vessel rocked so violently he feared they would both be thrown overboard.

"Keep your weight low, lad," Harry snapped, steadying the boat. "That's right. Bend your knees, sit here now. Take the oars, that's it. Hold them like this, see? Pull them up and round towards you. Nice and easy does it."

But nice and easy Caleb certainly was not. He tried his utmost to follow Harry's commands but the oars were unruly and untameable in his hands. Either he dug too deep and lifted himself clean off the bench, or he missed the water completely and fell backwards off it. It would have been comical had it not been so utterly humiliating.

And all the time – with each failed attempt – they were moving further from the land. They were in the middle of the river by the time that Caleb realized that there was now a great depth of water beneath him containing God alone knows what kind of monstrous creatures. His stomach began to heave. Sweat beaded on his forehead and fear must have shown in his eyes because Harry said, "You all right, boy?"

In answer Caleb emptied the contents of his belly over Harry's feet.

Without another word the ferryman turned the boat and rowed Caleb back to where his aunt was waiting with Dorcas.

His stint as ferryman's lad had lasted less than half an hour.

Looking pained beyond endurance, Anne helped Caleb from the boat back onto solid land. She said nothing. Dorcas was fretful now, tired and hungry. Busying herself with her grizzling child, Anne turned for home and Caleb followed, cold and miserable. Harry had been his last chance of employment in Fishpool. There was no one else in the village to ask for work.

Letty returned an hour later. Dorcas was sleeping in the room above. Anne and Caleb were sitting in a dejected silence when they heard the rowboat thump against the jetty. Then Letty was calling, "Captain Smith is asking for two new shirts. New coat and all. And I got some off the *Mayfly* needs mending."

A bundle of unwashed clothing – reeking of sweat – was dumped into the middle of the floor the moment Letty entered the house.

"You find him anything?" she said to Anne, jerking her thumb at Caleb but avoiding his eyes.

"No." Anne sounded defeated. Despairing even.

"Who'd you try?"

Wearily Anne listed everyone they had gone to in the village.

"Harry?"

"He would have taken him on. But Caleb became ill from the motion of the boat."

Caleb waited for a contemptuous remark but none came. He looked up to see Letty's green eyes were full of pity. Pity! He didn't want pity! Contempt would have been easier to bear. Contempt was what he deserved. He was an oddity, a misfit, a dark-skinned bastard. A landlubber with a pitifully weak stomach. No one here would want him.

All these ships! But not even a press gang would take him! Who'd have a lad who would spew his guts over the boots of the captain the moment he set foot on deck?

He dropped his head into his hands. He was a millstone about his aunt's neck. Her husband was absent at sea and she and Letty were so obviously struggling to make ends meet, yet he was unable to do a thing. Dorcas whimpered in fear each time he went near her. He couldn't even mind the baby!

Leaving him to his misery, the two women began to sort through the clothes that Letty had brought from Tawpuddle.

Anne was a seamstress: both fancy work and plain, linen sheets, damask tablecloths, ladies' dresses, gentlemen's shirts – whatever she could get she took. But it was Letty who did the heavy work. She now set the copper on the fire to boil and washed the shirts that were in need of repair before wringing them out and hanging them to dry on the line that stretched between the cottage and jetty. It was easier to believe that Letty was mistress of the house than Anne, thought Caleb as he watched them working. The two women were polite to each other. There even seemed to be some affection between them but there was little ease there. Indeed they were both excessively cautious, as if theirs was a relationship that might fracture and break with the slightest of knocks.

He watched Letty with some envy. She was energetic.

Competent. If he'd had her skill with the oars he'd be out earning his keep instead of having to sit here. Her every move made him feel more useless.

Yet when the laundry was done and Letty sat down to the mending Caleb was surprised to discover that she was as much use with a needle as Pa had been last winter.

When Joseph had decided to fashion a new set of puppets he'd carved heads and hands with ease. But when it came to the stitching of their glove bodies and costumes he was at a loss. It was Caleb who'd done all the sewing that was needed and he'd enjoyed it, crafting costumes that were bright enough to draw the eye but strong enough to withstand the energetic use to which Pa put them.

He watched Letty as she threaded a needle and sat punching it crossly from one side of the cloth to the other. Her hands, calloused from rowing, were ill-suited to the task. The thread seemed to have a life of its own under her control. It snagged and tied itself into knots and when it finally broke Letty cursed loudly.

"Patience," said Anne mildly. "Letty, you must not hurry the work. Small stitches, my dear."

Anne's words fell on deaf ears. Letty was not designed to sit still and sew. Her face turned constantly to the window and the sea beyond: that was where she wanted to be.

Watching her, Caleb lost patience. "That seam will not hold." Snatching the work from her, he pulled out her crooked, uneven stitches and began to mend the garment himself. He kept his head down. He didn't want to see more of Letty's pity, or meet his aunt's eyes. If Anne thought Letty's rowing was unseemly she'd no doubt feel the same about him sewing. The air seemed to thicken with tension as he worked.

When he was finished he handed the shirt to his aunt for inspection. The neatness of his stitching was enough to make both women's jaws drop. Looking at Letty's startled face, Caleb thought that God had played a poor prank on them both. Letty had a sailor's heart and stomach: if she'd been born a boy she'd no doubt already be at sea. As for him, he'd surely been granted a talent that should rightly have belonged to a woman.

There wasn't a word spoken, but that afternoon Caleb became his aunt's assistant. They laboured steadily in silence. Having seen Letty's sewing, Caleb knew that the day's tasks must have been finished in half the time they would usually have taken. There was still some daylight left when they were done. But whether Anne was more grateful or mortified by him working alongside her was hard to tell.

Caleb would have liked to walk outside for a while alone but he could hear the village children playing in the street, the distant cackle of the women at the well and the laughter of the men in the tavern. He felt too raw to expose himself to their gaze. Instead he stayed inside until nightfall and when Letty and Anne retired to the attic where Dorcas was already sleeping he curled by the fire once more with Pa's puppets.

He could pay his way at least: that was some relief. But he'd lived a roving life, enjoying Pa's lively company, his endless stories and easy laughter. He'd never imagined there would be an end to it. And now he felt himself to be so confined, so constrained within the cottage's four walls that it was like being slowly buried alive.

6.

By the time Caleb arrived at his aunt's he'd lost track of the days of the week. Indeed he'd been so shocked by Pa's arrest and all that followed he couldn't have said with any certainty even which month of the year it now was. But on the second morning he woke in Fishpool Anne declared that it was Sunday and to church they must go.

Caleb owned only the clothes he stood in and, after his long journey, it was not surprising that he was in no fit state to be seen by a parson.

Letty was sent for water from the well while Anne turned her attention to Caleb. From an upstairs trunk she fetched the few garments her husband had left on land. When Letty returned he was told to wash. The women kept their backs turned, but he still felt awkward. He and Pa had bathed in streams or swum in rivers. Having to manage with a jug and bowl in such a cramped space fearing that at any moment one of them might swing round and stare was a new and deeply uncomfortable experience. It made him sweat so much that the washing seemed pointless. When he was done he dressed hastily in borrowed clothes. The shirt was too large, as was the coat. The britches would not stay up without a length of cord tied about his middle. He was a ludicrous sight but he was at least respectably clean and that, it seemed, was all that Anne cared about. His aunt then turned her attention to her daughter and Dorcas was scrubbed until she wailed in protest. She was then placed in one corner of the room like a parcel.

Once Letty was washed to Anne's satisfaction and dressed in a threadbare, sun-bleached skirt, the four of them set forth.

Letty led the way to the church, striding ahead without a backward glance. She didn't want to be seen with him, Caleb thought, and Anne appeared to be equally embarrassed. She busied herself with Dorcas, avoiding the need for conversation with him or indeed anyone else. The villagers who trooped along the lane and up the hill chattered loudly and much of their talk, inevitably, concerned Fishpool's new arrival. Snatches of it reached Caleb's ears.

"Her brother's child."

"A convict!"

"A thief!"

"But who was his mother?"

"A whore?"

"A slave?"

"Wrong side of the blanket."

"Bad blood."

"The shame of it!"

"Disgusting thing!"

"I wouldn't want him in my house."

"They should put him on a ship. Take him back to where he come from."

"That's right. Send him to the jungle, I say."

No more sense than a gaggle of geese, Pa would have said. He'd have rolled his eyes at their stupidity. Mocked their accents, made some joke, flung his arm around Caleb's shoulders and begun to tell him an anecdote or story to stop him dwelling on their remarks. Together he and Pa would have shrugged off their talk as meaningless drivel. Anne walked ahead of him, her back stiff, her head turned towards the child on her hip. She said nothing: not to him, not to any of the villagers. All Caleb could do was fix his eyes on the road and keep walking.

The church was small, low-roofed, with a squat square tower of a kind Caleb had never seen before. It was as if there might have once been a steeple which had buckled and been slowly crushed by the weight of the vast sky.

The parson stood by the gate, greeting his flock by name as they arrived. Letty was no doubt already inside the building. Anne – who must have heard the villagers' comments as clearly as Caleb had – held back a little and flushed scarlet as she introduced him to the parson.

Caleb extended his hand in greeting, but the parson did not shake it. Instead he stared in evident horror at the open palm as if searching for evidence of the sinner's blood that must flow through Caleb's veins.

Disconcerted to be so obviously shunned, Caleb turned away and found himself face to face with the parson's wife – a small, mouse-like woman who began to babble with apparent nervousness.

"Your name is Caleb, is it not? I gather you have had a long journey to get here, and I am so sorry to hear of your dreadful misfortunes. Are you well enough now? Are you settled at your aunt's?"

Her eagerness to talk was as disconcerting as her husband's coldness. Caleb started to reply but was then distracted by the loud clatter of hooves and wheels as a large, open-topped carriage bowled around the corner of the lane and came to a halt by the church gate.

The mere sight of the vehicle caused both the parson and his wife to stand stiffly upright and Anne to turn and run with Dorcas up the path and into the church along with the rest of the straggling villagers.

Caleb did not move. He was intrigued to know who had such a powerful effect on these people. He'd never laid eyes on the wealthy gentleman who sat in the back of the carriage but still there was something about him that seemed familiar. The curve of his cheekbones, the line of his nose: both brought someone to mind, but the more he tried to remember who it could be, the more the memory eluded him.

There was a lady seated beside the gentleman, expensively but not elegantly dressed. Both bonnet and gown seemed designed more to scream aloud their vast cost than to show her face or figure to their best advantage.

Sitting next to the driver was somebody Caleb had no difficulty in identifying. It was the horseman in the powdered wig he'd encountered at Norton Manor: the man who'd suggested Caleb was the son of a whore and declared that Pa had died of the pox. The man who'd looked suddenly pensive when he learned of Pa's transportation...

"Who is he?" Caleb asked the parson's wife, nodding in his direction.

"That is Sir Robert Fairbrother of Norton Manor, and his wife beside him." Her voice was high and tight. "Your aunt was maid to her before she married."

"No, I meant who is the man beside the driver?"

"Oh ... that's William Benson, his steward. Why do you ask?"

"I passed him in the road."

"He would have been out on his master's business, no doubt. Sir Robert's estate is of large extent: it comprises every dwelling in Fishpool." Her voice dropped to a whisper and she added, "The parsonage, too."

Caleb didn't respond. He was watching William Benson, who'd leapt down to open the carriage door.

"You must go in now," the parson's wife urged Caleb. She flapped her hands at him as if trying to shoo him away. "Go quickly. Sir Robert likes his tenants to be gathered and waiting when he enters the church."

Does he indeed? thought Caleb. He did what he was told but with some resentment, walking steadily but not hurriedly up the path and sliding into a pew at the rear of the church beside his aunt. The moment the congregation heard Sir Robert and Lady Fairbrother enter the porch they bent their heads as if they were praying. Caleb was astonished. Who did this man think he was, that everyone in the village bowed down before him? Pa was afraid of no man. Well, he would be the same. Caleb sat stubbornly bolt upright until he felt a slap across the back of his head.

It was William Benson. "Show your respect, boy."

Furious, Caleb started to get to his feet, but Anne seized his arm, her fingers pressing into Caleb's flesh. Her face was deathly white and she looked at him desperately with eyes so like Pa's that Caleb's heart missed a beat. It was the same look Pa had given him inside the gaol. He forced himself to relax. To slump in the pew. To lower his head. From the corner of his eye he watched Benson strut down the aisle, proud as a bantam rooster. He was followed by Sir Robert and his wife, slow and stately as a pair of galleons in full sail. When they reached their family pew they settled themselves on silken cushions. While the rest of the congregation had to sit still and pay attention to the parson's every tedious word, Sir Robert and Lady Fairbrother shut their eyes and commenced a nap that lasted the duration of the service. After the sermon, the congregation prayed for the souls of the dead, and most particularly for those lost at sea – a long litany of names that meant nothing to Caleb. Sir Robert and his lady were not required to utter a word. They did not pray, they did not sing and at the end of it all they were gently roused by William Benson. They stood and the parson's flock kept heads bowed once more as the couple passed along the aisle towards the door.

The parson may have preached on the debt mankind owed to almighty God, but it seemed to Caleb that here, in Fishpool's small church, Sir Robert Fairbrother was far and away the more important deity.

7.

Time passed, and Caleb's life fell into a pattern.

Daily, Letty watched the ships sail over the bar and went in pursuit of those whose captains might be in need of new clothes. Daily, Anne protested when her stepdaughter jumped into the little boat and deftly turned its head into the currents that would carry her speedily to Tawpuddle. Daily, Caleb worked alongside his aunt all the hours of daylight. With two proficient stitchers in the cottage she was able to take in more sewing and finish it more quickly than before. Letty did the heavy work – hauling water, boiling shirts and sheets in the copper, wringing them out to dry – without a murmur of complaint, but Caleb could feel her resentment simmering beneath the surface. He might be paying for his keep but he was a cuckoo in the nest.

He felt he could breathe freely only when Letty was gone from the cottage. When she was there she wouldn't look at him, wouldn't speak to him. She'd barely said a word since that first night when he'd lost his temper so badly. He probably should have apologized but what did she expect, staring at him like that? He wanted to put it right for his aunt's sake if not for Letty's but didn't know how to begin. And the longer he left it, the worse it became. A chasm of silence yawned between them that grew broader and deeper with each day.

Dorcas, however, was a different matter. The child had grown used to his presence before the first week had passed. She'd happily crawl across the floor and play at his feet or hold up her arms so he could lift her onto his lap. Sometimes she fell asleep there and her trust, her simple, straightforward acceptance touched him more than he'd have believed possible.

Seeing her daughter becoming so fond of Caleb pleased Anne. As they sat side by side sewing for hours at a stretch the sharp edges of their initial awkwardness with each other softened.

His aunt, Caleb discovered, was an intensely private person – shy, reticent – so different from her brother! Pa had possessed the ability to fall into easy conversation with anybody, from bishop to beggar. Caleb, on the other hand, had never been able to converse freely with strangers. Oh, he'd tried a fair few times. But a fair few times were enough to put him off for life. People had looked at him as though he was a talking horse, or a flying pig. If they'd answered him at all they'd spoken slowly and very loudly, as if he was a total simpleton. Let them rot in hell, then! Other people's conversation was something he could do without!

But now, with Anne, he tried to imitate Pa's manner. He made observations, asked questions, told stories of his roving life with Pa. He tried to draw her out but she wouldn't speak of his father, however much Caleb tried to probe her. He came at the subject from every conceivable angle, but she never rose to the bait. One word. Two. Then silence. She would not speak of her past either, of her parents or of the childhood she'd shared with her brother. She wouldn't even speak of her time in service and only once said anything relating to her husband.

Caleb had tried a question he'd sometimes heard Pa ask – "Your husband. How did you meet?"

"Oh … at Norton Manor," she replied.

"He was a servant there too?"

"No! Edward has always been a sailor."

"So how did he come to be there?"

It was like trying to tempt a snail from its shell. Bit by bit he found out that Sir Robert Fairbrother – in a great show of charitable benevolence – held a gala day each spring for the poor and unfortunate of the parish. Children whose mothers had died in childbirth or whose fathers had drowned at sea; widows struggling to keep their families fed and clothed – all were invited to the manor for an afternoon's entertainment. Letty, having lost her mother, attended annually and one year had been escorted there by her father.

Edward Avery had seen Anne for the first time when she

was crossing the lawn bringing a shawl to Lady Fairbrother and ... well, he'd set his heart on marrying her there and then. As she uttered those words Anne blushed deeply and Caleb suddenly felt uncomfortable. He'd touched on something intimate and didn't want to know more. He didn't ask any further questions about his uncle and she didn't volunteer any further information.

The only subject on which they could talk freely was literature – the writings of Jonathan Swift and Daniel Defoe, of Alexander Pope and William Shakespeare.

Pa had taught Caleb to read when he was small but books had been a luxury they could never afford until last winter, when they'd drowned in a sea of them!

They'd been in Porlock's when Pa had heard tell of a country house a day's walk from the city. Its owner had died and the heir lived in the north of England and was unable to make the journey until spring, when the roads would be passable. The place had been shut up and the servants sent away: Pa had no qualms about making use of it. Standing outside, looking up at its grand facade, he'd said, "No sense in us freezing to death while a place like this stands deserted. We'll be keeping it warm for its owner!"

It had been an easy task to break in and during the cold, dark months they had lived in luxury. Feather beds, linen sheets, roaring fires. And the library! Poetry, prose, plays – a great profusion of literature at their disposal! It was there that Pa had carved his new puppets and while he worked

Caleb read aloud to him. They had been shipwrecked with Robinson Crusoe and travelled to strange and exotic lands with Lemuel Gulliver. They had laughed and wept over the comedies and tragedies of Shakespeare.

Caleb did not mention the country house to his aunt but he spoke of the books he and Pa had shared. While they sewed, he and Anne discussed whether Brutus was right to lift a knife against Caesar, and whether it was Macbeth or his lady who was more to blame for the murder of the king. It was in these moments he caught glimpses of the softly spoken, earnest and intelligent girl she'd once been. He could picture her and Pa debating matters of prose and poetry, for her mind was the match of her brother's.

Only once did Anne let down her guard. They had been talking of *The Winter's Tale*, of the jealous king and his doomed queen, of their baby abandoned on the shores of Bohemia. A silence had briefly fallen while Caleb re-threaded his needle. When he looked up, Anne was gazing at him, a strange expression on her face. She was in a kind of reverie as though she saw not him, but something beyond. When she came back to the present she started.

"I am sorry," she said. "I did not mean to stare. I simply look for your father in you."

"And do you see him?"

"Yes. Oh yes, indeed!"

Caleb smiled, relieved. To be like Pa was all he'd ever hoped for.

Anne said, "You are every inch his son. I wish…"

Her voice died away. She bit her lip. She seemed poised on the brink of speech.

Here was his opportunity! There was so much he wanted to know, if he could only ask the right question – one that would not startle her back into her shell…

But then they heard the familiar bump of boat against jetty and Letty was there, hot, tired, irritable, dropping a pile of stinking clothes onto the floor. Anne's head was already bent back to her sewing. Caleb threw a glare in Letty's direction. She didn't meet his eyes but the way her skin reddened told him she'd felt every ounce of his fury.

8.

The season slid from summer towards autumn, one day much like another, with only two events of consequence.

The first occurred one afternoon in late August. Letty was in Tawpuddle; Caleb and Anne were working in tranquil silence and Dorcas was sleeping when they were disturbed by a sudden knock on the door.

Lady Fairbrother's maid had been sent to the cottage to demand that Anne accompany her to Norton Manor immediately. It seemed a new gown was required and Anne – having been Lady Fairbrother's maid for some years and knowing her tastes and preferences – was to have the making of it.

Leaving Caleb to mind Dorcas, Anne went to the manor and some time later returned with a bolt of scarlet brocade, several yards of ribbons, a vast quantity of French lace and a small amount of money to pay for their labour. She brought, too, a gown whose style they were to copy.

"We must begin at once," Anne said, taking the

captain's coat that Caleb had been close to finishing from his hands. "She wants the gown delivered before the end of September."

"Can she not wait her turn?" Caleb asked irritably. The arrogance of these people was unbearable!

"Her husband is our landlord," was Anne's only reply.

And so they began. As their work on the gown proceeded the weather turned, the heated air cooling, the sea breezes bringing a damp, foreboding chill into every corner of the cottage, whispering of a long winter to come. Caleb's fingers were stiff and clumsy with cold at the start and close of each day, slowing him down. Besides which the nights were drawing in and they had fewer hours of light to sew by.

It was an intricate, wearying commission, but they were glad to have work. Gladder still when they learned of a second event that was of great significance to the whole of Fishpool.

The village went to sleep on the evening of Wednesday 2nd September and woke on the morning of Thursday 14th, yet this was no enchanted sleep or supernatural occurrence. A year earlier an Act of Parliament had decreed that England's calendar must be synchronized with those of other nations. In order to do so eleven full days must be struck from the year. Drinking coffee in Porlock's, Pa had explained the matter of the Gregorian and Julian calendar in great detail but Caleb had paid little attention. It involved politicians. Foreign nations. Who cared about numbering the days? It could make no difference to him and Pa.

He had given it no further thought at all until Letty returned from Tawpuddle with a rumour that William Benson would be collecting rent for the whole month of September as usual. No concession was to be made for the changing calendar. Every tenant had lost eleven days of work and consequently eleven days of pay, but Sir Robert would not lose eleven days of rent.

The news made Anne dizzy with panic. "How can we manage? We will be turned out!"

"It can't be true!" Caleb scoffed. "No man could be so unfair."

"Go ask Benson yourself," said Letty. "I just saw him. He's down along the end of the village."

Her jaw came jutting forward. They were the first words she'd spoken to him in weeks. Was this a challenge? Did she think he was too much of a coward to confront Benson himself? Well, he'd show her he wasn't afraid. Despite Anne's plea that he would let the matter lie Caleb left the house with Letty at his heels.

The steward was supervising the unloading of a small boat. Bales of wool, Caleb noticed. An odd cargo for a fishing vessel but that wasn't his concern. When he mentioned the rumour, Benson confirmed Sir Robert's orders. "The full amount, due on rent day, same as usual."

"But this was not meant to happen!" said Caleb. "Parliament decided—"

"Parliament?" With exaggerated slowness Benson turned and looked at him with feigned ignorance. In thick, yokel tones he asked, "Where's that to, then?"

"London," said Caleb.

"Oh. London. Near three hundred miles away. Terrible long walk, so I've heard."

Caleb felt every ounce of Benson's mockery but with Letty standing behind him he could not let the matter rest. "My father said Parliament promised that the common folk would not suffer..."

"Did he now?" Benson rubbed his cheek thoughtfully and appeared to consider. Then he asked, "Was that before or after he took to thieving?"

Caleb's hands clenched. He could wipe the smirk off Benson's face. Two blows, one either side. The man's head would be ringing for days.

But what would follow? Eviction? Arrest? How distressed Anne would be. She was fragile at the best of times and had he not already brought her trouble enough? Finger by finger Caleb unclenched his hands. As he did so Benson's smile grew broader.

"Word of advice, boy..." The steward leaned towards him until his face was an inch from Caleb's. Raising his voice so that the men who were unloading the boat could hear, Benson said, "If you want to keep a roof over that miserable hide of yours, you keep your head down and your mouth shut. And you pay your rent when it's due, the same as everyone else."

Flecks of his spittle hit Caleb's cheeks. The man was vile. Wiping his face, Caleb turned on his heel, almost knocking Letty sideways as he stormed away down the street. She ran to catch up with him.

"Parliament would not want their wishes thwarted," he raged.

Letty laughed bitterly. "You think them in London give a damn about the likes of us?"

He stopped. Looked at her. Caleb knew that she was talking sense, but anger had him in its grip. "He cannot get away with this! Is there no one we can tell? The Member of Parliament, perhaps?" He knew the suggestion was absurd even as the words left his mouth. He'd heard men talking about politics often enough in Porlock's. Hadn't Pa declared that government was run by the rich, for the rich? That as far as Westminster was concerned the common folk could go hang? Letty was shaking her head, looking at him with pity. She thought he was an idiot! And she was right. Tackling Benson had been the act of a complete simpleton.

"We've got a Member of Parliament around here, true enough," Letty said. Her mouth twisted into an angry grimace. "But there's only seven men in the borough entitled to vote for him. And I'll bet you can guess who they're in debt to."

"Sir Robert Fairbrother?"

She nodded. "And they won't say a word to displease him. So we'd best get working, hadn't we?"

They worked. Letty was out all the hours of daylight, knocking on doors, taking washing from whoever would give any to her, gathering wood, boiling the copper, scrubbing and wringing until her hands were red and raw. Anne sewed until her fingers bled, Caleb alongside her, stitching rage and loathing into every seam. To be counted a man and yet be so utterly powerless! His helplessness was like a bitter poison that spread through his veins day by day.

By labouring every daylight hour and by starving themselves enough money was saved. When rent day came Benson strutted along Fishpool's single street, rapping loudly on doors, yelling the names and amounts owing. As their jar of hard-earned coins was poured into his hands, it seemed to Caleb that the steward took an obscene delight in his work. He counted every last farthing, noting it down in his pocketbook before stowing the coins away in a large casket.

They were safe for this month at least, but before the day was done they heard that two families in Fishpool had been turned out of their houses: one whose father had been lost at sea, the second where four of the children had sickened and died and the parents been too maddened with grieving to care to work or eat.

A sad, sorry picture they made as they trailed out of the village to who-knew-where, their meagre belongings tied in one small bundle. Anne could not bear to watch or even to bid them farewell but sat inside, Dorcas clutched tightly in her arms, weeping softly.

"He is a monster," Caleb said, as he and Letty stood in the street, watching Benson urging the evicted families to make haste, to hurry, to shift themselves and get gone from Sir Robert's property.

"Maybe. Maybe not," said Letty. "He's following orders. I'd say he's more of a lapdog, dancing on his hind legs to please his master."

"He relishes it. The man is contemptible."

"He is that."

The scene was grim. Miserable.

And yet here at least was something that Letty and he could agree on.

9.

The onset of winter brought storms: rain that pounded on the roof, salt wind that rattled the shutters and knived into every nook and cranny. Inch by inch the countryside died. Days shortened. Nights became interminable. Sleeping, Caleb was tormented by vivid dreams of Pa, chained in the hold of a ship that heaved in dreadful storms on the wild sea. Pa, sick to the stomach, lying in his own filth, calling Caleb's name. Screaming. Weeping.

But one night in November there was a strange reversal and what filled his unconscious mind was not the bleak present, but the warm, golden past. Caleb's dream was full of colour, of sound, of sweet smells and summer sunshine.

He was small – five or six – and he and Pa were in a water meadow, thick with flowers, by the winding river. Pa was trying to teach him his letters, but Caleb was making little headway. He could make no sense of the strange symbols Pa had scratched with a stick in the gravel at the water's edge. His head ached with the effort and he was on the verge of bursting into tears of angry frustration.

But then the sunlight caught Pa's signet ring. It glinted, dazzling his eyes, and at that moment Caleb recognized the letters that were engraved at its centre. He had always thought the design was of two interlocking horseshoes, but now he saw it was two letter Cs, back to back. They were the initials of Pa's father, Charles Chappell, but at five years old Caleb didn't know that. He knew only that those shapes suddenly made sense.

Grinning he took Pa's hand, pointing – "That is a C," he declared. "C is for Caleb."

Pa had hugged him tight, telling him he was proud, proud to have such a son. What man could wish for more? "C is for clever too. Clever lad!"

In the morning he woke not in a fevered sweat, but in a warm glow of contentment. He could feel Pa's presence. It was as if his father was there with him still, that Caleb would only have to open his eyes to see Pa's smiling face. That sense did not leave him when he rose, but wrapped itself around him like a cloak when he left the house at first light.

High water had been an hour before dawn. Letty had developed a racking cough so Anne sent Caleb in her place to see what had washed up overnight. Driftwood for the fire, she hoped, plenty of it. The more wood Caleb could find, the more tolerable the coming winter would be.

He walked along the marshy shore where the river spewed its contents into the sea. It was a leaden grey, bitter morning, the chill air pierced by the shrieks of seabirds. The souls of lost sailors, Letty called them, and it had the ring of truth to it. There was something in those cries that smacked of grief.

Far out to sea, totally obscuring the island in the bay, clouds squatted heavy on the horizon, big-bellied, big-arsed, angry bruise-black.

And then came a sudden shift of light. Through a gap between the clouds the rising sun sent slanting beams across the water. The sea turned deep blue against the dark sky, the sand russet and copper and gold, the marsh grass emerald-green. A squall of wind blew an icy shower over the water and then a rainbow was arcing over the bay from one headland to the other. There was an awful, raw beauty to the scene that made Caleb draw in a sharp breath.

He stopped near the sandbanks that humped across the river's mouth forming a bar at low tide that ships couldn't cross. It was like a line of beached whales, Letty said, although as he'd never seen a whale and couldn't imagine a creature so vast he didn't know whether her comparison was a true one or not. But he'd lived long enough at his aunt's to know that after a high tide the flats near the sandbanks were strewn with debris. Flotsam and jetsam drifted in massed hordes. Clumped seaweed, branches, sometimes — after a flood — what seemed like whole forests of uprooted trees.

But today, the sea had given up nothing. Nothing at all. Indeed it was strangely calm, the waves barely breaking although it was clear that a storm was on its way. The marsh flats were washed clean, with no trace of anything laid down by the tide. Caleb skirted the dunes and looked along the beach where the wet sand reflected the sky so it was hard to tell one from the other.

The beach was as empty as the flats. There was just one thing. A dark shape in the water, rising and falling in the slight swell. The moment he saw it he knew it was a corpse.

A man. Drowned. Dead. No doubt about it.

A cold hard lump formed in Caleb's belly. He wanted to turn. Walk away. But the corpse couldn't be left there. He was alone, so the task fell to him. He must wade in, drag the body onto the sand to stop the sea carrying it back out again.

His feet were like lumps of lead as he walked. The sand was waterlogged, and he sank ankle-deep, his sucking footprints filling with seawater, step by step. By the time he reached the body the tide had ebbed a little and it was no longer floating weightless, but lying heavy and sodden, waves breaking over its back.

It was face down, arms beneath its chest, hair slicked across the cheek and wound around its neck like a rope. A noose.

Caleb's mind was frozen with shock. It took some minutes for him to realize that the body would need to be carried off the beach and given burial but he couldn't manage the task single-handed.

Help. He needed help. But who could he go to? Who in this godforsaken place would help him? Letty? She was unwell. Anne? The sight of a dead man would reduce her to hysterics. Who then?

He was standing, wondering, when the seventh wave came. He'd heard people in Fishpool talking about the seventh wave. He'd thought them fools – who counts waves, for God's sake?

But now one so much larger than those that had gone before hit Caleb, almost knocking him off his feet, soaking him from the waist down. It crashed over the drowned man, tugging him as it ebbed, pulling him onto his side.

One arm came up, a bloated hand, stiff fingers pointing at the rainbow, tracing its line across the sky.

A ring on the third finger. Glinting gold. Two C's entwined.

Caleb's legs gave way, crumpling like paper. He was on his knees in the water, heaving his guts onto the sand.

PART 2

1.

After Caleb's retching had ceased he got to his feet and stood bent over with shock, arms wrapped across his stomach.

The corpse's features were distorted. Bloated. Made unrecognizable by their immersion in the water.

But there was no mistaking the ring.

However much Caleb longed to be mistaken, however much he yearned for the truth to be different he knew that Pa was a man of his word. He'd kept his promise. He'd come back. But he'd come back dead.

Turning away from the body and the sea Caleb looked about him. Not a living soul in sight. Yet there – on the horizon – its squat tower poking just above the brow of the hill – was the church. Church. Graveyard. Parsonage. That was where he must go. Trembling, sobbing, gulping in air, he willed himself to move. He tried to go quickly but it was like running in a dream. The ground was soft as quicksand, his limbs were heavy as iron: each step was unutterably wearying. He could not catch his breath. He staggered, limped, hobbled.

He did not look back.

Even if he had, his eyes were so full of tears he would not have seen a man emerging from the cover of the dunes.

A man who now crossed the sand and squatted down beside the corpse.

2.

By the time Caleb reached the parsonage he was almost unable to stand. A maid coldly informed him that the parson was attending on Sir Robert Fairbrother at Norton Manor. His sobs of distress brought the parson's wife to the door and, seeing his condition, she took him indoors and made him sit down in the parson's study.

"I dreamed of him! Last night. And then I found him. On the beach. He's dead. My pa! Dead! Oh God!" Saying the words aloud brought on another bout of sobbing and retching. Caleb tried to master himself but could not. All dignity, all self-respect had been left on the sand with Pa's corpse. It was some time before he managed to tell the parson's wife exactly what had happened. She paled so dreadfully that he thought her in danger of swooning like Anne, but despite her mouse-like appearance it seemed she was made of sterner stuff. Although her voice shook as she gave instructions she did not faint away. Despatching one maid to find men to carry the body from the beach to the outhouse she then sent another girl running to fetch Anne. A third maid was ordered to the kitchen to make a posset of warmed cream, laced with brandy and egg, which the parson's wife then pressed into Caleb's hands.

It took an effort of will for him to drink it. His stomach was reluctant to hold anything but, sip by sip, he started to edge it down. He was only halfway through when the men arrived with Pa's body. He could hear them outside, their boots scraping on the cobbles, voices raised, grumbling, arguing with each other.

"You ain't taking your share of the weight."

"I am."

"You ain't. You're a lazy old bugger, you."

"Where do we put 'un then?"

"Out here, she said."

"Don't bang him around like that!"

"He's past caring now."

"Ain't you got no respect?"

So mundane. So ordinary. It was unreal, this couldn't be happening – that wasn't Pa being bumped and heaved and deposited in an outhouse as if he was no more than a sack of wheat.

It seemed an age before the sound of hooves outside announced the parson's return.

His wife went out to meet him in the yard. Through the window Caleb watched him dismount. He could not hear their words but saw the parson frown and shake his head as she told him of the grim discovery. And then Anne, Dorcas and Letty arrived on foot with the maid. Their faces were strained, shocked. There was a muttered conversation in the yard after which all of them came into the study.

At the parson's invitation Caleb related what had happened that morning. He was a little calmer now, his story less garbled, more coherent. There was a long silence when he finished the telling. He expected Anne to break down with grief as he had done and for the parson to utter words of sympathy. Wasn't it a churchman's duty to comfort the bereaved?

Instead the parson cleared his throat, exchanging a glance with Anne that spoke of severe embarrassment. And then horror was piled on horror as it became clear that Caleb's tale was not believed.

"You found a dead man, Caleb, but it wasn't your father," the parson said. "I know you're missing him, lad. That kind of sorrow can do strange things to a person's wits. It sometimes makes people see things that are not there."

Caleb was confused to begin with. Why was he being contradicted? He looked to his aunt but Anne would not meet his eyes. Letty, seized with a fit of coughing, had her face turned away. "It was him!" he cried. "It was Pa!"

"It was not," the parson insisted. "Joseph Chappell was transported. He'll be in the colonies by now."

"I know what I saw!"

"You are mistaken, boy. Your mind is playing tricks. You

told my wife you dreamed of him last night. Isn't that so?"

"Yes, but…"

"Well, then. You didn't recognize his face, did you?"

"No, sir." Caleb recalled the bloated features, the flesh so corrupted by the sea that the man looked scarcely human. He feared he might begin to retch again.

The parson sat down in front of Caleb and assumed a tone of utmost patience as if he was speaking to a very small child. "And so tell us once more what happened. You were gathering driftwood. You looked along the beach. What did you see?"

"A dead man."

"How far away?"

"Fifty yards or so. I knew at once it was a corpse."

"But you can't have," the parson said calmly. "You couldn't have seen clearly, not from that distance. You'd have seen a shape, nothing more. You would have thought it was seaweed. Driftwood. A barrel, perhaps. You can't possibly have known it was a dead man until you got closer. Not unless the idea was already in your mind. Come on, boy: will you not admit it? You saw what you wished to."

"I would never have wished to see Pa like that!"

The parson urged him to think again. "The past few months have been difficult, I know. There's no one in Fishpool who doesn't pity you. It would be no disgrace to admit you were mistaken."

Once more, Caleb glanced at his family. Anne was

white with shock, Dorcas looking wide-eyed and fretful in her arms. Letty was frowning, her brows drawn so fiercely together they made one line across her forehead. None of them had spoken a word.

Again Caleb said, "I know what I saw."

The parson was done with patience. Now he did not trouble to conceal his irritation. "This is absurd!"

"I saw his ring."

"There was no ring, Caleb! The dead man was not your father. The very idea is ludicrous. Impossible!"

"May I see him?"

"What?"

"May I view the body?"

"There is no need. You are quite distressed enough – I will not allow you to completely unhinge your mind. Are your wits already turned so inside out that you would not take my word on this?"

Challenge a man of God? Caleb could not. And yet he couldn't let the matter rest. "If he was not my father ... then who was he?"

The question drove the parson into a temper. "A common sailor, no doubt. It takes but a small slip for a man to end up in the water. You'd do well to remember how easily a man can drown, Caleb, if you continue to live with your aunt."

If he continue? The parson's words seemed heavy with menace. If Caleb had to leave Fishpool, where would he go?

The workhouse? The lunatic asylum?

The parson turned to Anne. "His wits are addled. In time, he will come to his senses. Take him home for now and make sure he doesn't talk to others the way he's talked to me. He must not speak of this. I won't have the whole of Fishpool running wild with foolish rumours."

It was too late for that, Caleb thought. The maid must have heard him telling the parson's wife that he'd found Pa's body on the beach. She'd gone running to Fishpool to fetch Anne and she'd have passed the gossips at the well. There would be more whispering. More sideways looks. The thought wearied him beyond belief.

Perhaps he'd have yielded. Perhaps he would have believed the parson and given up the idea that the man he'd found was Pa. He might have bowed to the pressure that was being brought to bear upon him had it not been for one thing: a change in Letty's demeanour.

The parson was talking still, telling Anne that the dead man must have gone into the water soon before high tide. "It is always the same tale. A few months at sea and a crew comes home with a raging thirst. A night in Tawpuddle's taverns and one too many draughts of ale. A dark night. No moon. He probably fell from the quay or from the bridge and the river's current carried him out into the bay and onto the beach." The parson said he'd make enquiries, discover from the Harbour master or one of the many seamen in port who the dead man might be. Perhaps if he could discover his name, it might soothe Caleb's troubled mind. He spoke as if Caleb was deaf and dumb or as if he was not in the room.

It was when Caleb turned his head away that he caught sight of Letty's expression. He'd thought her earlier frown had been directed at him, but no... She was perplexed, observing the parson as if puzzled by something. Then she became annoyed. Her lips thinned into a line like a thread pulled tight against the cloth and then she was staring at the parson with ill-concealed distrust. Finally she gave the smallest, slightest shake of the head.

Letty was no friend of Caleb's. Yet now she fixed him with a stare so penetrating it was as though she had pierced his very soul. He felt suddenly certain that Letty knew he was speaking the truth.

Anne, apologizing over and over again for the trouble Caleb had caused, took their leave of the parson. Caleb got to his feet and followed his aunt. As they reached the door Letty sped ahead of him down the path, eager to get away, but Anne hung back, standing on the step, continuing to murmur how dreadfully sorry she was about the morning's events. Nodding his thanks to the parson's wife, Caleb darted after Letty, catching up with her in the lane out of sight of the parsonage, where he seized her by the arm with such sudden force that she was thrown off balance and flung against the hedge.

He did not say sorry. Too many apologies had been

made that morning. Anne's footsteps were fast approaching. Before she was within earshot he demanded, "You shook your head, Letty. I saw you. Why?"

Caleb startled the words out of her.

"The parson's lying."

3.

Caleb wasn't comfortable with Letty. He felt they'd been like two dogs circling each other, hackles raised, the whole time he'd been at his aunt's. Yet in the days that followed his discovery of Pa's body he burned to speak to her. He would have been utterly overwhelmed by sorrow, but the thought that the parson had lied filled him with rage, and rage was so much easier to bear than grief. He was desperate to hear more from Letty, and there were times when she seemed to hover on the brink of conversation, but then Anne would appear and Letty's jaw would clamp shut. He watched. He waited. A chance would come to talk to her. When it did, he promised himself he would be ready.

That chance was a long time coming.

Anne's remedy for Caleb's supposedly addled wits was to keep him occupied. No doubt the parson had advised her – exhaust the body and the mind will have no time to dwell on unsavoury matters. At first she used Letty's cough as an excuse, giving him the tasks that her stepdaughter usually carried out. From before dawn until after dark she had him gathering driftwood for the fire, drawing water, filling the copper, running errands, washing shirts, delivering orders, doing endless chores in addition to the sewing by which he earned his keep. His competence with a needle meant that demand for their services had increased. There was no shortage of things to keep Caleb occupied.

As he walked from Fishpool to Tawpuddle and back again on his aunt's instruction he caught the tittle-tattle of the women at the well – as indeed, he was meant to. They were gripped by Caleb's discovery of the drowned man and his lunatic delusion that it was his father's corpse.

"Buffleheaded fool!"

"Simpleton!"

"Lost his marbles, he has!"

Loudly they speculated about whether he should be admitted to an asylum and if he might run mad during the next full moon. Their fascination with him seemed limitless.

"Better bar our doors, I reckon."

"Keep the children inside."

"Who knows what he might do?"

He pretended deafness each time he passed, refusing to give them the satisfaction of seeing him break his step. But one morning the gossips stopped him in his tracks.

"That drowned 'un got a name, so they say."

"Thomas Smith, I heard."

"Sailor, he was."

Caleb turned. He loathed these women, yet the temptation to know more was too much. "Who says so?" he asked.

For the very first time they did not look through him but answered directly, "The parson. He just come from paying a visit to your aunt."

"And what else did he discover?"

With relish one of the toothless crones informed him that the parson's guess had been right – Thomas Smith had stumbled on the Tawpuddle quayside and fallen in the river after a bellyful of ale.

"Why didn't he swim to shore?" Caleb asked.

"Lord love you! No sailor can swim!" laughed one of the women.

"Especially not after a night in the tavern!" wheezed a second.

"What would be the use of it?" cackled a third. "If your ship goes down, 'twould just prolong the suffering, staying afloat."

"Best to get it over with!"

"And so the river carried him out?" asked Caleb.

"Looks like it."

"Did the parson speak of any family?"

"No. He wasn't from around these parts."

So that was that. It seemed that "Thomas Smith" had no one to mourn or miss him. How very convenient. He'd been buried the day before in the churchyard, with only the parson and his wife present.

Now that they had Caleb standing before them the women were hungry to hear every detail of the corpse's discovery. They smiled. They simpered. But they were like crows pecking at his thoughts and he refused to oblige them. Anne was expecting him back, no doubt poised and ready with another chore. Besides, his mind was too full for chatter. Nodding to them as courteously as he was able, he made his excuses and went on his way.

4.

The following Sunday Caleb found himself facing a strange ordeal in Fishpool's church.

The entire village was gathered as usual and the parson was delivering his sermon, rambling and repeating himself, talking in tedious circles. Sir Robert and Lady Fairbrother dozed, as was their privilege, while the rest of the congregation was condemned to a purgatory of boredom. At last they came to the prayers: ones for the souls of the dead, and most particularly for those lost at sea.

"Thomas Smith" had been added to the long litany. The name dropped like a stone into a still pool. The moment it was uttered, ripples of curiosity spread the length and breadth of the church.

When the service was done at last, Sir Robert was gently roused by William Benson. Without even a nod at the parson he and Lady Fairbrother proceeded down the aisle, looking neither to left nor right, bestowing neither look nor greeting on any person present. Every head was lowered respectfully, every back almost bent double as they passed by.

The fact that Anne had been Lady Fairbrother's maid had always seemed to lend her an even greater degree of repulsiveness, for both would turn their heads to the side as though a foul smell emanated from the place in which Caleb's aunt sat. Or perhaps it was his presence next to her that provoked their reaction.

That Sunday Caleb expected them to glide past in their customary fashion and indeed Lady Fairbrother did so. But from the corner of his eye he saw a pair of gentlemanly legs stop and then turn towards him.

Not wishing to invite another blow from William Benson, Caleb kept his head lowered. It was not until he was addressed that he looked up.

"You, boy. Caleb Chappell."

The moment he raised his chin, Sir Robert's eyes latched on to his.

Caleb had once heard tell of how a rabbit could be transfixed by the gaze of a weasel, and unable to flee though its life was in peril. He had thought it foolish, but in that moment he perfectly understood how the creature felt.

Sir Robert spoke again. Before the whole congregation he asked, "You found Thomas Smith, did you not?"

"I found a man, sir," Caleb said carefully. "I hear his name is Thomas Smith."

"And do you doubt it?"

"I could not say who it was. I did not know Thomas Smith while he lived, so I wouldn't recognize him dead."

"The parson has discovered he was Thomas Smith, and he is a man of God." Sir Robert tilted his head slightly, waiting for a response.

There was a moment of silence. Then Caleb said, "Indeed, sir. And I put my trust in him."

It was an adept move. Caleb referred to the Almighty but Sir Robert took him to be speaking of the parson. His eyes continued to bore into the lad, skewering him to the pew so that he could neither move nor turn his head. Letty had been right, Caleb thought: Benson was a mere lapdog. This was the pack leader. The wolf.

There was menace in every line of that aristocratic face. Sir Robert had no need to say aloud that Caleb must think no more, know no more, discover no more about Thomas Smith. His eyes warned him off so powerfully that words were unnecessary. He held Caleb's gaze for a few seconds longer. And then at last he turned away and Caleb could breathe again.

Only when the gentleman was out of the church and in his carriage, only when the sound of its departing wheels clattered on the cobbles was the rest of the congregation permitted to stir.

Caleb's heart was pounding, his mind racing, every inch of his flesh prickled with fearful excitement. Sir Robert had meant to silence him, humiliating him in front of the entire village like that, but all he had done was convince Caleb that something was deeply amiss. Why would a man like Sir Robert Fairbrother concern himself with a drowned sailor, much less discuss the matter with the likes of him? There was a mystery here, some secret evil was afoot. He had caught the scent of it, and now his blood was up.

He was aware of the parson standing in the porch watching him as he rose from the pew. When he reached the church door the parson's wife enquired after Caleb's well-being with what appeared to be sincere concern. He was braced for the parson's less sympathetic enquiries into his state of mind but was mercifully saved by one of the village crones – a talkative old maid – who engaged the couple in a long, rambling account of her various ailments.

Caleb noted the mound of fresh earth in the far corner of the churchyard. A new corpse had joined the silent army of the dead but was it Pa or the drunkard Thomas Smith? How was he to discover who truly lay in that grave?

Letty – who had now recovered from her cough – went on ahead because Anne had asked her to go to the river's mouth and gather cockles. Caleb would have gone in pursuit of her but his aunt put her arm through his to keep him beside her.

Dorcas toddled along in front, but she had only recently taken her first steps and suddenly stumbled over her own feet and fell, cracking her head on a stone. The wound was small but bled profusely, as cuts to the head often do, and the little girl started crying with shock and pain. The noise she was making would surely wake the dead!

Releasing her hold on his arm, Anne ran to Dorcas. She was distracted. Here, at last, was his opportunity. Running, ducking swiftly through the side gate, he left the churchyard and went in pursuit of Letty.

He found her on the sand. The tide was ebbing fast, beaching fishing vessels, turning them onto their sides, and the stink of salt and sodden timber was overwhelming. Letty had a rake and a pail and was already hard at work along with maybe a dozen others. When she saw Caleb approaching she frowned.

There was nowhere in the village that they would not be noticed. Nowhere they could go that the gossips would not see, and discuss, and remark on them being out alone together. Caleb did not doubt that their whispers would reach his aunt's ears before they returned home and yet here was his chance. He had to take it.

"My aunt has sent me to help you," he said loudly for the benefit of the other cockle-pickers.

Letty's frown deepened. Her fingers tightened around the rake. She said nothing.

He bent to pick shells from the sand she had turned over. "The parson's lying," he reminded her quietly. "Those were your words. What did you mean?"

She straightened up at that and thrust her chin out as though accepting the challenge. "I know this river," she said. "I know this shore. Currents. Tides."

"Well," Caleb said. "What of it?"

"Look, see... Whoever he was, he didn't go falling in the river off Tawpuddle quay."

"Does it never happen?"

"Oh, it happens often enough. We get a fair few every year. Drunken sailors lose their footing, fall in, drown. But they get washed up on the far side of the river, opposite Fishpool, this side of the bar. With your man? I'd say he died a long way from shore. The river didn't carry him out. The sea carried him in." Caleb must have looked sceptical for she added hotly, "I'm telling the truth."

"And so am I," he countered. "I know what I saw."

She sniffed. "There's a fair few gentlemen wear rings. How do you know it was your Pa's?"

"It was unmistakeable. It belonged to his father." He described the insignia.

"You knew the ring. And yet you didn't know his face? Your own pa?"

"No. It was..." He could not begin to describe the corpse's features. The very thought made his gorge rise. But there was no need to tell Letty: it seemed she already knew. She nodded, sparing him from having to say more.

"Look," she said, "you might have known the ring. Doesn't mean the man wearing it was your father. I hear men get hungry in gaol. He sold it, maybe. Traded it for bread."

"Impossible. The ring was part of him. It would not come off his finger." Caleb recalled with a stab of grief how the ring had lodged tight beneath Pa's knuckle. Over the years his skin had grown around it like the bark of a tree.

"Fair enough." She rubbed her face with the back of her hand then said, "He'd been in the water a while if you couldn't recognize him. Days. Water's cold this time of year. Might even have been weeks."

"Then he can't have fallen in the night before he was found. It was Pa, I'm certain of it."

"I want to see the proof."

"The ring? But the man is buried."

"Well, then," said Letty, as if nothing could be simpler or more straightforward. "We'll just have to un-bury him, won't we?"

5.

"Un-bury him?" Caleb echoed. Struggling to keep his voice low, he asked Letty two questions. "How? When?"

Her answers came back neat as a pat of butter. "Tonight. The parson keeps the gravedigger's shovel in his yard. Moon's full, so we won't be needing a lantern. We'll wait until the village is asleep. Then we'll go find out if the drowned man was wearing a ring or not."

"He will be."

"Perhaps. You're not to speak a word to anyone, do you hear me? Not anyone."

"Who do you imagine I would share this secret with?" Caleb was exasperated. "Even if I were a blabbermouth... Letty, there is not a soul in this village I could talk to!"

She looked at him. For a moment her expression softened. And then she was fierce again, stern and hard, but her words were at odds with her face. "Me. You've got me to talk to now."

* * *

The rest of that Sunday passed slowly. They said nothing more to each other but Caleb was acutely aware of Letty's every move. When night fell his aunt took Dorcas and climbed the ladder to bed as usual. Before Letty followed she gave him a look that told him her resolve had not wavered. Tonight they would be gravedigging.

He didn't think he liked her. He certainly didn't understand her. But whatever her faults, Letty was in possession of a great deal of courage, and Caleb knew he had need of that just now.

There was no watchman to call the hour. No church clock to chime. It was a matter of waiting for the night to pass. Praying for the village to sleep, and sleep soundly. Waiting and praying, praying and waiting, all over again.

A full moon there may have been, but its light did not penetrate into the cottage. There was some small glow from the fire's embers but that was all. Caleb lay in the dark and listened to the breathing of the family above becoming slower and deeper.

When Letty moved, she moved quietly, but sound behaves differently in the dark. Each creak of floorboard, each rustle of cloth is magnified. A breath becomes a shout, a footfall akin to the blast of a cannon. Letty walked across the attic floor slowly. With every step she took he was in an agony of suspense, thinking his aunt would wake at any moment and ask what her stepdaughter was doing. As she descended the ladder each rung groaned in protest under her weight and yet neither Anne nor Dorcas woke. Together Caleb and Letty padded across the slate floor and slipped from the cottage into the street.

He followed where she led, not up the road they usually walked to church, but along a path that skirted the marsh flats and then climbed through scrub up the hill to the parsonage. When they reached the house and she took the shovel from the yard the iron blade grated against cobbles, making a sound so harsh that Caleb expected the parson to peer from his window and demand to know their business.

As they crept towards the churchyard their breath hung like smoke on the cold night air. Caleb was sure he could hear trees sighing, leaves dying, the whisper of bats' wings, the slow slither of worms through soil. The village slept, but the world did not. Everything was alive. The very walls watched them.

Their noses would have led them to the place even had there been no moon. The scent of wet earth, freshly turned, was strong.

Caleb took the shovel from Letty. Was it not his father whose rest they disturbed?

He began to dig, but he was as inept with a shovel as he was with a pair of oars. He dug deep, sinking the blade so hard into the heavy clay soil that he could not at once lift its load. His hands slipped on the shaft and the earth tipped back into the hole.

Letty pushed him aside. She was deft and efficient, making light work of it. She dug swiftly, piling dirt onto the side of the hole. She was waist-deep when the shovel struck something other than earth. Cloth. Flesh.

With the change in sound came a stench. Putrefaction. Decay. Caleb fought the urge to vomit but Letty, it seemed, had a stronger stomach than he did. She did not even wrinkle her nose.

There was no coffin for this poor soul: there had been no one to pay for it. He was wrapped in a pauper's winding sheet and Letty had come ready with a knife. She slit it open and reached inside for the corpse's hands. Grasping his dead wrists, she held both up for Caleb's inspection.

The moon, however full, does not shine as bright as day, no matter what the song says. Yet, even in that cold, grey light he saw that the parson had not lied.

On the third finger of the corpse's right hand there was no ring.

Indeed, there was no finger.

The digit had been severed: hacked with a knife, the bone broken, the flesh ripped away.

Such brutality spoke of urgency. Of desperation.

It spoke of villainy.

Letty wasted no more time. One glance at Caleb was all: a look of naked fear. Then she was herself again, brisk and business-like, filling in the grave while Caleb helped push earth back in with his bare hands, covering the corpse, treading down the soil so the disturbance would not be observed. He followed her every whispered instruction. The shovel must be wiped clean on the grass. Returned. Their hands must be washed in the river, every trace of churchyard dirt removed from their persons. And all this without making a sound. They must both slide unnoticed into their places, as if they had done nothing but sleep through the long night.

The next day Caleb would have to go about his aunt's business in his customary fashion as though he was not burdened with the knowledge that Pa, his Pa, his beloved father, truly was dead.

And that someone was prepared to go to great lengths to conceal the fact.

6.

Knowing he was right and his wits were not addled was no comfort. What he and Letty had uncovered was deeper and darker and more dangerous than any sickness of the mind. Whoever had been so determined to hide Pa's true identity that they had taken a knife to his dead hand would not hesitate to do the same to Caleb's living flesh. There was a secret here that someone wished to protect and it would be wise to wipe the entire incident from his mind. For his own safety, for Letty's, he should forget it.

But that night as he lay by the fire's glowing embers, clutching Pa's puppets to his chest, Caleb could not rid himself of the sight of that corpse: bloated, stinking, and now mutilated. Wrapped in a pauper's winding sheet, rotting in the cold dark earth, lying in an unmarked grave with nobody to weep at his funeral, nobody to mourn his passing or honour his memory. The parson had not commended the soul of Joseph Chappell into the keeping of the Lord but that of the mythical Thomas Smith. Would the gates of heaven be closed against Pa in consequence?

There is power in a name. Through the years of his childhood Pa had always encouraged Caleb to find the right names for everything that he felt. Names could tame emotions, confine fears, govern passions. Language was what separated mankind from the brute beasts, Pa said. Words were what connected mankind to God.

But now there were none. None at all. There was no word, no phrase, no sentence even that was big enough to describe the grief, the anger, the fury that tore at Caleb's heart. Pa's life had been taken and that was hard enough to bear. But this? To steal away his name was beyond enduring! Pa was the best of men, the best of fathers: his name should be honoured. Men should speak of him with respect; they should know of his passing and mark it with tributes and words of praise. Not this. Never this. Joseph Chappell had been wiped out, annihilated. Nothing could be done for Pa. Nothing, nothing, nothing!

Unless...

Caleb sat up suddenly. The sack of puppets rolled across the floor.

Suppose he found out how Pa had drowned? If he could uncover the truth... If he could see justice done... Why, then he could return to Pa his name. Did he not owe him that much?

Pa had promised to return, come hell or high water. Well, Caleb would make a promise of his own: he'd discover by what strange, twisting path his father had been washed up on the very beach he walked upon. It would be done, whatever the risk, whatever the cost.

But having made his solemn vow, he hadn't the slightest idea how to proceed.

7.

At around noon the next day Caleb went out to gather driftwood but one glance over the marsh flats showed him that the sea had delivered much more than he alone could carry. He returned to the cottage, calling for Letty to come and help. Anne looked a little troubled, but they were desperately short of firewood. Necessity overcame any other concerns.

A slow, steady drizzle soaked them while they worked but they had at least a chance of some conversation.

"Who would have severed Pa's finger?" he asked her. "The men who carried his body to the parsonage? Who were they?"

Letty frowned, considering. "It was Stanley and George. They'd have done whatever they were told to, I reckon, but they're not good at keeping their mouths shut. They'd have likely said something by now."

"But who else? The parson?"

Letty was already shaking her head. She had evidently

been giving the matter as much consideration as Caleb and she had the advantage of knowing the people concerned so much better than he did. "You're taking it from the wrong end."

"How so?"

"When you found him – your Pa – how long did it take you to fetch help?"

"I ran. But I was distressed and the sand was so sodden – I didn't move fast."

"And you left him lying there?"

Caleb bridled. "What else could I do?"

She shrugged. "Nothing. You did what you needed to. But anyone might have come by, see? Cut his finger off before they come and get him. Stanley and George – well, let's just say they're not the sharpest men in the village. Whether there was a ring or whether there was a missing finger, I don't suppose neither of them would have noticed."

"But you said the parson was lying."

"And so he was. Lying about the tides, I meant. He doesn't know anything about the river or the sea – he was talking off the top of his head."

"But why would he lie about a sailor going in the water at Tawpuddle?"

"I don't know. But maybe he never saw the ring. That finger could have been off before he came riding home – anyone could have stopped him along the way, told him you'd lost your mind. I don't know that he even set foot in the outhouse, did he, to see for himself?"

"He named the man as Thomas Smith."

"Did he though? He said he was going to make enquiries. Doesn't mean he did it himself. He'd have sent a servant, I expect. I reckon someone's feeding him stories, telling him there wasn't a ring, saying it wasn't your Pa and you're soft in the head, that it was this Thomas Smith, and him all too willing to believe it."

"Who could be spreading such lies?"

"Don't know. Truth is, could be just about anybody."

A silence fell between them. Caleb, suddenly daunted by the scale of the task he had set himself, had nothing more to say. Letty had filled a basket with wood, yet she did not return to the cottage. Instead she stood, looking out to sea, her eyes seemingly fixed on the island in the bay. He noticed that her mouth twisted – as if she wanted to ask something more, but couldn't quite bring herself to do so. He didn't press her. He'd learned from Pa that silence can sometimes be used to great effect.

Years ago he and Pa had eaten in an inn and when they rose to leave Caleb had discovered that the bottle – which had been brimful of coins – was missing. The innkeeper called all his people together and invited Pa to question them, but Pa merely stood and slowly, slowly, slowly looked from one to the next. At last the kitchen lad broke down in tears, and retrieved the bottle from where he had hidden it.

Later, Pa said, "If you shout, if you accuse – why then, folk will defend themselves by instinct. They'll bluster and lie and convince themselves they're telling the truth. But if you say nothing people feel they need to fill the silence. It plays on their guilt, their fears. They credit you with all manner of thoughts whether you're thinking them or not. And then they feel the need to explain themselves."

It was a powerful lesson that Caleb had taken to heart. So he stood on the marshy ground not taking his eyes from Letty's face but uttering not a word until the quiet stretched out to breaking point and she felt compelled to ask, "When did he sail, your Pa?"

Caleb was taken aback. "I don't know. They told me nothing at the gaol."

"He was in Torcester, wasn't he?" Letty persisted. "Convicted back in the summer, you said."

"Yes."

"I expect he left for the colonies not long after."

There was another long pause while Letty chewed her lip. Caleb had the impression that she knew something – that she was thinking, speculating, considering how much to reveal. Pa would have let her stew in her own juices so he did the same.

At last she spoke again. "Where'd he sail from?"

"I don't know. I left and walked here like he told me to. I know nothing of what happened to him afterwards."

Yet another pause. Yet more lip chewing. And then

Letty sighed. "I hadn't ever seen it before. Can't get it out of my head. I was down that way, see? Must have been a couple of weeks or so before you showed up. I watched a ship loaded. Cloth. Bales of wool. Nothing out the common line. But then there was this group of convicts, brought up from someplace."

Caleb was aghast. "And all these months you have said nothing of this? Did they come from Torcester?"

"No... At least I don't think so. Barnford, some folks said, though maybe that was wrong. You know what gossip's like round here: empty as a barrel of air, most of it. There were others said they'd come from Tordown but probably no one knew for sure. It was just a group of felons, no one cared who they were or where they were from. They were cargo: same as salt cod or bales of wool. I don't suppose even the crew knew their names. Didn't seem to matter. There were twelve men. Might be your Pa was one of them."

Caleb struggled to understand. Could it be that while he'd been walking, following every twist and turn of the river, Pa had overtaken him on a journey to the county's north coast?

If Pa had come by road, if the convicts had been loaded onto a cart ... why then, they could probably have made the journey much more quickly than Caleb had been able to. That his father should have sailed from the port so close to Anne's home was a strange chance. But though Tawpuddle was not the nearest port to Torcester it was the largest, so perhaps it was no stranger than anything else that had happened since that market day.

To think of Letty watching Pa loaded onto a ship, regarding him with the indifferent curiosity of a stranger, was terrible. "If you'd seen him, you wouldn't have known him."

"No, I wouldn't." When she looked at Caleb her eyes were full of misery. "Their own mothers wouldn't have recognized them. They were covered in filth. I've never seen men in such a sorry state."

They were both quiet for a while, Letty haunted by the memory of what she had seen, Caleb trying to imagine it. At last Letty broke the silence. "I'll tell you something peculiar. They were in manacles, fetters, all those men, and none of them fitted properly. Those irons were dug right into their skin. Every one of them was bleeding. They were put down in the hold. Chained up, like slaves."

The thought was unbearable. "Perhaps Pa found a way to escape. He could swim. Perhaps he thought he could make it back to land."

"Maybe. But last night ... that body ... his wrists weren't marked. The skin must have healed. I'd say he'd been out of fetters a while before he went in the water."

"Pa was a skilled man. Good with his hands. Perhaps they found a use for him. Could they have unchained him? Made him work? Could he have taken a chance and jumped overboard?"

"It's possible."

"How else could he have got in the water?"

Letty considered. "Died on board maybe," she said thoughtfully, but then threw her hands up and blew out a mouthful of air in exasperation. "That doesn't explain it either! When a man dies on board ship he gets sewn into a canvas shroud. They weigh it down with stones, so it'll sink to the bottom." She stared out to the horizon.

For a moment Letty had a look of Pa: Pa concentrating, settling himself before starting one of his tales. Perhaps once again he was looking at this wrong. The finding of Pa's body was the end of this story. In order to place events in their correct pattern, in order to make sense of the whole he should begin at the beginning.

He had little hope that she would recall the name of the ship: dozens of vessels sailed in and out of Tawpuddle on a daily basis and the one she had seen had departed four months or so ago. But he would not know the answer unless he asked the question.

"Do you recall the name of the ship the convicts were loaded on to?"

Her answer came back at once. "The *Linnet*."

He laughed in surprise. "Your memory's extraordinary!"

"It's not the kind of thing I could go forgetting." Letty's tone wiped the smile from Caleb's face. "The *Linnet* is the ship my father sailed on."

8.

For some moments Caleb was speechless. Was this a joke?
But no ... she seemed sincere. Barely controlling his temper,
he said, "Letty, why didn't you tell me this before?"

"Because of Anne." Letty's voice was a whisper.

"Anne? What has she to do with this?" he demanded.

When Letty lifted her face there was such anguish on
it that Caleb's anger melted away. "Nothing. That's just the
point." She began to talk, the words coming thick and fast
as though she wanted to spit them out before they choked
her. "Anne doesn't ever come and see Father off – the sea
scares her stiff and she hates watching him sail – so she
didn't know there were convicts on that ship and I didn't
want to tell her. You know how she is. She feels things so
deeply, she's so soft-hearted! I thought it best to let her
think there was nothing unusual about the cargo his ship
was carrying because she'd tear herself to pieces thinking
of those convicts. There was something shaming about it,
Caleb, something dirty and vile for all it's a legal trade.

I didn't know what it might do to her so I decided she didn't need to know anything about it. I knew Father wouldn't say anything – I saw the look on his face when they were loaded on board: he was mortified, but he doesn't get a say in what a ship carries. So I kept quiet, but then you came along talking about how your Pa had got himself transported and how you'd walked here and I started wondering if one of those men might have been him, but I couldn't say anything then either because how could I tell Anne that maybe, just maybe, her husband was carrying her brother off to America like he was a piece of salt pork? And how could I tell you that maybe, just maybe, my father might be the gaoler of yours? I didn't think there was any sense saying anything because it wasn't like I could change any of it." She drew a breath and then exclaimed, "And it might not be true! I don't know where those convicts were from, don't know their names, don't know anything for sure. I just kept hoping and praying I was wrong."

Letty was sniffing now and swallowing as though she was trying to hold tears at bay. He felt the urge to put his arms around her but feared she'd push him away. Instead he said awkwardly, "I wish you hadn't carried this for so long alone."

"Well," she said, wiping a hand across her face. "It's out now."

"It is. And I will find out what happened. It may be hard but I need to know the truth. I think you do too?" Her face was pale, her expression grim, but she nodded. "How would I find out if Pa was on the *Linnet*?" he continued. "Do they keep records of such things?"

"In the customs house, yes. The officers write down everything that goes out from Tawpuddle. Everything that comes in too. They're over the ships like rats, poking into every nook and cranny, checking the cargo. They've got to tax it, see, for the king. Bill of lading, they call it."

Caleb recalled the phrase: he'd heard it the day he'd first arrived in Tawpuddle. He remembered the place he'd stopped at to ask the name of the town, where men sat in a line at desks and one had demanded if he was off the *Mary-Louise* and if he'd brought the bill of lading – that must be the customs house. "I'll go there, then. Yes, that would be the place to start."

It wouldn't be easy, he thought, and it must be done secretly. No one but Letty could know. But here at last was a definite task: a firm course of action. He felt his mood lightening.

Taking a deep breath, Letty picked up her basket of driftwood. Caleb shouldered his. Together they walked back to the cottage.

Having made the decision, Caleb wanted to go to the customs house at once, but it was in Tawpuddle and he couldn't leave his aunt's house without good reason. He and Anne had a job hemming linen sheets for a trader in the town and it was three long, frustrating days before the task was completed to her satisfaction.

When the sheets were at last finished, Anne tied them into a bundle. To Caleb's annoyance she'd decided to deliver them herself, but Dorcas was fretful that morning, tired and tearful yet unable to settle or to rest, so Caleb volunteered to go in Anne's place.

He made the delivery. He collected the payment. And then he made his way towards the customs house.

Everyone in Fishpool knew each other's business inside out and back to front. It would no doubt be the same in Tawpuddle. He could not be seen to be lingering outside the place without people noticing and if word got around that he was looking for information concerning his father he could be in the gravest of dangers. And so he strolled along the quay as if he'd been bred to a life of idleness, seeming to admire the many ships whose masts bristled from the water like the spines of a hedgehog.

The tides had been a mystery to him when he first arrived – he'd found the constant shifting of water strange and unnerving – but after several months at his aunt's he'd got their measure and had timed his arrival carefully. Now, at high water, the port was at its busiest, bringing ships in while others prepared to sail the moment the tide turned. Cargoes would need to be inspected, accounted for. Letty had told him that Tawpuddle's fishing fleet was due to depart for the cod banks of Newfoundland that very day and it seemed she was right. The quay was in chaos and the customs officers were fully occupied.

He was careful not to get in anyone's way. As well as the customs men there were plenty of seamen whose families had gathered to watch their men sail. Sweethearts clinging to their lovers; wives holding tight to their children while they bade their husbands goodbye; children embracing their fathers as if for the last time.

When Pa had sailed there had been no one to call farewell or wish him a safe voyage. How lonely, how desolate it must have been. Caleb tried to shake free the picture that Letty had planted in his head: Pa, filthy and in shackles. He could not allow himself to think of that now. He needed to concentrate on the task ahead.

When he drew near to the customs house he noticed that the door of the building was ajar and the place apparently unmanned. He glanced to the left, as if his attention had been caught by something of interest in the high street. Heart in his mouth, he crossed over, apparently making for the chandler's. But as he passed the customs house he slipped inside, pulling the door closed behind him.

He coughed noisily. No one emerged to see who'd come in. He was alone.

A line of desks. Rows of shelves, groaning under a weight of thick ledgers. A ticking clock, loud and ominous in the empty room. His forehead began to prickle with sweat. He didn't know what he was looking for, or where to begin. He wished Letty was with him but she wasn't. He had to rely on his own wits now.

Lying on the desk was an open ledger. It seemed as good a place as any to start. Pa had taught him to read but printed words were one thing – to decipher these men's handwriting was more time-consuming. Their letters looped and curled and wound back on themselves as much as the river. Taking a breath to steady himself, he ran his finger along the line of writing and gradually made sense of the thing. The name of the ship and the date of sailing were written at the top of each page, and each bill was kept in strict chronological order. He started to turn back through the heavy pages but this volume went back only two months so there was no mention of the *Linnet*.

It must be in one of the volumes standing on the shelves then. Acutely aware of the clock's ticking he crossed the room, frantically scanning their spines, and found that – thank God! – the customs men were meticulous in their approach to record-keeping. It did not take him long to locate the correct volume and, heaving it down, he began leafing through the pages. Eventually he found the sheets from the month of July, when Letty said the *Linnet* had sailed.

There had been a vast number of vessels going in and out of the port that month. It took him some time – time in which his palms itched, his heart pounded and the sweat began to trickle down the sides of his face – before Caleb found what he was looking for.

There it was. Black ink on cream paper.

"Outwards, Port of Tawpuddle, in the ship the *Linnet*, British-built about 70 tons. Luke Slater, a British man, captain for this present voyage to Maryland in America with ten crew besides."

The crew's names were listed. One of them was Edward Avery – Letty's father. And then came the details of the cargo.

"365 bushels of Spanish salt

4 boxes cutlery ware

2 casks haberdashery

17 bales containing Brocade, Broadcloth, Stockings,
    Duffles, Kerseys, Serges

5 casks nails

1 hogshead cordage

1 box Lace and Silks

1 box Hats

7 bales Irish Linen

7 bales wool

6 hampers wrought pewter

on account of Sir Robert Fairbrother."

The name jerked in his head like a fish caught on a line. Sir Robert! Was he, too, linked to the *Linnet*? Did Letty know of this? Caleb was gripped with sudden fury. Was this another secret she'd kept? Why hadn't she told him of it?

Forcing himself to keep calm, he read on:

"12 convicts brought from Torcester: Jack Lancey, Mark Andrews, Thomas Sinnett, John Kingscot, Henry Meddon,

Edwin Hampton, Robert Buckleigh, Walter Coombs, William Hockin, Edward Braddick, Richard Brendon, Joseph Chappell."

Joseph Chappell.

Caleb traced Pa's name with his finger. To see it written gave him a grim kind of satisfaction. It was true then: Pa had sailed for the Americas from Tawpuddle shortly before Caleb had arrived at his aunt's house.

It was a start. He would get to the bottom of this. Slowly, inch by inch, Caleb would creep towards the truth. He would find out why Pa's body had washed up on the beach almost five months after he had sailed.

And he would expose the villain responsible for it.

9.

His mind on fire with the implications of what he'd read, Caleb failed to notice that one of the customs men had finished his inspections on the quayside. Only when he heard a hand on the door latch did he look up.

The man outside had paused and was greeting a passing acquaintance. Neither had seen him, but Caleb couldn't leave the building now without both of them doing so. There was no time to close the ledger or return it to its place. He fled. There was nowhere for him to go but up the narrow staircase, nowhere for him to conceal himself but flat on the floor, under a sideboard. He lay there and tried to steady himself as one by one the customs men returned from the quay and took their places at their desks. If he didn't grow calmer they'd hear the noisy hammering of his heart.

There he stayed, expecting to hear a cry of rage when the officers saw their ledgers had been disturbed, expecting them to begin a search and for him to be dragged out by his heels and compelled to explain himself. But there was nothing. Through a crack in the floorboards he watched the movement of the men below. One of them closed the ledger Caleb had opened, and replaced it on the shelf. He didn't even remark on it being out of place. There was the occasional hum of conversation, the scratching of pens on paper, the creak of floorboards as they went about their work. Slowly his frantic heartbeat steadied. All he could do was lie there and wait and watch.

He became fascinated by the men who were going about their work. They all seemed to be orderly, decent, respectable people, ensuring regularity of business and fairness in administering the king's taxes. Mariners came and went, passing over papers for signature, checking records. Those newly into port from long voyages were weary, stinking of the sea, eager to be off home to their families. Those about to depart were on edge, impatient to get underway. But then a ship's captain entered, declaring he had brought in the *Charming Sally*'s record for their inspection. When the ledger was laid on the desk directly below Caleb's peephole he saw that coins had been slid between the sheets. Coins which were then deftly palmed by a customs officer before he signed off the record as accurate and agreed. He had not had time, surely, to read a single line. The captain bade him a cheerful farewell and left. As Caleb lay there in his dusty hiding place that long afternoon the same thing happened time and again. It seemed to be quite routine for a captain or first mate to slip a few coins between the sheets of his ship's record in order to get the signature the law required.

Dishonesty. Corruption. Caleb's lip curled in distaste. Oh, he knew there were pickpockets and thieves in the world: he'd kept a sharp lookout for them every market day in Torcester. But Pa had looked upon such people with a kindlier eye than Caleb. "Some are rogues, it's true," he'd said. "But most are poor and desperate."

It was the wealthy whose morals Pa had more often questioned. "Look around you. Magistrates, ministers, members of parliament, even the king – all of them skimming a little cream off the top for themselves. None of them get called thief! None of them swing on Gallows Hill. There are plenty of men in the city of Torcester who steal from those who have nothing. Only they call it business."

Caleb might be an innocent in the ways of seafaring men but he knew a bribe when he saw one. For all their apparent vigilance the customs men could be bought. By the end of the afternoon Caleb had begun to wonder if there was an honest man in the whole of Tawpuddle.

He stayed hidden until the day's end. When the men left the building, they locked him inside. His only means of escape was an upstairs window, through which he squeezed, praying for the darkness to conceal him. Hanging by his fingernails from the ledge, he dropped into the yard, sinking knee-deep into a midden heap.

It broke his fall, but landing in such extremes of filth was a high price to pay for keeping his ankles intact. As he looked in disgust at the decaying dung and fresh excrement into which his feet had disappeared he thought he caught a movement out of the corner of his eye. He froze, scanning the shadows. A soft thud. A scrabble. A crunch. And then a cat emerged, a mouse dangling from its jaws. Thereafter all was still.

He extricated himself from the heap. There was no time to get clean. He must return to his aunt's, and quickly. He'd been gone the greater part of the day and she'd want to know what he'd been doing. Letty might have thought up some tale to tell Anne. Or she might not. He felt strangely uncertain about her since he'd seen Sir Robert's name on the *Linnet*'s bill of lading. Why had she kept it from him? Could she be relied on? He didn't know. Perhaps he'd better invent some plausible lie for Anne himself.

But there were no questions asked on Caleb's return. Indeed, Anne barely looked at him. She was beside herself with worry.

Dorcas, who had been fretful and unwell when Caleb left that morning, had worsened. The child was lying by the hearth, tossing and turning in a high fever.

10.

Dorcas was slicked with sweat, her skin burning to the touch, but shivering so violently that her teeth chattered. When he entered the cottage the sight of her was enough to drive all thoughts of the customs house from Caleb's mind. Almost all. Letty glanced at him and he gave her a brief nod to confirm what she'd long feared. A look of suffering passed across her face that pierced him to the core. How foolish he'd been! She wasn't a child: playing games, keeping secrets. He'd been so wrapped up in Pa's fate that he'd given no thought to Letty's feelings. Her father was caught up in this murky business and the pain and shame weighed heavy on her. But she would not let Anne see any of it. Her face cleared almost at once. Her jaw was thrust forward. He realized then that her expression of furious indifference was an armour she donned to protect herself. He'd seen beneath it now and would be more careful with her in the future.

Soon after Caleb's return, Anne tried to carry Dorcas up to bed, but the girl screamed out in pain when she was touched. Anne sank to her knees, panic-stricken, frozen with fear. It was Caleb who fetched down the straw mattress from the loft; Caleb who stoked up the fire and put a kettle of water on to boil; Letty who tried to make Dorcas comfortable as the fever grew stronger, who washed her down when she soiled herself and wrapped her in clean linen. And all the while Anne sat mute and trembling and pale as death.

A fever is a terrible thing: terrible for Dorcas to endure, terrible for the rest of them to watch. Caleb had never seen anything like it. The child tossed and turned and whimpered. None of them slept that night.

Caleb longed to seize the disease, to fight and wrestle, to kick and pummel it into submission, but he could do nothing but sit and pray and hope that dawn would bring Dorcas some relief.

It did not.

By first light Dorcas was even worse. Caleb and Letty looked at each other, seeing their alarm reflected in the other's eyes. The child's colour was ghastly, her eyes bright but unseeing. She shrank away when they tried to touch her. When Anne rose to her feet, saying she would fetch fresh water to bathe Dorcas, her legs buckled beneath her and she fell to the floor. Her brow was sheened with sweat, her palms clammy. Caleb lifted Anne as gently as he could and laid her beside her daughter on the mattress.

That day, Letty and Caleb shared the invalids' care. First, Letty went to the well while Caleb tended them by the fire. Later he gathered wood and she took his seat, watching, praying.

Neither mother nor child would eat, so Caleb spooned what little ale they would take into their mouths. Letty moistened their brows with cooling water until both went into spasms of shivering and Anne begged that they stoke up the fire for she was cold, so very cold.

As the day wore on, Anne and Dorcas slept in snatches, giving their nurses a little time to rest and talk.

"Sir Robert's name was on the bill," Caleb told Letty quietly. "You didn't tell me he had an interest in the *Linnet*."

She looked puzzled. "It's no secret."

"I thought him just a landlord."

"He owns more than half the ships that sail in and out of Tawpuddle. I'm sorry ... I thought everyone knew that."

"He's the *Linnet's* owner?"

"Yes. It was his father who had her built thirty or more years since. She was the finest ship in Tawpuddle, in her day, but she never once sailed to the Americas in all those years." She paused for a moment. Sighed. Shook her head. "There was something wrong from the moment Father signed up for that voyage. I knew it, but I couldn't put my finger on what it was. Benson came looking for him. Took him off up to the manor. That had never happened before. Usually Father would pick his own ship down on the quay at Tawpuddle: sign on with a captain he liked. He was glad of Sir Robert's offer of work, he said, but he was unsettled after he took it. Restless, right until the day they sailed. He's a good man, Caleb, and a patient one: I'd never known him raise his voice even. But all that changed. Suddenly he was so quick to anger, so slow to calm down, not like himself at all. He never said what ailed him even though I almost wore my tongue out asking. Then I heard the talk. The *Linnet* had been fitted out for the crossing, see, but word was that she wasn't sound. I told Father, but he said they were all damned fools, that the *Linnet* was fine – couldn't anything be safer than a grand old girl like her. I had to take his word for it. Only then I saw her sail…" Her voice trailed away.

"And what of it?" Caleb prompted.

"Her rigging was old, her sails were ragged. She hadn't been fitted out at all. She was low in the water, too. Overloaded, I'd have said. Father's been at sea since he was eleven years old: there's nothing he doesn't know about it. I never thought to see him set sail in a ship that looked like it wouldn't last the voyage. So why did he?" Letty looked towards Anne, who was tossing from side to side and mumbling fretfully in her sleep. Kneeling beside her stepmother, she carefully replaced the blanket Anne had thrown aside. "I never told her, of course. It would have frayed her nerves to pieces."

They were both silent a while. Caleb perceived that Letty had been as deeply troubled these past months as he had. Secrets had eaten away at her and she'd had no one to share them with. Well, all that was different now. But why would an experienced mariner like Edward Avery sail in a ship that was not seaworthy? It was lunacy. No sane man would do it willingly. But maybe Edward had not been a willing crewman…?

Caleb had seen enough of Sir Robert Fairbrother to know how much power he wielded over his tenants. Even the parson's living was in his gift. Perhaps Letty's father had been threatened – forced – into joining the *Linnet*'s crew. He checked that Anne still slept then asked Letty softly, "Could pressure have been put on him? Is it possible Sir Robert forced your father into something against his judgement?"

"Sir bleeding-high-and-mighty Robert could have forced anyone into doing anything if he chose. But why would he? Why would anyone send a ship out to sea that isn't sound? He's a rich man but not so wealthy that the loss of the *Linnet* wouldn't be a bitter blow. There isn't a man on Earth would want to risk a ship going down."

She did not have to remind Caleb what the loss of a vessel could mean. Hadn't such a catastrophe ruined his grandfather?

Letty continued, "I saw Sir Robert down on the quay the day she sailed. First time he's ever bothered to see one of his ships off."

"Did his face give anything away?"

Letty shook her head. "He's a hard man to fathom – doesn't show anything most of the time. He lost a child a few years back. The boy was took with fever. Died. When they came to bury him, Lady Fairbrother was screaming and crying – you could hear her right through the village. She was beside herself. But him? By all accounts he stood there and watched them lay his boy in the vault and never even shed a tear."

Letty stopped, for the same thought was passing through both their heads: fever was no respecter of rank or wealth. If it could take a rich man's son it could as easily take Dorcas and Anne.

It was some time before Letty added, "I'll tell you something else. William Benson was there with Sir Robert on the quay when the *Linnet* sailed. You know what he's like – face like a slab of slate most of the time. But that day, when he saw the convicts going on board, he started grinning from one ear to the other. He was excited, like he was in on some big secret."

Caleb's head had begun to ache. He rubbed at his temples. "Whatever it is – your father will tell us what happened to Pa. This mystery will be resolved when he returns."

"Maybe," said Letty, dabbing her sister's forehead. "Pray God we're all still alive to see that day."

11.

Letty fell sick two days after Anne. At first she was tired – so tired she could barely lift a bucket or put one foot in front of the other. Then the fever took hold: sweat poured off her body, and her eyes became glazed and distant like those of her sister and stepmother.

Caleb – who remained in stubborn good health – was left to nurse all three, to cool their foreheads, to clean them, to wash their soiled linen and to spoon drink into their mouths, to collect wood for the fire and fetch water from the well. To pray and pray and pray for the Lord to preserve them, for he had not realized how much this family meant to him until he feared he might lose them all.

Dorcas was plagued by dreams but what ran through her head he could only imagine. Stroking her hair from her face, he told her over and over again, "I am here, I am here. I will protect you." But she remained lost in a nightmare landscape of her own and he could not reach her.

His aunt in her delirium would suddenly seize Caleb by

the arm and demand, "Is it you?" Her hands would reach for his cheeks, pulling him down until his face was within an inch or two of her own. She seemed almost ready to kiss him, but then, discerning his features, her own would fall into lines of disappointment. On one occasion she demanded, "Where is he? Where is your father? Where's he gone? Where's he gone?" She was clearly distressed but Caleb had no answer that would soothe her. What was he to say? That Pa was lying in the graveyard under a false name? Or the truth as the parson would have it – that he was in America doing Lord alone knew what? How could he tell her that her own husband had been part of the crew that had carried Pa away? Caleb was so dumbfounded by all he knew – and all he did not – that he spoke not a word.

And Letty? Letty was the most terrifying of the three. When she sank into the delirium she said nothing, but simply stared at Caleb with furious eyes and a jaw clamped so tight shut he feared she would bite through her own tongue.

One morning when they were all sleeping he left the house to draw water from the well. He might have hoped for some neighbourly feeling, some measure of sympathetic concern, but he encountered only enmity and suspicion. "Why had he alone not sickened?" the gossips asked each other in voices pitched plenty loud enough for him to hear. "He must have carried the contagion to his aunt's. A lad like him couldn't be a healthy thing to have in a house. Hadn't they said so since the bastard arrived? Perhaps it was divine judgement. Punishment for some terrible vice. Didn't the parson preach last Sunday about the sins of the fathers? What could he have meant, but to warn the village against the darkie?"

The next day, worse came. The gossips decided it was witchcraft. Sorcery. Heathen devilry. Caleb had – until the fever came – gone to church every Sunday but "if you think about it, well then … a darkie can't really be a Christian, can he? He probably doesn't even have a soul. There surely can't be men like him in heaven? Leaving sooty handprints on the angels' gowns? God wouldn't allow it!"

Caleb had never felt as lonely or as miserable as those interminable, exhausting days and nights he tended Dorcas, Anne and then Letty. A week passed. They lay senseless and helpless upon the floor and still he did not sicken, and yet watching them suffer was perhaps a worse torment.

When – after almost two weeks – it was plain that all his nursing was not enough, Caleb went running to bring help from Tawpuddle.

The surgeon who came back with him would not even enter the house. He looked at Anne and Dorcas and Letty from the safety of the doorway and announced that he could work a cure, but that he would not lift a finger unless he was first paid.

Caleb cursed himself. He should have expected this. Pa always said that physicians were charlatans and surgeons were butchers, both as likely to kill their patients as to cure them. But Pa was dead and Caleb was desperate. He handed over the hard-earned money they had so carefully set aside to pay the rent. He had no choice. If they died what point was there in keeping a roof over his own head?

With brutal roughness the surgeon bled his patients until the basin was filled once, twice, three times. And then, as he left, he pressed a bottle of medicine into Caleb's hands and instructed him to dose them with it three times daily. What was in it he would not say, but when Caleb uncorked the bottle it looked and smelled as though it was nothing but watered-down treacle.

They were all three quieter that night but that was worse than when they had been calling out in their delirium. He sat listening to their rasping breath, dreading that each inhalation would be the last, that each exhalation would turn into a death rattle.

For two more days and nights they seemed to hang between this world and the next and Caleb, too, was suspended in a twilight region from which there was no escape.

And then came midwinter. The longest night. He sat, unable to believe that the sun would ever rise. He was trapped in everlasting dark. Everlasting solitude.

When at last the sky began to lighten on the morning

of the third day that followed the surgeon's visit all three lay still as death, their skin white and waxen, their lips a pale violet. *How am I to pay for their funerals?* was Caleb's first thought. *I cannot let them go to a pauper's grave!*

But then one by one he saw they breathed still and that their colour was so pale because they had lost the ruddy rash of the fever. It had departed, and carried none of them with it.

For the first time since Pa had been taken he sat, wrapped his arms around his knees, buried his face and wept like a child.

Their misfortunes were not over when the fever broke. All three were helpless as newborn kittens for many days afterwards. Caleb's sixteenth birthday passed unremarked. Christmas likewise came and went and they could not even attend church, but slept and slept with Caleb watching over them.

As the invalids started to gain some strength and he no longer feared to leave them alone, Caleb went in search of work. He knocked on the door of every house in both Fishpool and Tawpuddle to offer his services, not simply as a tailor, but for any task they could offer. He would have done anything: swept pigsties, scraped cattle byres, dug night soil from privies. Anything. He went to the butcher's, the draper's, the baker's, the chandler's, the tailor's. He even stood on the quay and talked to captains and first mates. But he had not Letty's power of persuasion, or perhaps he was not picking the right vessels or the right men, for no one would give him work.

Each night he returned home empty-handed, footsore, his heart heavy with failure. He was able and willing to provide for his family yet it was the one thing he seemed unable to do!

Caleb said nothing of the surgeon's visit or what it had cost. Neither his aunt nor Letty recalled it and he didn't wish to harm their recovery by making them fear being turned out of the house for want of rent. He watched Anne and Letty and Dorcas gaining in strength and vigour, saw the pinkness returning to their cheeks, and all the while he felt sick inside. When life resumed some semblance of normality he couldn't keep the lack of money secret any longer. Rent day was fast approaching and when his aunt went to the jar and shook it she was aghast to find it made no sound.

Caleb, hanging his head in shame, had to explain that he had run to Tawpuddle for the surgeon.

Letty turned on him in fury. "Everyone knows the man is a quack! Were you out of your mind? What made you send for him?"

His temper matched hers. "I couldn't stand by and watch you die."

"No more you could." Anne was conciliatory. "Hush, Letty. Caleb did as he judged best. We will hear no more of it."

There were no more reproaches, but they all knew that very soon William Benson would come and demand Sir Robert's money. Though still weakened by her illness, Letty was once more out in the rowing boat fetching what sewing jobs she could find. Anne and Caleb worked in a frenzy on whatever scraps she brought back but the money they earned was nothing like enough. Not a word was said, but it seemed likely that at the turning of the year they would be forced out of the cottage and onto the street.

The knock on the door came a day early, but William Benson was not there to demand Sir Robert's rent or to evict them. He had brought news.

The *Linnet* had been lost at sea.

12.

When William Benson knocked on the door, Caleb was in Tawpuddle delivering the shirts that he and his aunt had patched, but he knew something was amiss as soon as he walked back into Fishpool. There were people out of doors, bunched in groups, talking, arguing. A common enough sight on a summer's day, perhaps, but not in the middle of winter when a bitter wind was being funnelled down the street. All fell silent as he walked by. He knew they would begin whispering again as soon as he had passed and so he kept his ears open, but he caught only snatches, piecemeal fragments that made no sense.

"Wasn't no surprise."

"None at all."

"What was he thinking of, fitting her out like that?"

"Old girl should have been broken up."

He was uneasy even before he walked into his aunt's house and found Letty sitting staring into the dying fire, Dorcas huddled on her lap. When the little girl saw Caleb she struggled to escape her sister's iron grip. A white-faced Letty released her reluctantly and Dorcas toddled towards him, outstretched arms clamping around his neck as he lifted her from the floor.

"What's wrong? Where is my aunt?"

Letty's eyes shut for a moment. Her mouth became pinched, as if she was struggling to contain her emotion. Then she said quickly, "The *Linnet*'s gone down."

"Down?"

"She got halfway to America, or near enough. Sank in a storm in the middle of the ocean."

Caleb exhaled heavily. "Oh dear God! Your father…?"

"Is alive and well," said Letty dully. "The crew was saved, every one of them."

"Saved?" He felt awash with relief. "Thank the Lord! But how…?"

"They lowered the rowboat. Got picked up by a ship bound for Bristol. It brought them into Tawpuddle this very afternoon. You must have just missed seeing them." Her voice was entirely without expression.

Caleb crouched down beside Letty, Dorcas still cradled in his arms. "You seem distressed. Is this not good news? Your father is alive!"

"He is. And I'm grateful for that – of course I am. But you haven't heard it all. William Benson came to tell us the crew are at Norton Manor right now. They were taken up there straight from the ship. They've got to give an account of the sinking. Sign affidavits, he said, in front of the magistrate. It's all got to be written down to keep the records straight. Anne went running along there right away, she was that desperate to see Father. Left me alone with Benson." For a moment her composure slipped.

A fist squeezed Caleb's heart. "What did he say? Did he harm you?"

"No. He just hung back long enough to tell me that you and me were to go there too as soon as you came home."

"Did he say why?"

"No. But it wasn't an invitation, Caleb. It was an order."

Dorcas started to wriggle out of his arms. Setting her down on the floor, he stood up. "Do they mean to tell us what happened to Pa, do you think?"

"The truth?" Letty shook her head. "I doubt it. They don't know how much we know, remember? After Anne had gone Benson told me the convicts had been chained in the hold: that all twelve went down with the ship. He said it like it didn't mean anything much, that he was just passing the time, exchanging a morsel of gossip. But he watched me when he said it. Watched me to see how I'd react. All twelve, Caleb. He was very particular about that. He said they're at the bottom of the sea, every single one of them."

Caleb's heart was thumping. "Did he mention Pa's name?"

"No. But neither did I. Because we're not supposed to know he was on the *Linnet*, are we? If you hadn't got into the customs house, looked at that bill of lading, we'd be none the wiser. Were you seen, do you think?"

"I thought not..." Caleb recalled the cat in the shadows. It was possible someone had been lurking there.

"Well ... if you were it can't be helped." Her voice cracked a little. She looked beaten.

Letty had the courage of a lion. To see her so troubled now was profoundly disturbing. "There's more here," he said. "You've not told me it all. What else did Benson say? Did he threaten you?"

"No! If he'd threatened me I'd have told him what for. No ... it was worse than that. He put on this big, broad smile. Said how it was nice to see Dorcas looking so well, after she'd been so sick. Then he said little ones are such a worry – accidents can happen so quickly, a life can be snuffed out in the blink of an eye. Like a candle, he said. If anyone else had been listening they'd have thought it was innocent enough. But I reckon it was a warning. It felt like one."

"You think he knows what we have discovered?"

"Maybe he does, maybe he doesn't." She rubbed her face with her hands. "Maybe he's just passing on the message he was told to deliver. I couldn't say. But I reckon we're being told to keep in line, not make waves, not ask questions. Someone doesn't want us saying what we know." Though the child protested, she pulled Dorcas back onto her lap and held her there tight for a few moments. Then she got to her feet and tugged a shawl around her head and shoulders, wrapping Dorcas into its folds. "Best we both remember that, for her sake. Keep it to ourselves if we want her safe. We've got to leave now. We mustn't keep them waiting."

They were agreed. Whatever happened next, they must play the part of ignorant innocents. And now they could delay no longer. They had been summoned. To Norton Manor they must go.

13.

Caleb knew nothing of shipping or the sea, but he understood the nature of drama well enough. What passed at Norton Manor that evening was a piece of theatre: perfectly stage-managed and expertly delivered. He and Letty were players, but as they had been given neither script nor directions they were little more than marionettes being jerked along on a length of string.

They were ushered towards the kitchen on arrival. A large pine table had been moved to one side and several chairs stacked upon it to make room for the families of the crew who were gathered there, whispering amongst themselves, awed to be in so grand a house. There were so many of them that the room was full, the air hot and sticky. Caleb and Letty were asked to wait with Anne by the door that opened onto the corridor. In hushed tones she told them that the crew were already gathered in Sir Robert's study, awaiting the arrival of Narcissus Puddleby, the magistrate from Tawpuddle. The families were not permitted to see or speak to any of their men until the business was done.

Caleb glanced around at the faces of those who stood in the kitchen. Women, mostly wives, he presumed, although maybe there were some mothers too. Children of all sizes. One or two men: fathers maybe, or sons and brothers. He saw little joy or relief on any of them. What was more evident was shock. Nervousness. Apprehension. This was not the reunion they had expected with their loved ones.

It was a good half an hour before the clatter of hooves and wheels on cobbles announced the arrival of the magistrate's carriage. Looking along the corridor, Caleb saw Narcissus Puddleby, a short, squat dumpling of a man, enter the house. Sir Robert left the study to greet him, shaking him warmly by the hand and throwing an arm about his shoulders as though they were old friends. No one who saw them could doubt that the magistrate was as much Sir Robert's man as William Benson. Catching Caleb's eye, Sir Robert smiled as if to underline the point.

Caleb expected the official business to take some time. There had been eleven men on the *Linnet*'s crew. Piecing each man's account together to arrive at a semblance of the whole truth might take hours. Caleb was prepared for a long, weary wait.

And yet in no time at all the study door opened, the men emerged and were directed towards the kitchen. There were no noisy exchanges as families were reunited, no rapturous embraces, no cries of joy, no tears: just whispers, pressed hands, fond looks. They should have met on the quayside, Caleb thought, where they could behave without inhibition. Men could have gone to the tavern to celebrate their safe return, or back to their own homes. But Sir Robert had decreed otherwise. All was as muted and decorous as he could have desired.

Letty's father was the last to leave the study, lagging behind the rest of the men. He looked so like his daughters Caleb couldn't doubt who he was even before he broke into a run, coming along the corridor and sweeping his wife right off the floor and into his tight embrace. His face showed signs of tremendous strain, which relaxed only a little as he held her, eyes shut, face bent towards her neck, breathing her in, oblivious of his surroundings, not even greeting Letty or Dorcas and only setting Anne back down when William Benson laid a warning hand upon his shoulder.

Sir Robert was advancing in his stately fashion down the corridor towards them with Puddleby trotting at his heels. Edward Avery, Anne and the rest pressed themselves against the wall to let him pass. In the kitchen, people squeezed together to make room. When he was at the centre of the throng he cleared his throat and then addressed them.

"This has been an appalling tragedy," Sir Robert said clearly. "Yet I will not have it compounded by speculation or idle gossip. These men have suffered enough. I wish you all to hear the account of the event that has been authorized and approved by the magistrate."

He ushered his man forward. The magistrate unrolled a length of parchment and began to read.

"I, Narcissus Puddleby, magistrate duly admitted and sworn, do hereby certify that on the thirty-first day of December in the year of our Lord 1752, came before me Luke Slater, master of the *Linnet*, along with ten of his crew, who have put their names to this paper. All are agreed to the following particulars of their voyage.

"They did set sail from the port of Tawpuddle on the sixth July last, laden with bale goods, besides twelve convicts, men from Torcester gaol, bound for Maryland."

Caleb kept his face utterly neutral but beside him Anne cried out, her hand raised to her mouth in horror. "Convicts?"

It seemed this was news to no one but her. While Letty and Caleb merely acted the part of ignorant innocents his aunt truly was one. Anne was upset. Severely so. "Edward?" she whispered, turning to her husband. He put his finger to her lips to silence her, for Sir Robert's eyes were on them and the magistrate was still speaking. Anne flushed and then grew pale. Her husband put his arm about her waist. Letty took her hand.

"Having the wind hard against them for much of the crossing, they could make but slow progress. On the fifth day of October last, being in the middle of the ocean, the wind began to blow hard from the north. The sails were split by the sudden gale and, it coming on to dark, new sails could not be put on and they thought it most advisable to come to anchor until the next morning. But before daylight a mighty storm arose, so furious that the anchor came home whereupon they let more cable slip even to the utmost end. They made it fast about the bit but it was dragged away and the vessel was driven before the wind and on towards a jagged reef. A colossal wave then fell upon them, picking the vessel up and breaking its back upon rocks before tearing it asunder. The ship began to sink and the convicts, being chained in the hold, could not be reached..."

Anne pressed a hand to her lips to stifle a cry. Her distress grew with every word that Narcissus Puddleby read and she didn't yet know the worst, thought Caleb. His own heart ached in anticipation of the wound that would shortly be inflicted on hers.

Anne was not alone in her horror at the convicts' fate. To go down with a ship, to be chained, unable to escape, to drown in such conditions was worse than any sailor's nightmare, and that of their loved ones too. There was a murmur of sorrow, a wave of pity that rippled through the room.

Indifferent to it, the magistrate continued. "The crew had no choice but immediately to lower the rowing boat over the side of the ship and betake themselves to it. They remained in it, tossed by wind and waves, all the hours of darkness. In the morning, the wind being to the westward they were blown once more before it and were providentially observed by a brigantine named the *Celandine*, out from Philadelphia bound for Bristol, who very compassionately came to their assistance and took them on board from the rowing boat, which was likewise in danger of sinking in a very small time..."

The magistrate concluded by saying that captain and crew had sworn the disaster to be an act of God and that the loss of convicts and cargo was total and unavoidable. To this every man had set his hand.

This was the sworn testimony of them all. And yet from the start the picture conjured by their words did not make sense to Caleb. He was no sailor, but he could not understand why a storm of sufficient violence to down a large vessel, to break it open on the rocks, to pick it up bodily before plunging it to the depths, would not likewise overwhelm a rowing boat weighed down by a crew of eleven.

It was a dreadful tale. But it also struck him how very neat an account it was. That the entire crew – eleven men who would have been running hither and thither and struggling to prevent the sinking of the ship in a great howling tempest – had all seen and heard and done the selfsame things at the selfsame moment, that they should all be so perfectly in agreement was suspicious in itself, was it not?

He recalled Pa's tale of the three blind men who had – for the very first time – chanced upon a horse. The first took hold of only an ear and remarked, "Aha! Now I understand.

A horse is small enough to fit in the hand, and is as soft as velvet." The second had only its hoof, and assured him, "No … a horse is hard and has an iron edge." The third, grasping only its tail, declared, "Fools! You are both wrong. For a horse is long and hairy."

The story had been told to amuse him, but Caleb knew there was a moral that lay at its heart. There was no such thing as the whole truth. "If something happens, Caleb – a fire, perhaps, or an accident? – ask five men what happened and you'll get five quite different stories. Some notice one thing, some another. There will be five different truths, not one, and each of them as fragmented and incomplete as the other. Man cannot know everything there is to know. Distrust anyone who tells you he has all the answers to life's mysteries, for God alone sees the whole."

He looked around the room. Every man of the *Linnet*'s crew had fixed his eyes dead ahead and was staring into space.

Caleb knew that if he glanced at Letty he would see his doubt reflected in her eyes. So he did not. They exchanged neither word nor look and kept their faces perfectly composed, aware they were being scrutinized by both William Benson and Sir Robert.

With Puddleby's account concluded there seemed no more to be said on the matter. But then Anne asked guilelessly, "Sir Robert, forgive me… May we know the names of the convicts? Poor souls! We must pray for them!"

There were a few muttered words of approval from the other crewmen's wives.

Sir Robert raised his eyebrows. "Do not waste your breath. They were villains. Sinners! I have no doubt their punishment came from God, for as you see the honest men were saved from the tempest."

Anne's voice was mild as ever, but when she spoke she did not yield to Sir Robert. "Are we not taught 'judge not, lest ye be judged'? I would wish to pray for every man who drowned." Again, there was a murmur of support amongst the families.

Sir Robert now displayed some irritation. "You are too tender-hearted, madam. Their names? Regrettably, I do not know them." He turned to the ship's captain. "Mr Slater, are you aware of the felons' names?"

Luke Slater straightened his back as if standing to attention. "They were listed on the bill of lading no doubt, Sir Robert, but I have not seen that since the day we sailed."

Sir Robert turned to the magistrate. "Mr Puddleby, are you aware of the felons' names?"

"Why yes. I had the bill copied before I left Tawpuddle. I have it here."

And so the names were read, each one sounding like the tolling of a bell.

"Jack Lancey, Mark Andrews, Thomas Sinnett, John Kingscot ..."

This is it, thought Caleb. *Any moment now I will be called on to act my part.*

"Henry Meddon, Edwin Hampton, Robert Buckleigh …"

I must make it convincing. They must believe I know nothing of this.

"Walter Coombs, William Hockin …"

Shock. Display utmost shock. Make it sincere.

"Edward Braddick, Richard Brendon …"

Here it comes. Help me, Pa.

"… Joseph Chappell."

Caleb took a sharp breath. He widened his eyes. Looked at Letty in startled confusion. Popped open his mouth just a little. He didn't need to do more because Anne turned to her husband.

"Joseph Chappell? Edward…" Anne clutched his arm. "Edward! He's my bro— but you don't know…! Joseph, I…"

"Do you know the man?" Edward Avery asked in great astonishment. His eyebrows had shot ceiling-wards in a display of surprise but his voice, thought Caleb, sounded too loud, too theatrical to be entirely credible. His words seemed intended for the gathered crowd, not his wife alone.

"Anne?" he repeated.

She did not answer. Her eyes fluttered, she staggered sideways and then fell to the floor in a faint.

There was a collective gasp from the people assembled in the kitchen. Suddenly the family were centre-stage in a drama of operatic scale and the audience were gripped.

Cradling his wife's head in his lap, Edward Avery looked to Letty for the first time that evening. "What is this about, my girl?"

Holding Dorcas tight, speaking through her sister's hair in stiff, wooden phrases, Letty told her father, "It seems your wife had a brother. They've been estranged these many years. He was taken for a thief back last summer. Transported. Oh Lord, Father! Looks like you had him on your own ship and didn't know it! This is his son."

It was Caleb's turn to feign amazement. "I came here when he was taken, Uncle. How strange that he should have been on the very same vessel you sailed on! My poor Pa! Drowned! Is it true? Did he go down with the *Linnet*?"

"He did! Alas! Alas!"

The audience began to whisper. "Anne Avery had a brother! Her own husband did not know it! And him a felon! Fancy that!"

"Both men on the selfsame ship and neither man known to the other! How extraordinary! A full-grown nephew – appearing from nowhere! And a darkie at that!"

Far from curtailing tittle-tattle this sensation would give the scandalmongers meat enough to feed on for a century. And, thought Caleb, if the gossips were kept busy feeding on his family, no one would be asking questions about the sinking of the *Linnet*. What a lucky chance for Sir Robert. How very, very convenient…

As the scene played out, Caleb fervently hoped that his acting was better than his uncle's. For while Anne's feelings were utterly sincere, Letty's father was a different matter.

Sorrow and concern for his wife were writ large upon Edward Avery's features and Caleb didn't doubt for a minute the depth or extent of those emotions: any fool could see that Edward's heart bled for Anne's suffering.

But surprise at the existence of Joseph Chappell?

Real astonishment at their close connection?

No. There was not a trace of it.

14.

The evening had been beautifully orchestrated from beginning to end, Caleb thought bitterly as they were ushered out of the house and into the cold night air. Pa would have been impressed by the slick deftness of it. As they walked back to Fishpool in the moonlight he turned the question over in his mind: what was the purpose of it all? What had Sir Robert hoped to achieve by this charade?

Firstly, he supposed, it had given an authorized version of events. Signed by every member of the *Linnet*'s crew and sanctioned by the magistrate, the affidavit could never be questioned. It had also been made plain to Caleb that there was no higher authority to which he could appeal. The law in these parts was in Sir Robert's pocket.

He seethed with anger. That man, that high-born, titled man, with his vast estates and carriages and money and grand house and fine clothes, had stood there and lied in his own kitchen like the lowest of criminals! With no qualms, with not a moment's remorse or regret, he had declared that he was entirely ignorant of the convicts' names. And yet he must have both known them and known that they'd come out. If Anne hadn't asked her question someone else would have. Every week in church the congregation of Fishpool prayed fervently for the souls of the drowned. Sir Robert had expected the question to come – why else would Puddleby have had a copy of the bill of lading so conveniently to hand?

And the result? The names of the convicts were common knowledge and Pa was declared drowned and dead, dragged down to the bottom of the sea by his convict's chains. Caleb was now expected to grieve publicly for a man he'd privately mourned for weeks. He was expected to swallow the lie that Pa had been lost in the middle of the ocean halfway between England and the American colonies along with the other felons. This would be the received truth from now on, unless Caleb could prove otherwise.

There was besides the matter of his uncle to consider. Edward Avery walked a little ahead, his arm around his wife's waist, his hand upon Letty's shoulder. She was carrying Dorcas and the child was asleep in her arms. They looked like a family happily reunited, and yet Caleb could see from the stiffness of Letty's back that she was profoundly ill at ease.

Edward Avery had said he was unaware of Pa's existence, and yet how could that be true, for he'd betrayed not an ounce of amazement?

That Anne herself had never told him she had a brother

wasn't in doubt. Her fit of fainting, her appalling distress, her grief: this part of the scene alone had not been acted. So if she'd never told Edward about her brother, who had?

It wasn't hard to fathom the answer. All the men had been closeted in Sir Robert's study for some time before Caleb and Letty had arrived and then they'd all stayed in there even longer waiting for Narcissus Puddleby. There would have been plenty of opportunity for someone – William Benson or Sir Robert himself – to inform Edward Avery of Pa's relation to Anne. It must have come as a huge shock – they'd have wanted to tell him in private to give him time to compose himself before he saw his wife, lest he accidentally let something slip.

Edward would have been told of Caleb's unexpected arrival in Fishpool too, of his discovery of the body on the beach and of his insistence that the drowned man was Pa. They'd have impressed on Edward how vitally important it was that Caleb was not believed, for he was the fly in the ointment that threatened all their plans – he had to be discredited. Oh, it was ingenious, Caleb had to admit that. By formalizing this version of events, everyone but Letty would doubt his sanity. There seemed no hope now of ever doing anything to change it.

But there was Pa, lying in that unmarked grave. Surely every man on the *Linnet* must know what had truly happened to him? Yet they were all apparently sworn to silence.

Caleb's head thumped. He felt as though he was engaged

in the elaborate steps of an intricate dance. So many lies, so many deceptions, so many people involved! If he put a foot wrong he risked catastrophe.

If he'd only had himself to consider he wouldn't fear the consequences of seeking out the truth. Indeed, that night he felt he could happily have beaten his uncle to a pulp and forced it from him. But there was Letty. And there was Benson's threat to Dorcas. He couldn't risk her safety.

And so they made their way back to the house in silence. It was only when the door was closed behind them that any of them spoke and then it was simply for Edward Avery to declare that the hour was so late they must all retire at once to bed.

Letty climbed the ladder to fetch down a blanket for herself and Dorcas. They'd sleep below, she said. She added no more but Anne gave a blushing glance in her husband's direction. A man and wife so long apart would wish to be alone together and Letty's thoughtful act seemed mere courtesy but Caleb knew – or suspected – a different motive.

Dorcas settled at once, but Letty and Caleb stayed awake, whispering to each other about the evening's events. Talking to her, hearing her agree with his own impressions, brought Caleb some relief.

It was a long time before the muffled noises from the attic ceased. At last Letty and he could hear nothing but the slap of water against the jetty outside, and the soft breathing of the child that lay between them. The threat that had been made to Dorcas lay heavy in both their minds. When the little girl turned, mumbling in her sleep, they both reached out a hand to soothe her. In the dark their fingers entwined. Letty seemed as startled as Caleb was, for she drew in a sharp breath. But she didn't pull back. Instead she gave his palm a gentle squeeze, which he found enormously comforting. The rest of the night they lay, hands held together in a protective shield over Dorcas.

15.

The following day dawned bright and clear. With Edward home and a change in the weather there came a lightening of the household's mood.

While Edward Avery had been at sea, his family on land had barely scraped a living. Anne, Letty and Caleb had worked long and hard but at best they had been able to afford to eat only the most meagre of foodstuffs: rye bread, broth made from vegetables and only rarely a scrap of bacon to throw in the pot. There were days when even those few things were beyond their means. Caleb spending the rent money on a useless quack had worsened an already desperate situation.

But the head of the house was back now and none of this troubled him in the slightest. Though his voyage had ended with the sinking of his ship it seemed it was not the catastrophic disaster for Sir Robert that it had been for Caleb's grandfather. Edward slept late, but when he finally descended the ladder from the attic the first thing he did was press a fat purse into Anne's hands.

She was too astonished to say anything. It was Letty who remarked, "The *Linnet* sank. She was lost ... and her cargo besides. How could you be paid?"

"Sir Robert is an honest man, and a generous one," Edward answered. Letty and Caleb exchanged an astonished glance but he continued, "He has promised that he will not see men who have suffered so much on his behalf go hungry. Nor their families neither. No ... he looks after those who are loyal to him, and that's the truth."

And so their fortunes were suddenly turned on their heads. They – who had seemed so cursed – were blessed, declared Edward Avery. Had not Caleb's tender care brought the women through the most dreadful of fevers? Had not he himself survived a shipwreck? Had not they all escaped the prospect of certain eviction by his timely return? Joseph was lost, it was true, and that was a sorrow they would all struggle to bear. But nonetheless, they also had cause for celebration, he said. Before noon he jumped into the boat with Letty and together father and daughter rowed to Tawpuddle. They came back laughing, fresh-faced, cheerful. Calling Anne and Caleb down to the jetty, they unloaded onto it a great ham, two loaves of fresh baked bread made from fine white flour, a huge wheel of cheese and a jar of chutney. They had besides a new shawl for Anne, blue ribbons for Letty's red hair, a doll for Dorcas. That night they consumed a veritable feast.

And it was not for that evening alone that they ate well. The following day Letty and Edward went once more to Tawpuddle and came back with more food of marvellous quality, and there was plenty of it for them all.

Days of this strange plenty turned into weeks and Caleb had never been so well fed. They ate meat at every meal and not just the cheapest of cuts that must be stewed for a night and day to render them edible. Beef. Mutton. A chicken. White bread, eggs, milk, cheese. His clothes grew tight, and when his shirt split altogether it seemed there was plenty of money to purchase cloth to replace it. Indeed there was sufficient to make him a thick woollen coat besides. All the while, his Uncle Edward was cheerful, friendly. Caleb had feared he would be regarded as an intruder but the reverse seemed true. Edward often remarked that it was pleasant to have another man about the place. Frequently he thanked Caleb for all he had done for his family while he'd been at sea. He was generous. Affable. Apparently free of care.

And yet Caleb noticed that Edward's mind would sometimes wander, his mask sometimes slip. Staring into the fire, his uncle's face would twitch as if he experienced a sudden stab of pain. Looking out to sea, staring fixedly at the island in the bay, his mouth would purse as though he was tasting something bitter. Caleb would catch Letty's eye and both would hold their breath and wait for Edward to say something that might betray his secret. But there was nothing. He gave every appearance of enjoying the company of his family, of enjoying the bread and ale put before him. Yet the more his uncle held his tongue, the more Caleb was convinced that he was a puppet going through the motions for his master.

Ships came and went in and out of Tawpuddle but Edward did not sign with another crew after a short time on shore as Letty said he had in past years. She was puzzled by her father's behaviour. Weeks turned into months and he stayed at home.

"He's become a man of leisure," she said on a rare occasion she and Caleb found themselves alone. "He has the look of a soul in hell some days, but whatever happened on the *Linnet* he's profited handsomely from it."

"As have we all," Caleb said dryly.

"I don't like it. True enough, it's a pleasant thing to have a full belly, but I don't know… Makes me feel dirty, somehow."

Caleb shared every ounce of Letty's unease and yet he could not help but like his uncle. Having no son of his own, Edward sought his nephew's company and it was impossible for Caleb to avoid giving it.

Pa had always stood between him and hostile strangers and now Letty's father stepped into that role. Or he would have done, had he been required to. Caleb noticed with wry amusement that the change in their family fortunes had a substantial effect on the people of Fishpool. Where once there were insults and whispers behind Caleb's back, now there were greetings and smiles to his face. It seemed that a little ale could go a long way when it came to acquiring men's good opinion. Some evenings his uncle would take him to the tavern. Edward would buy drinks for the folk assembled there and then Caleb would sit with him listening to sailors' tales: stories of gigantic squid that would rise from the ocean's depths and wrap their tentacles around a hapless ship. "Twenty, thirty feet long each one of them, thick as the arms of half a dozen men, with suckers as big as your head. They'll snap a mast like it's kindling wood, break the ship's back and drag her down to fill their gaping maws."

There were tales too of flying fishes that leapt out of the waves and soared through the air with rainbow wings glinting in the sunlight; of mermaids that appeared by the side of boats, faces staring up from the water, arms languidly beckoning to those who watched them, their unworldly beauty tempting captains to steer their ships too close to rocks where they would founder and perish.

As they walked home late one evening, Edward, who had drunk a little more than usual, put his arm around Caleb's shoulder to steady himself. It was high tide, and together they paused a while watching the moonlight play on the water.

"I heard singing once, Caleb," Edward said. Without the tavern's noise to contend with his voice was rich. Warm.

"I was down in the belly of the ship when the sound echoed through the timbers. It filled my head; made every muscle shake, every sinew tremble. I clapped my hands over my ears but there was nothing I could do to silence that singing. I could feel it, Caleb; it was in my blood, in my bones. I thought my end was come: that this was not a single mermaid but teeming hordes, a great army of them, bent on our destruction. But when I came on deck my eyes beheld something stranger even than that. Great fishes – whales – their tails wider than the whole of Fishpool, lifting from the sea, slapping down on its surface when they dived, coming back up and blowing great plumes of smoke and water from their heads. And they were singing to each other." He sighed. Shook his head. "Singing of what, Caleb? There was a melody to it, but were there words? Can the beasts talk to each other? Could we learn their language? I wonder."

His uncle had a mariner's rough speech and manners and yet the scope of his imagination, the wonderful stories he told, had much in common with Pa. The two men would have been friends, Caleb realized. He missed Pa so very much – he could not help but enjoy his uncle's company for it lessened the terrible ache of his father's loss. And yet there was a shadow lying over everything.

When sober, Edward was guarded in his speech – he never mentioned the *Linnet*, or Joseph Chappell, or anything relating to his past. But ale loosens the tongue. Sometimes

Edward went into a kind of reverie and would become talkative.

"Anne was the comeliest creature I'd ever set eyes on," he told Caleb one evening. "So dainty. So ladylike. But so very sad! The very first time I saw her she was crossing the lawn at the manor. I'd taken Letty up there in her clean frock, ribbons in her hair. And then there was Anne, bringing a shawl, her Ladyship snapping at her for not coming fast enough, and Anne close to tears. I wanted to wrap her up, put her somewhere safe, somewhere warm and dry where folks couldn't harm her, where no one would shout or make her cry. I've never wanted to do anything but keep her safe, see?"

Once he exclaimed, "She had a brother! I can hardly believe it. Why did she never tell me? She closed up tight as a clam when I asked. Did he do something that shamed her? I wonder." His thoughts then seemed to turn in another direction and he cried, "Oh Lord, then what would she say of this?"

On another occasion he lost his temper, suddenly slapping the tavern table and declaring, "Her father was a fool! Putting all his money into one ship? That's the surest way to lose a fortune!" Then he softened and sniffed. "But if he hadn't, if he hadn't, why then she'd never have looked twice at me. I've done my best to keep her, but a man like me ... you try to rise above your station, you get doors slammed in your face every way you turn. She should be sitting in a parlour, stitching samplers, having servants running everywhere doing her bidding, not slaving for every man wants his shirt mending!"

Sometimes his tone became pleading, desperate – "Benson said we'd be turned out. That Anne would end her days in the workhouse and Letty and Dorcas with her! How could I tell him no? But what would Anne say? If she knew what would she say?"

Caleb asked him gently, "Knew of what, Uncle? What is it that troubles you?"

But speaking broke the spell. Edward's eyes focused on Caleb's face. Tears spilled out over his lower lids and down his cheeks and chin. He wept into his tankard, but said no more.

One night towards the end of March they returned from the tavern with Edward unusually drunk. Caleb had his arm about his uncle's waist and was trying to support him but Edward slipped from his grasp, stumbled and fell to the ground. Kneeling there, as if in prayer, he cried out, "Fools! Do gentlemen in Torcester know nothing of the sea? They cannot! I saw their letters. There, on his desk. Poor, trusting fools! Simpletons! They have been deceived in him. And I...? Oh dear God, I have sold my soul to the very Devil!"

"What letters? What men?" asked Caleb. But Edward vomited and afterwards was so dizzied, his legs so weak, that Caleb could do nothing but drag him home. He was not able to climb the ladder so Caleb simply made him comfortable by the fire, where he fell into a deep slumber.

To his relief Anne was already in bed and sleeping, but Letty had waited up. When Caleb told her what her father had said she whispered, "What in God's name is it all about? It's no good. We've got to find out."

"Do you really want to?" he asked. "We've been threatened, Letty. Think of Dorcas…"

"I know. But if we do nothing we'll have to live with those threats for ever. I feel them stifling the life out of me. Out of all of us. I can't stand it!"

"We might hurt your own father," Caleb reminded her.

"I know that too." He could see that loyalty and morality fought for control of Letty's heart. At last she said, "Your pa's dead, Caleb. Mine is tangled up in it somehow, but I feel in my bones it's against his will. Father's a good man – always has been. But now there's a cloud over him. I've got to know what's going on. Can't see how else to help him. I want him back the way he was."

Caleb took a long look at Letty. He felt dimly that there was more to this than she was telling him, that for reasons he didn't entirely understand she was throwing her lot in with him. Their fates were tied. Whatever her motives, he felt hugely grateful.

The next day Edward's eyes were reddened and he complained that his head ached. Anne persuaded him to climb the ladder and rest. He stayed in bed that morning to sleep it off, but his dreams were full of distressed murmurings and from time to time Caleb thought he could hear weeping.

Piecing together the fragments his uncle had let slip had kept Caleb awake. He had a burning desire to go to Norton Manor, to stride into that damned study, to seize Sir Robert by the coat, to demand the truth. But if he did that, the dogs would be set on him. People like him did not simply go strolling up to a grand house. People like him had to wait to be summoned to the homes of the wealthy and influential, and being summoned by Sir Robert seemed as likely as a pig growing wings. There was nothing he could do, he thought.

Yet later that morning, circumstance provided him with an astonishing opportunity.

Sir Robert was a pitiless landlord and yet, in a great display of patriarchal benevolence, he hosted a gala each May Day. The event was fast approaching and Letty was – as usual – invited to attend. While her husband lay ill in bed Anne brought the matter up, wondering aloud whether she and Caleb should make her stepdaughter a new gown for the occasion.

Letty immediately said she would not go in any case, no matter how well she was dressed. "I've had enough of those damned galas to last me a lifetime."

Anne was visibly shocked. "But you must go, my dear," she said gently.

Caleb could see Letty trying – and failing – to control her irritation. "What?" she said. "Go curtsey and smirk and say 'thank you kindly' to a man who'd throw us on the street without a second thought?"

"But it's expected…"

"I'm not a child any more, to be bought with a plate of pudding. I'll not bend and scrape to him." Without another word she left the cottage, ran down the jetty, stepped into her rowing boat and hauled herself midstream. Whether it was to remove herself beyond the reach of Anne's persuasion, or to stop herself saying something she might regret, Caleb couldn't tell.

Anne sighed and fretted. How was she to explain her stepdaughter's absence? If he noticed it Sir Robert would be offended! And her Ladyship! Nothing good could come of Letty's refusal. She must talk to Edward. Maybe he could persuade his daughter to change her mind.

Caleb didn't hear a word. An idea had taken hold, one that made his heart beat faster and his skin prickle into goosebumps.

When the *Linnet*'s crew had been gathered in the kitchen Sir Robert had pulled all their strings. Indeed, they had been compelled to dance to his tune ever since. Yet now maybe Caleb could indulge in a little theatrical trickery of his own…

Letty might choose not to attend the gala and he couldn't blame her. But was it possible that a showman and his puppets might be invited to Norton Manor to bring a little laughter into the lives of the poor unfortunates of the parish...?

16.

Having lived so lavishly for so long, it was inevitable that the money would eventually begin to run out. The day after Caleb had decided to revive Pa's show there was a knock on the door and William Benson was summoning Edward Avery to Norton Manor.

Letty's father came back later that afternoon looking troubled but declaring that although he'd enjoyed being on shore and had treasured the time he'd spent with his family the sea was calling him. His purse was growing thin and so, along with the captain and the crew of the *Linnet*, he'd signed to the *Lady Jane*, a ship newly built for Sir Robert. She was being fitted out for a voyage to the colonies and would sail as soon as she was made ready. He'd have a few weeks more at home and then the *Lady Jane* would be gone, and him along with her.

The question of Letty's attendance at the gala was instantly forgotten. Anne was anxious and wearied by the very thought of having to make ends meet without her husband so Caleb told her that he'd been a burden long enough. Of course he'd continue to assist her as long as she wanted but he'd also see if he could do anything with Pa's puppets. The summer was coming and there would be fêtes and festivals; he was sure he could earn a little money at these in addition to sewing for his supper.

He needed to practise, of course. If an audience was to give money the show must be honed and polished to perfection: he couldn't simply waggle dolls and expect to amuse a crowd. He needed to rehearse and for that he needed space and privacy but where could he go? His uncle solved the problem. Edward knew a man – a fellow drinker at the tavern – who had a barn to the west of Fishpool that would stand empty until the harvest was brought in. Caleb could set up the show there and no one need be troubled by the noise.

Yet Caleb also needed a director: someone who would watch and tell him straight if his performance was lacking. Who better than Letty? She'd looked at him sideways when he said that, clearly wondering what he was up to, but readily agreed to help him.

Anne and Edward swallowed his tale whole and so, one bright spring morning when the countryside was just starting to emerge from its long winter sleep, Letty and Caleb carried the theatre and the sack of dolls to the barn. It was time for Pa's puppets to see the light of day once more.

* * *

It was strange unpacking the theatre without Pa. Caleb untied the rope and peeled back the sacking. The cover badly needed washing – it had lain unaired, unused for so long that black mould had bloomed like storm clouds across it. The curtains were similarly blemished. This could be rectified later, but the frame was another matter. If the wood had warped after being left so long in the damp corner of the cottage it would be far more difficult to put right.

The sight, the feel of the timber struts in his hands brought memories flooding into his mind. Feeling apprehensive, Caleb took the lower frame, stood up straight and gave it a flick. It unfolded in one easy movement and Letty's mouth dropped open; and when he repeated the trick with the top half and slotted both together she laughed aloud.

"It's marvellous, Caleb! Why have you never showed me this before?"

"Wait until you see the puppets."

For months they had remained in their sack. Caleb had slept almost every night curled around them but he had not been able to bear looking at them until now.

Their cloth bodies were folded over their faces to prevent their paint chipping. He lifted each one out, straightening it, smoothing its costume before laying it gently on the ground. "This is Punch," Caleb told Letty. "Here is Judy, his wife. Here is their baby, poor ugly thing. He could crack a looking glass, couldn't he? This is the jester, the only one who can keep Punch in order. He sets Mr Punch to mind his sausages, but look, here is the dragon who eats them. This is Jack Ketch, the hangman."

"Does Punch get hanged?"

"No! Punch outwits him. He outwits everyone. The judge, the hangman, even the Devil. He beats them all over the head with his slapstick, here, see?"

"He does what I'd like to. Is there a puppet of a landlord?" asked Letty. Caleb shook his head. "Shame. I'd love to see Punch beat the hell out of one of those. Or maybe the landlord's lapdog." She ran her fingers over their faces, captivated. "You made these?"

"No, Pa did. I mean to say, he carved them. I sewed their bodies."

"They're wonderful."

He was pleased to have Letty's admiration. It was consoling. Looking at the puppets lying on the barn floor, he thought they looked like a line of corpses. Poor dead things! Without Pa they were nothing. Joseph had given them such life that even after a show when he took the dolls off his hands they seemed animated. Indeed, Punch had always oozed with such delightful wickedness that it wouldn't have surprised Caleb if the puppet had sat up and talked to him.

Pa had often said that Punch had a mind of his own. There would be things that happened during a performance – someone fresh from the tavern would call out from the crowd, a man might heckle, yell abuse. As quick as lightning Punch would throw back a retort that bent folk double with laughter. Afterwards, if Caleb complimented Pa on his quick thinking Joseph would say it was nothing to do with him: Punch had reacted, Pa was a mere conduit. There had been a magic there – an alchemy – that could not be explained.

And now Caleb had to attempt to capture it.

When Caleb took Punch from the ground he was a painted doll – a grotesque wooden gargoyle with a hooked nose and hunched back. Seeing the puppet so limp and lifeless paralysed Caleb for a moment. It seemed Punch's spirit had died with Pa. Caleb was not up to this! Whatever made him think he could do it?

He took a deep, steadying breath. Rallied. He had to be up to it. For Pa's sake, and for his own. It was the only way he'd get access to Norton Manor.

Movement, he reminded himself: that's the key.

Caleb slid his right hand into the glove, his first two fingers in Punch's head, his thumb in his left arm, the two remaining digits in his right. Caleb held the puppet above his head and attempted to wake the heart and soul within the wooden doll.

But his palms were too small, his fingers too thin to support Punch's head. It lolled to one side like a hanged man and flopped about uselessly. When Caleb tried to make the puppet clap its hands it was as though its arms were broken.

He could have wept. He was useless! He couldn't begin to catch Pa's magic. He might more easily have scooped up the moon's reflection in a fishing net.

He glanced miserably over to Letty, mortified by his failure.

But she wasn't looking at him. In fact she hadn't even noticed what he'd been doing. Letty was crouched, staring at the puppets on the ground with fascination. Suddenly she reached for Judy. Slid her hand into the glove.

Caleb hated the story of Cinderella. So many powerful enchantments used just so the heroine can marry a prince? It had always seemed the most disappointing of endings. But what Caleb saw then was truly like a moment from the fairy tale. The glove fitted Letty's strong, oar-calloused hand as well as the glass slipper fitted Cinderella's dainty foot.

Caleb knew it was a common fault amongst inexperienced or poor showmen to hold a puppet so that its head is thrown back and it looks only at the sky. But without instruction Letty was holding Judy so that the puppet's eyes were focused directly on him. And then Judy's voice erupted shrill and clear, "About bleeding time! What d'you mean, leaving me in the dark the whole damned winter?"

Caleb addressed Judy, a broad grin breaking across his face, "I apologize most sincerely, madam." He gave her a small bow. Then, "I have your husband here. Would you like to see him?"

He handed Letty Punch, holding him so she could slide her hand into the glove. Judy protested, "Ooooh not him! Worthless good-for-nothing old devil! Put him back in the sack!"

Caleb watched with delight as Punch began to live again. The puppet moved a little slowly at first, stiffly, as if he was waking from a long sleep. But second by second, minute by minute, he became his own ribald, seditious self again.

Punch flung his arms wide. "Give us a kiss, Judy."

"Certainly not."

"Just one little kissy. Kissy, kissy, kissy. Come on."

"You filthy devil!"

"You like it."

"I love it!"

Letty and Caleb had been oppressed by fear and secrets for months. To share some moments of utter nonsense was as unexpected as it was delightful. Joy, laughter, happiness: they had been hidden away with the puppets the whole of that long winter. To feel those sensations again was intoxicating.

But there was work to be done. All too soon Letty took the puppets from her hands and gave them to Caleb with a sigh. "We've got to get on," she said. "Go on, get in the theatre. Show me what you can do."

With a shake of the head, Caleb thrust Punch and Judy back towards her. "You must do it."

"What?" Letty had never looked so surprised.

"I can't, Letty. The puppets die in my hands. Yet you make them breathe."

She frowned, staring at him angrily, thinking he was mocking her. He could read what ran through her head as clearly as if she had spoken her thoughts aloud: a woman getting up in front of a crowd, a woman as an entertainer? He couldn't be serious! The word "actress" was the same as "whore", wasn't it? If her father knew what Caleb was suggesting he'd forbid it. And Anne? She'd have a fainting fit! And yet, oh dear God, those puppets were lovely to work. She'd heard tell of women who got away with performing, ones who had the courage to brazen it out…

"No one will see you, Letty," Caleb told her. "You'll be hidden inside the theatre. No one need ever know it's you." He was alight with the possibilities Letty's talent offered. "Don't you see? This is the perfect solution! You can do the show at the gala. It will be our secret. They'll think I'm in there and while you're performing, I can slip into the house and find out what I can about the *Linnet*. I can look at the papers in Sir Robert's study."

"But me … to perform…?"

"You have a gift that I could never match. Pa always said a skill like that is given by God. Surely he means you to use it. Come, will you do it?"

He held the puppets out to her. Her eyes gleamed, but still she paused. She looked at Caleb once more then read the challenge in his face and responded by snatching the puppets, unable to resist their lure.

It had taken Pa years to perfect his craft. Years to hone his timing, to develop the routines that delighted both bishop and beggar. Letty had only the month of April, but she was a natural. How Pa would have loved her!

There is a secret trick to making Punch's squeaking voice. Pa had learned it from the Italian who had crafted his first set of puppets. A small object is placed near the back of the throat and pushed up hard against the roof of the mouth with the tongue. A *linguetta*, the Italian had called it, and Pa said the same although Caleb had sometimes heard other Punch men call it a "swazzle". The air is squeezed through it when the user talks, and this changes the pitch and volume of the voice. Pa had once tried to teach Caleb the skill but the thing had made him gag so much he'd nearly vomited.

Letty had no such problems. Caleb placed the rectangle of silver and linen tape in the palm of her hand and, once he'd explained the principle, she popped it into her mouth and into position. Taking a deep breath, she tried her first, experimental blast. When Caleb had attempted it some years ago all that had emerged from his throat was a hiss of air. But Letty now emitted an ear-piercing shriek in Punch's falsetto. The noise – the sheer volume – she produced would have made Caleb leap out of his skin had he not anticipated it. It startled Letty so much that she spat the *linguetta* out in alarm.

"Was that me? Did I do that? Dear God, Caleb, I scared myself half to death! Why didn't you warn me?" They both collapsed into peals of laughter at her reaction, but when Letty had recovered herself a little she slid the thing back into her mouth and began to try words, phrases, sentences. She sang bawdy ballads and pious hymns in the squeaky, comical voice of Mr Punch. She took to it like a duckling takes to water five minutes after it has hatched. The *linguetta* made her drool to begin with, admittedly: spittle ran down her chin until she grimaced at the absurd repulsiveness of it, but she never once gagged or choked.

Caleb explained the show's basics and Pa's rule of three – the same joke once, twice, three times before the punchline on the fourth – and Letty revelled in developing each routine under Caleb's watchful eye. Her show would not be the same as Pa's of course. It was rough, unvarnished. But she had a natural feel for the rhythm of the comedy, for its wild, anarchic mayhem, and for its violence. In her hands Punch's fight with the Devil was a hundred times more gleefully brutal than Pa's had ever been.

Caleb stood out front: the conductor to Letty's orchestra. He made suggestions, recalling things Pa had said and done, fine-tuning each separate act in the drama. He told her where to make a longer pause, to let the puppet appear to think, to let the crowd anticipate what would happen next.

As the day wore on there was a wild, creative excitement in both of them. Caleb had not realised how very much he'd missed the puppets. They had been so much part of his life they'd been almost invisible to him, but to rediscover them now was like having part of his father back.

There was besides the thrill of seeing Letty blossoming into something quite extraordinary. For the length of that day she was freed from the constraints, the grindingly hard labour, the boredom of ordinary life and consumed with the pleasure of discovering something she excelled at, that she seemed to have been made for.

The work was intense. Absorbing. By sunset they were tired but deeply at ease with each other. To discover they were bound by something other than the shared knowledge of villainy was a marvel.

After that, they rehearsed daily. As the month went on Caleb began to feel that there was something sweet in the air. The future seemed to hold an unspoken promise.

It was easy, almost, to forget the purpose behind it all.

17.

It was not possible for Caleb to revive Pa's show without the gossips noticing. He had expected – indeed counted on – their spreading word of it. It came as no surprise that everyone in Fishpool now took him for a showman. What did amaze him was the sudden elevation in his status. As his aunt's assistant he had been the object of contempt and derision. The colour of his skin had been deplored. Despised. Yet now his supposed foreignness gave him an aura of mystique, of exotic rarity. He became an object of fascination. For the first time since he'd arrived the women who gathered at the well spoke politely to him. They smiled. Some of them even flirted! The children who'd once pelted him with stones now pelted him with desperate pleas to see the puppets, to watch a show. And before long the housekeeper of Norton Manor sent a maid with a request that he perform at Sir Robert's May Day gala, and give some amusement to the poor unfortunates of the parish – a request to which Caleb very graciously agreed.

* * *

As luck would have it, the gala was taking place on the very same day the *Lady Jane* was to sail on the evening tide. Anne was frantic with preparations to ensure her husband had all he required for the forthcoming voyage; Dorcas, sensing a change in the air, was tearful; and Edward Avery was distracted, silent. It was a relief for Caleb to escape to Norton Manor.

Letty must not be seen – that was vital to the deception. Caleb had to appear to be performing alone so while he proceeded along the road and then the carriageway she crept through the woods, keeping low to the ground.

On arrival, a maid showed Caleb to the middle of the vast lawn and told him this was his place. He looked up to the sky then protested as politely as he could, "Unfortunately, the sun will strike the audience in the eyes and they will not be able to see the puppets. My apologies, but I cannot put the theatre here."

He then appeared to give great thought to the matter of where would be best to set the show, finally deciding on the spot that Letty had described to him before he'd left: backed up against a line of bushes whose lush growth would conceal their coming and going.

He set up the theatre. Opened the frame, slotted the two halves together, pulled on the cover and then hung the puppets on their hooks. As he finished, there was a rustling in the undergrowth. Letty had arrived, and stepped swiftly inside before she could be seen.

The audience assembled shortly after. Every servant in the house was there by the looks of things, along with the parson and his wife. William Benson stood behind his master. Sir Robert had condescended to join the audience of skinny women, pinched with hunger, and children, scrubbed clean but with eyes too large in skull-like heads. He and his wife had strolled across the lawns and now each held a nosegay of sweet-smelling herbs, presumably to mask the stink of poverty that hung over the rest of the audience. Lady Fairbrother, gaudy as a parrot, was wearing the gown that Caleb and Anne had stitched. For her to be dressed in such a showy manner in front of such a company grated on Caleb, but he was all smiles, bowing low to Sir Robert and his lady, showing them the respect they thought was their due. He had a job to do. Nothing must distract him.

It had been his father's habit to begin the show by first addressing the watchers, for Pa said that every crowd had a different personality. It was his way of gauging them, of seeing where troublemakers might be, of assessing whether they needed whipping up or calming down. Pa's introduction determined the pace of the show and sometimes its content. Routines could be changed or swapped according to the mood of each individual audience.

And now Caleb had to fill Pa's shoes.

He felt a moment's blind terror. What was he doing? Hadn't he always hated crowds? What was this madness? He was the bottler, not the showman!

His hands had bunched into fists. But he was not Caleb now, he told himself. He was being Pa. Acting a role. The part must be his armour.

Taking a deep breath to calm himself, Caleb donned Pa's personality like a coat. Stepping forward, he introduced himself with elaborate theatricality: "Good afternoon, ladies and gentlemen, boys and girls. Let me introduce myself. My name is Henrietta…"

An exchange of glances. A gasp here and there of both confusion and embarrassment. A few muffled giggles.

"Oops! Oh dear me!" he said. "Sorry. I'm a little nervous. I've never done this before, you know. That's a girl's name, isn't it? Yes, I made a mistake. I'll try again. Good afternoon, ladies and gentlemen, boys and girls. My name is Betsey."

Now realizing the joke was deliberate the children giggled louder. Adults smiled and Caleb suddenly saw why Pa had loved performing. There was power in it. He had the crowd in the palm of his hand. It could become intoxicating.

"Wrong again! Whatever is the matter with me? I'll try once more. Good afternoon, ladies and gentlemen, boys and girls. My name is Charlotte. Oh no!"

He was applying Pa's rule of three and it was working. Repeat once, twice, thrice, then change on the fourth. Rhythm and timing were everything.

"I'll try again. Ladies and gentlemen, boys and girls, my name is Caleb – I got it right that time! I am Caleb

Chappell. Welcome to the Hunch and Roody show!"

There were three variations on this deliberate mistake too. Caleb welcomed them to the Lunch and Booby and then the Munch and Pooby show – before finally giving the correct introduction. By this time some of the children were screaming with laughter and making Lady Fairbrother wince at their noise.

Telling the crowd that Mr Punch could not wake without a rousing cheer and a round of applause, Caleb then stepped back, as if into the theatre. But Letty was already in there, and with a wink she started the show with the loud sound of Punch's snoring.

As was always the way, the crowd cheered to rouse Punch from his slumbers while Caleb, knowing Letty was absolutely in control, slipped unnoticed through the bushes and made his way swiftly towards the house.

So long as the show continued he need not fear discovery. The servants had been given permission to watch, so for its duration the manor was empty.

He remembered enough of the layout to go at once to the study but on the way passed rooms of overwhelming opulence. *Look at all this*, they screamed. *Imagine how much this cost! Look at this wealth, this power. Do you really think you can do anything to harm the man who has so much?* The rooms seemed intended to intimidate, to make Caleb feel that he was a speck of dirt, a blot on the page, a smear on the glass – something that needed wiping away. But he would not be cowed: he was not the villain here, and he had waited far too long for a chance to prove who was.

In the study was a desk as Letty's father had described. Its surface was clear but in its drawers there was so much paper to be sifted through! So many records, so many ledgers, so many letters relating to Sir Robert's business affairs!

From across the lawn came the children's delighted shrieks and the loud laughter of their mothers. Punch had been woken and was now bidding "How d'ye do?" to the jester. Every time Punch bowed, the jester struck him upon the head. Letty had been skilled in the barn, but now – with a crowd – her performance had clearly moved up several notches.

But he couldn't allow himself to be distracted by thoughts of Letty – he had to move swiftly. Caleb pulled open one drawer, then another. Nothing of interest. The third, to his relief, was full of papers that related to the *Linnet*. There was a copy of the bill of lading and of the affidavit sworn before Narcissus Puddleby. There was also a copy of the contract for the transportation of the convicts. He skimmed the document. It seemed Sir Robert had been paid by His Majesty's Government no less – paid very handsomely! – to carry the twelve men across the ocean.

And there was more – so much more! A pocketbook detailing notes of payments to members of the crew – surely these sums were way over and above what any sailor could have expected to earn for a voyage? Each man had signed, or made his mark, on the page beside his name, acknowledging receipt. It had the look of a pact with the Devil, Caleb thought – it should have been written in blood. Here was the evidence that the crew's silence had been bought with a good deal of money. But what were they keeping quiet about?

Caleb leafed through more papers. There were many letters, correspondence back and forth between Sir Robert and a group of gentlemen who gave their communal address as Porlock's Coffee House in the city of Torcester. Porlock's – Pa's favourite hostelry. It seemed a strange co-incidence. Surely it must mean something? But what? He couldn't make head or tail of any of this. The nature of the business contained in the letters was mystifying. He must calm himself. Sit down. Read each one slowly, thoroughly, from beginning to end.

As he worked his way through he began to see that Sir Robert had paid to each of the Porlock's gentlemen a small amount of money. They, in return, had agreed to underwrite the risk of the *Linnet*'s voyage, covering the value of both the vessel and cargo in the event of her accidental loss. What did it mean – to underwrite a risk? He'd never heard the phrase before. It was nonsense. Jibberish.

His palms were damp and clammy now. He was going nothing like fast enough. And he was getting nowhere!

Everything he looked at added to his confusion.

He then came across a letter that mentioned a sum of money paid to Sir Robert by these same Porlock's gentlemen upon receipt of the magistrate's signed affidavit. It was a vast amount. Pa could have worked his entire life and not made half that sum. Why had a group of men who drank coffee together given Sir Robert a fortune? The letter stated that it was to cover the cost of the *Linnet,* but she had been a leaky tub, Letty said – thirty years old, or more. She couldn't be worth that much, could she?

He spread the documents on the desk, willing himself to make sense of them. In his own grandfather's day the loss of a ship had resulted in ruination. Had times changed so much? Something new was afoot here, something he couldn't grasp. These papers seemed to show that Sir Robert had been paid for his sunken vessel. Had Caleb understood that right? It seemed unlikely. Impossible. And yet there was no other explanation.

Rifling frantically through the drawer for anything that might throw more light on the matter Caleb saw that pushed into the back was a silken handkerchief wound into a bundle. It looked as though it had been dropped there absent-mindedly and forgotten about. But to find such a thing in this particular desk amongst these carefully ordered papers could surely be no accident? The handkerchief was embroidered with Sir Robert's initials and contained something hard and heavy. Cupping the bundle in his palm, he started to unfold the silk. One corner, the second, then the third. When he pulled back the fourth to reveal the contents, Caleb gagged.

A finger. Mummified now, the skin dried hard as leather but still clinging to the golden ring. Two interlocking *C*s gleaming as brightly as ever they had.

He swallowed, desperate to quell his nausea. For a moment his hands shook. But only for a moment. This new discovery had driven a piece of flint into his heart. He would have vengeance.

The distant screams of delighted children drifted through the open window. Out on the lawns Punch was already fighting the Devil. The routine should have been swift, rapid, the stunning finale to the show, but Caleb was aware that Letty was drawing it out, unable to finish until he was there to take the bow.

He must go. Wrapping Pa's finger in the handkerchief and placing it in his pocket, cramming the papers back in the drawer, he left the house. Hurrying through the bushes, appearing at the back, he whispered, "I'm here," before lighting the hellfire flame's candle and holding it in place as he had once done for Pa.

Letty looked exhausted. But right on cue she blew and a cloud of powdered resin ignited in the air. Clapping his hands, taking his final bow, the show was done. On the playboard, Punch waved goodbye to the crowd and then Letty collapsed into a heap on the floor of the theatre while Caleb stepped out front and took the applause that rightfully belonged to her.

Lady Fairbrother approached him. Looking over his head, she deigned to ask, "Was it very hot in there?"

Caleb was breathless and sweating from the speed of his return, but her Ladyship took the cause to be his recent "performance". "Oh … yes, my Lady, the theatre lacks air."

"It was an impressive show. May I see inside?"

"Ah no!" he said hastily. Then, with an attempt at a smile, added, "A showman must keep his secrets."

"Very well," she replied stiffly. Caleb had offended her, but he cared nothing for that. Sir Robert himself now walked slowly forward to congratulate Caleb and then to inform him that the sequence with the Devil was a trifle too lengthy and could do with a judicious trimming. "Cut out the gristle and the whole dish will be more appetizing." His eyes travelled from Caleb's face down to his toes and then back up again. "I suppose you will be leaving your aunt's shortly. No doubt you intend to travel far and wide like a gypsy. You will be well suited to a vagrant's life."

The insult required no answer so Caleb gave none. Not out loud. But *I will have you, Sir bleeding-high-and-mighty Robert,* he thought. *I will see justice done.*

Caleb bowed while the lady took her husband's arm and together the couple walked away, proceeding slowly across the lawns, William Benson at his master's right hand, the parson and his wife trailing meekly behind.

After many more warm shakes of the hand, many congratulations and expressions of gratitude from the widows and the children the crowd dispersed. Food was the next on their list of that afternoon's delights and all were eager to fill their bellies. Who knew when they would eat so well again?

Caleb was finally alone with Letty. She was flushed from her success but hadn't forgotten the purpose of the visit. There was no time for them to talk. Caleb simply pressed the silk package into her hands. "Keep this safe," he said. "But do not look inside."

"What is it?"

"Pa's ring, still on his finger. I found it in Sir Robert's desk."

Her eyes widened. "And you took it? For God's sake, Caleb! What'll happen if he sees it gone?"

"We must move quickly, that much is certain. Go on home. After the *Lady Jane* has sailed, then we can decide what's to be done."

Letty looked grim, but she slipped the bundle into her pocket, buttoning it up safe. And then she left the way she had come, furtively, through the woods, unseen.

Caleb packed the theatre and puppets but his mind was so taken up with other things he made a poor job of it. It was only when the sack was tied that he realized he'd left Pa's hellfire pipe and tinderbox on the grass along with the bag of powdered resin. There was no time to repack.

Wanting to get away quickly, he stowed them in his pockets and then hoisted the theatre onto his shoulder. He'd been unable to do that last year, he recalled suddenly: he must have grown over the winter. Carrying the sack of puppets in the opposite hand, he walked away from Norton Manor.

He'd found out many things about Sir Robert's business but so little of it made sense – and he still didn't know what had happened to Pa. The frustration of that gnawed at him. Pa couldn't have been chained on the *Linnet* when she sank and now he had the proof of that, but what the Devil had befallen him? Pa's body still lay in the churchyard under a false name. He'd hardly made any progress! He had no idea what to do next and there was no one he could go to with the information, no one in authority he could trust.

He stored the theatre and puppets in the barn. Until he'd spoken to Letty, until they'd agreed a course of action, he must behave normally. He'd return home and then go off to see the *Lady Jane* sail. Letty would no doubt row to Tawpuddle with her father. He would walk – take Dorcas along, maybe, if Anne would allow it.

Pausing for a moment on the crest of the hill, he looked out to sea. It had been a fine day. The cliffs were sheened pink and yellow with wild flowers; water and sky were a brilliant blue and the island, which had looked so bleak and godforsaken all winter, was topped by a line of green vegetation. But now the heat had become oppressive and great clouds had begun to billow, hanging like anvils above it. A storm was approaching and he wondered if the departure of the *Lady Jane* would be delayed. The captain surely wouldn't wish to sail head-on into a tempest? Caleb felt a glimmer of optimism. He might yet have a chance of talking to Edward Avery face to face and demanding the truth. The discovery of Pa's ring gave him fresh resolve.

Caleb wasn't halfway home when he heard a sound. Someone was running, hard and fast, coming up swiftly behind him. He turned. But before he could see who it was he was struck on the head. Struck so hard that all sense was knocked clean out of him.

18.

If this is death, was Caleb's first conscious thought, *it is sadly disappointing.*

He was curled up, folded in on himself like a newborn baby. There was blackness – not the cool, clear blackness of night, but a muffled, smothering dark. And there was pain. So much of it! Pain everywhere, in every part of him. He had died, but this was not heaven: that could not hurt so savagely. He was damned to hell. Yet there was no flaming pit, no smell of sulphur, no horde of demons. Nothing, but the enveloping dark and the pain.

And then movement. A violent jolt that made his head explode with agony. He screamed, or tried to. His mouth was stoppered with a cloth, balled and pushed so hard between his teeth that it was close to choking him. He longed to tear it out, but could not move, so tightly was he confined on all sides.

Panic – that most futile of emotions! – overwhelmed him. If he'd been free to run it might have lent an extra spur to his flight. Trapped, it did nothing but reduce him to a helpless terrified wreckage. Tears streamed down his face, his nose ran: he was going to suffocate. He had to get out! He struggled. Wrestled. Strained. But he couldn't move even a fraction of an inch.

Pa's voice in his head: *Be calm. Slow down. Take a breath.*

But his arms were tight across his chest. He couldn't fill his lungs.

Shallow breaths, then. But slow. Count. In. Hold. One, two, three. Out. Release it slowly. Now the next.

Do as Pa would do.

Come on, Caleb! God gave you a mind; he meant you to use it. So think. Use your reason!

Caleb forced himself into a state of relative calm. Where was he? Captive. In something small. A trunk perhaps. Or a chest. No. The sides were not flat. They curved against his back. Damnation, his back! The skin must have been scraped off as he'd been forced inside this thing. It smarted, sticky with sweat and blood. Rough, heavy timber against his raw, screaming flesh. *Take a breath.* Stinks like a tavern. But not ale. Something stronger. Whisky? Rum, maybe? Was he confined in a barrel?

Sound was muffled, but that regular, steady beat... It was the plod of a horse's hooves on the earth road. The creak of a harness, the turning of wheels. He was on a cart then, being carried along. By whom? To where? What did his captor intend to do with him?

He could see nothing. Smell nothing but rum and sweat and fear. His ears strained for clues.

The thud of hooves changed. They were no longer on a dirt road: cobbles now. There were people in the streets — snatches of conversation, shouts of greeting. And water? Was that the sound of water?

The cart stopped. Cries of seabirds. Men calling. Yelling orders. The chatter of women. Children. Crowds of people. The creak of rigging. The flap of canvas in the wind.

Another sudden jolt as the barrel was lifted, thumped to the ground, then pushed onto its side. Rolled over cobbles. Pain and dizziness rendered him almost unconscious. The barrel was righted, but this time it was upside down. Now his feet were uppermost. Caleb was on his head, neck nearly breaking under his own weight. Blood pounded in his skull, and poured from the wound made where he had been struck.

He had known many things in the past few months: hunger, fear, loneliness, grief. But he had never experienced such intense physical anguish as he did then.

And yet through that screaming haze of pain came a sliver of hope. As the barrel had rolled across the quayside a cork stopper had become slightly dislodged and a tiny crescent of light cut through the blackness inside. He struggled, each move a blinding, piercing new agony — and managed to get a single finger to it. Pushing the cork out, the crescent turned into a perfect circle of daylight.

He could see nothing through it, but could hear a little

more clearly the sounds of a ship being made ready to sail. And then he caught Letty's voice. Fretful. Anxious. "But where is he? He said he'd come."

Hearing her, Caleb redoubled his efforts to escape. But the barrel was suddenly hefted high and he no longer knew which way was up, which was down. With the last of his strength he pushed his finger through the hole, hoping that Letty or someone, *anyone* – customs officer, sailor, child – would see it, would demand to know why a barrel containing a man was being carried on board.

But there were no shouts. No questions. No cries of surprise or alarm. Simply another crushing thud as barrel hit deck. The slither of ropes lashing it down. For a moment everything was still. And then the slap of waves on the hull, orders yelled, feet running to and fro, the crack of canvas as sails were hoisted. The shouts of mariners as the ship cast off and got underway, shrill cries of "Farewell!" from the women and children on the quay.

One of the voices deeper than the others. So achingly familiar, it jerked his heart from his chest.

Letty!

Bidding goodbye to her father.

And then nothing but the creaking of the ship's timbers as the *Lady Jane* carried Caleb from the land.

19.

Caleb was no sailor. The river was calm as they left Tawpuddle but even the boat's slightest motion made him sick to the stomach. He'd emptied his belly over the ferryman's feet all those months ago. If he did the same now the cloth balled in his mouth would prevent its escape: he'd die a choking death in the barrel.

He squirmed and wriggled, performing the most extraordinary contortions, scraping his already injured head, but couldn't extract it. Yet maybe the barrel being rolled over cobbles, getting lifted, dropped, lifted and dropped again had somehow dislodged it. Or maybe the sheer force of his reaction to the ship's movement was sufficient. Either way, on the journey down to the river's mouth he heaved out the cloth along with the entire contents of his stomach.

And then the ship passed over the bar. On the Tawpuddle side of it the river had been almost tranquil, but on the other the sea stirred like a vast beast rousing from its slumber. The swell carried the *Lady Jane* up to the peak of a wave then threw her over into the valley of the next.

There is no misery quite like the sickness that comes from being on board ship. Though he tried, no effort of will could conquer it. As Caleb endured its ghastly, life-sapping pangs he prayed for his life to end swiftly. Had his captors tossed the barrel overboard he'd have welcomed the drowning waves' embrace. He retched and heaved, heaved and retched and even though belly and guts were utterly evacuated the retching and heaving did not cease. He'd never felt such exhaustion. And each spasm set his wounded head pounding until he felt it had surely split in two.

A pitiful heap of misery, he was scarcely able to hear the conversation of the men on deck, much less to make sense of it. What did any of it matter? The sickness had robbed him of curiosity, of fear, of everything.

It went on for an hour, maybe two or more: to Caleb it seemed an eternity. The swell was already high and growing higher. The ship's timbers groaned and protested at every slapping wave.

But at last there came a slight lessening of the sea's violence. Caleb heard chains rattling and guessed that the crew had dropped the anchor. Had he slept? He didn't think so. He listened. There was nothing but the wind and the sea. They were not in port then. And yet they had stopped.

There were sounds of great activity on deck. Sails were furled. The captain gave the command and a second anchor was dropped. With the ship at rest Caleb caught snatches of the crew's conversation.

"We was told to do it tonight. Get the lot stowed on shore, he said."

"Too much swell. I'll not risk the men."

"Sir Robert won't be best pleased."

"Sir Robert won't know. Sir Robert ain't taking the risk. Sir Robert ain't never tried rowing there."

"Thought it was meant to be finished by now."

"Been harder to build than they thought."

There were protests. Grumbles. Then someone – the captain? – said, "We'll wait for this storm to blow over. The cliffs will keep us from the worst of it. We won't get no thanks if we lose the cargo in this swell."

Grunts of relief. "What do we do with this 'un?" A sudden kick at Caleb's barrel. Despite the sickness, he listened hard.

"I'll not do it." It was the voice of Letty's father.

"You'll do as you're bid, Edward, same as the rest of us. We're too deep in this now to go thinking of getting out. You want to see us hanged? We was told to get rid of him, and that's what we'll be doing. You heard what Benson said: we unload *here*, then we sail for Maryland. There'll be slavers who'll take him."

Caleb's head swam. His blood chilled. They planned to sell him? He'd rather die!

"He's been hit bad. What if he don't make the crossing?"

"Bury him at sea. We weigh him down good and proper. Don't want him washing up on the beach like his father did."

For a second Caleb's nausea was forgotten. Pa! They'd disposed of Pa too? Had they murdered him? He should have beaten his uncle to a pulp when he'd had the chance. He'd do it now. Burst from the barrel. If only he didn't feel so damned dizzy.

Having agreed to rest at anchor until the storm blew itself out, the men fell to drinking. There was nothing else for them to do. Caleb heard Edward Avery offer to take the watch. The others must have gone below for he heard nothing more.

Whether he slept, or whether pain drove him into unconsciousness, Caleb didn't know. He was only aware that some hours must have passed, for it was dark when the barrel lid was pulled open.

Cold, fresh air hit his skin so hard he felt he'd been slapped. His end had come. This was it.

But in the moonlight the face that stared into his with fearful intensity wasn't a sailor's.

"You stink!"

Letty?

Caleb's vision blurred. He shut his eyes. Opened them and saw her father was beside her. Seizing the back of Caleb's shirt, Edward pulled him from the barrel.

Collapsed upon the deck, every muscle, every inch of

skin screaming in protest, Caleb tried to make sense of what he saw. They were anchored close to cliffs. Strange cliffs that didn't run in both directions the way they should. There was just a piece of them – a chunk, broken off from the rest and dropped in the ocean by a giant hand. Sea washed all around it. Odd. And how had Letty got here? Did she come aboard in Tawpuddle? Was it her who'd hit him? Had she planned to sell him into slavery all along?

He would have accused her. Weakness alone stopped the words leaving his mouth.

"Can you climb down the ladder?" she demanded.

Still Caleb couldn't speak.

It was Edward who answered his unasked questions. "Letty rowed out here, God bless her. To rescue you. You got to get into her boat. Now."

"Do you mean to kill me?"

"Lord love you, Caleb, I've done some bad things in my time but murder's not one of them. I don't intend it ever should be."

"What will you tell the others?"

"I'll think of something."

Letty took Caleb's hand and was tugging him across the deck. "There isn't time for talk. We got to get off now before they see us. Come on. Shift your arse."

Clouds scudded across the full moon but there was a moment's respite. A moment's glimpse of the rowing boat that bobbed at the bottom of the rope ladder. Letty's boat.

Seeing it brought sudden clarity to Caleb's befuddled mind. She had rowed that tiny thing across the open sea in pursuit of the *Lady Jane*. She must have seen his finger poking from the barrel. Great God in heaven, she was a marvel. She had no equal, not in the whole of Creation!

Her father was embracing her, clutching her so tightly to his chest Caleb feared Edward might crack her ribs. He released her and there was one last searing look between father and daughter – one so tender, so full of sorrow that Caleb had to turn his head away. Then Letty went over the side, climbing down the rope ladder as nimbly as a monkey.

And now it was Caleb's turn.

He began his descent, but his fingers were stiff as claws. His numbed feet slipped and he fell, thudding into the boat, almost upsetting it.

Under her breath Letty cursed. The wind was rising with each passing second.

There were pinpricks of light in the far distance. But Letty did not turn the boat towards them.

"We can't make it back to shore. Not now. Storm's getting worse. We got to get to the island. We can wait it out there."

The island? That broken chunk of cliff was the island! The familiar dot in the bay looked so different from here.

Letty heaved on the oars but the wind was against them and she could barely make any headway.

"Come on," she said, "you've got to help."

Keeping his weight low, Caleb clambered over, took an oar and tried – tried desperately – to control it. But he was more hindrance than help to her and after his oar almost slipped its rowlock Letty cried, "Leave it be. Sit still else you'll have us over."

Caleb could do nothing but watch as she battled the sea, jaw clamped tight, hair plastered across her face as the rain began to fall.

The *Lady Jane* was at anchor perhaps half a mile from the island and Letty had covered but a fraction of the distance when there was a great clap of thunder and the ocean was lit by a flash of lightning. Rain cascaded from the sky in torrents.

But wind and rain were the least of Letty's concerns. "They've seen us!" Another bolt of lightning lit up the men on the deck pointing, yelling. And now the crew were scurrying up the rigging, setting the sails, weighing anchor, coming in pursuit.

Suddenly the wind veered around and began pushing the rowing boat hard towards the island, the force of it throwing Caleb from the bench. It was a help to Letty, but sail is faster than oar. She could not hope to outrun the *Lady Jane* but it didn't stop her trying.

Half a mile distant, quarter of a mile, the beach within sight, but the *Lady Jane* was close now, five hundred yards, four hundred, closer with each heartbeat. Another flash of lightning and it was plain that there was some sort of struggle taking place on deck. There were yells. Shouts. A scream. A man was fighting for his life.

"Father!" Letty paused at the oars. The *Lady Jane* was almost upon them.

And then a wave as large as a house took hold of the rowing boat, flipped it into the air and turned it upside down.

Caleb was tossed to one side, Letty to the other. The water was icy cold but it woke Caleb, cleared his head, numbed the pain.

He could not row, but he could swim. Letty was a sailor: she'd never learned. Once, twice, she went down before he could reach her. Each time she bobbed back up, screaming, gasping, thrashing. If she went under a third time, that would be the end of her.

Pa had once told Caleb that there is danger in swimming towards a drowning person. In their desperation they will seize you so hard they are likely to take you both down.

Caleb swam behind, hoping she wouldn't notice him until he had hold of her hair. But a wave knocked her sideways and seeing him so close she lunged for him. There was nothing for it but to put both hands on top of her head and push her under as though he meant to drown her.

The shock made her limp. He was able to get his hands beneath her arms and then to tug her up to where she could breathe again.

"Lie back. Kick, Letty. Kick!"

Progress was slow and hard, the deadening cold making their limbs sluggish. Letty's skirt was tangled around her legs, dragging her deeper. And all the while Caleb could see the *Lady Jane* coming ever closer. She was going to run them down, they would be ground beneath her hull. Caleb strained against the might of the sea, struggling to keep Letty's head above water, desperate to evade the ship.

A flash of lightning. Thunder. Another flash. She loomed above them...

And then a flash brighter than any Caleb had ever seen knifed across the sky and hit the *Lady Jane*'s mast, hurtling down its length, crackling over the deck. A direct strike, as though from the very hand of God.

There was an explosion deep within the ship's belly, louder and more terrifying than any clap of thunder.

Gunpowder!

The thought had a fraction of a second to pass through Caleb's head before great shards of timber blasted outwards from the hull. Jagged spears hurtled through the storm. The air itself was like a fist that punched them towards the rocks thrusting out of the sea, savage and sharp.

Caleb kept swimming, but Letty was a dead weight now, so limp he feared she'd been killed by the explosion. What was left of the ship tilted to the left. Her sides were split, gaping wide to the sea. She seemed to pause, as if stunned by what had befallen, before the water rushed in and devoured her.

And now Letty recovered the use of her limbs. She kicked hard towards the rocks, screaming at Caleb to do the same. Had she taken leave of her senses? She'd be torn to shreds! He had to keep her from them. They fought each other, going under, gasping, wrestling, struggling. They were almost upon the rocks when Caleb felt a strange and alarming sensation.

Suddenly the water seemed to thin and become insubstantial as air. The *Lady Jane* was pulling them towards her. They were being sucked down. And Letty knew! She knew it would happen! That's why she'd tried to reach the rocks. In sheer desperation he hurled her at a jagged outcrop, pushing her against it. It tore flesh, ripping great slashes across Letty's hands but she held on. The sea dragged at Caleb and he grasped Letty's skirts to save himself.

Another flash of lightning showed Letty clinging to the cold, jagged stones. Caleb clinging to her legs. Both of them watching the *Lady Jane*'s mast disappear beneath the sea.

PART 3

1.

Through long hours of darkness Letty and Caleb were blasted and bludgeoned by the twin forces of wind and sea. But little by little the tempest abated and, though the rain continued, the thunder and lightning passed on towards the mainland. Tides ebb and flow even in a storm. Inch by inch the sea level waned.

By dawn the rain had stopped, the tide had gone out and they were able to climb slowly, unsteadily, along the rocks and down to a shingle beach. From the mainland the island had looked like a flat stretch of barren rock, but now Caleb saw that it curved like a horseshoe around a tiny bay.

They moved stiffly, as though they had aged a lifetime in that one night, their shredded clothes sodden, their bodies chilled to the marrow. There was a cave at the foot of the cliffs and there inside its mouth was a small quantity of driftwood that had escaped the worst of the storm. Shreds of rope were mixed in amongst them that would serve as kindling. By some miracle the sea had not stripped Caleb of the contents of his pockets: he still had Pa's hellfire pipe, the bag of powdered resin, the tinderbox. His hands were so cold it took an age to strike a spark and when it did the rope would not catch. Letty was standing, moving from foot to foot, rubbing her hands, chafing her limbs to restore a little heat to them, her eyes on the sea, searching. Her voice, when it came, was little more than a whisper.

"Did they all go down, do you think? Every man?"

Caleb forgot his attempts to light a fire. He was on his feet, arms about her, holding her tight to his chest, his face buried in her hair. He longed to lie to her – to assure her that there was hope, there was a chance that Edward had survived, that she would one day see her father again alive and well. But he could not. He knew full well that no man could have lived through the destruction of the *Lady Jane*. As did she.

Gulls wheeled and shrieked above their heads while Letty wept. She seemed small, fragile as Anne, broken with grieving.

The birds' cries were eerie. Mournful. But then they changed, cackling in alarm as they spun away, startled by something. He turned his head to see what had disturbed them.

And saw that he and Letty were not alone.

Drenched as they both were, half frozen, cut and bruised by the rocks, their state was nothing compared to that of the wretched souls who emerged from the shadows of the cave.

Cries of birds ... souls of drowned sailors... "Ghosts," he breathed.

Caleb's arms tightened around Letty in sudden panic. She broke free, and let out a whimper of fear – a noise he had never expected to hear from her and which filled him with sudden courage. No harm would come to her while he was alive.

As the spectres came closer he saw their feet made impressions on the sand. Not ghosts then: living, breathing men. But in what a wretched state! Clothes in tatters, hair matted, ribs clearly showing through their skin. And their eyes told a story of deprivation and despair. Were they shipwrecked sailors: stranded and slowly starving?

They came closer, crowding in around Caleb and Letty. Suddenly the tale of *Robinson Crusoe* filled his head: savages, pursuing his man Friday. Cannibals, killing their victims, feasting on human flesh, dancing on the beach. These men were clearly desperate – who knew what they might be capable of? He and Letty should run. Where to? There was nowhere on this godforsaken rock to hide! And no way to get off it either.

One of the men extended his hand. Caleb flinched, expecting to be struck, but then he realized the man meant only to greet him. He pressed his palm to Caleb's and shook it. The voice that emerged from the stranger's mouth croaked like a rusty gate, but his words quelled Caleb's wild fears.

"Jack Lancey at your service."

Caleb looked at Letty as, one by one, the other men gave their names: the names they had last heard recited in Sir Robert's kitchen by Narcissus Puddleby. A list of dead men.

"Mark Andrews."

"Thomas Sinnett."

"John Kingscot."

"Henry Meddon."

"Edwin Hampton."

"Robert Buckleigh."

"Walter Coombs."

"William Hockin."

"Edward Braddick."

"Richard Brendon."

There was a pause. "And Joseph Chappell?" Caleb surveyed the ragged assembly. "Joseph Chappell is missing."

At the mention of Pa's name the men began talking all at once. "You know Joseph?"

"You have seen him?"

"Did he make it to land?"

"Is that why you've come?"

"He made it to shore! God be praised."

"Have you come to rescue us?"

Hope lit their faces. It broke Caleb's heart anew to have to tell them of Pa's death. "Joseph Chappell was my father. I found his body on the beach five months ago."

There were sighs of despair. Groans of pain. Murmurings of grief and sorrow and words of heartfelt sympathy.

Caleb cut through them. "Tell me, please," he said, "what in the name of God happened to him?"

Jack Lancey began to speak, the others adding to his story as it went on. Standing there, drenched and dripping, in that early summer dawn, Letty and Caleb clinging to each other for warmth and comfort, the sorry tale was laid before them.

The convicts had left Tawpuddle chained in the *Linnet*'s hold, bound for Maryland. None of them had expected to see the light of day until they reached that foreign shore but they had not been more than two hours at sea before the *Linnet* had come to rest at anchor.

"They took us off the ship," said Jack Lancey. "Lowered the little rowboat over the side. Put us in. Stranded us here."

"We was marooned. Every one of us."

"They said we wasn't convicts no more. We was slaves now."

"We'd be here until the day we died."

"Only Joseph wouldn't accept it, see? He said he didn't work for no one but himself."

"He made a raft. Took him weeks, gathering up bits of driftwood and the like. And then one day he put out to sea on it. Said it could only be three or four miles to the mainland. He meant to paddle the whole way. He'd get us help, he said."

But Pa knew no more of the sea than he did, thought Caleb. The raft must have broken up. Maybe Pa had been washed from it by the waves or caught in a rip tide. Keeping his promises to Caleb and the convicts had killed him.

Letty was sobbing quietly beside him. There was nothing to be done for Joseph Chappell or Edward Avery. There on that bleak island beach Letty and Caleb held each other and wept for their dead fathers.

2.

Following the dreadful chill of the night's storm, a hot day seemed in prospect. The clothes on their backs began to dry and, as the sun rose higher, Caleb and Letty were slowly warmed through. Grief may be overwhelming, but in time the living body makes demands that refuse to be ignored. Both were bruised and sore, their flesh torn and grazed, their limbs aching and weary. Added to which now came a raging hunger.

The convicts had been marooned on the island for almost ten months. Jack Lancey had informed Caleb that supplies had been brought from the mainland from time to time. Meagre rations, but enough to ensure that they did not starve. The *Lady Jane*, they presumed, had been bringing fresh food. Now she had gone down and all her cargo with her. If they were to eat, Caleb decided, they must make use of what was on the island.

The beach was backed by cliffs. Thomas Sinnett pointed out a narrow path that zigzagged up from there to a plateau of land at the top. It was steep, he said, with a sweet freshwater spring halfway up, but the rest of the climb was scarcely worth the effort. The land was coarse, growing with brambles and bracken so thick a man could barely pass. "There be rabbits up there, but you don't stand a hope in hell of catching the buggers."

Henry Meddon agreed. "Food enough all around, I'd say. Just no means of getting none."

It appeared that the convicts had all been city dwellers. Builders. Labourers. Stonemasons. They were skilled men, but lacked the knowledge to feed themselves from the land. The wandering, nomadic life that Caleb had led with Pa now served him well. He climbed the steep path to the top of the island, battling through the undergrowth, and saw from their droppings that rabbits were plentiful – in fact there were several within a few feet, nibbling the grass in broad daylight, untroubled by the sight of him. There being neither foxes nor hawks to hunt them the population had multiplied and they had lost much of their natural wariness. With no gamekeepers or man-traps to stop him Caleb intended to harvest as many of them as he could.

It took some time for him to fashion snares. Shreds of washed-up rope plaited together for a noose; driftwood for hook and stake; a bent branch of gorse to make the whole thing taut. He'd watched Pa do it often enough, but Pa had made it look easy. Without proper tools and with limited materials the task took him five times as long, but before noon he had set half a dozen crude contraptions along the animal trails that criss-crossed the island and by nightfall he had three fat rabbits. A swift blow to each one's head with a stone and then Caleb reset the snares so he could catch more overnight. Letty, meanwhile, who had neither line nor net to fish with, had instead scraped mussels and whelks from the rocks.

The convicts had not been left with the means to light a fire, for that might have been seen from the shore. Such food as they had been provided with had been dried, cured or salted, but they could not now eat raw rabbit or shellfish.

As evening drew in they debated the merits of lighting a fire with Pa's tinderbox.

"If it gets seen it might bring help," said Jack Lancey. He seemed cheered by Caleb and Letty's presence – as if their arrival might bring an end to his enslavement. Caleb wished he could share Jack's optimism.

"Bring danger, more likely," replied Letty. "Leastways to Caleb and me. I don't suppose anyone on land saw the *Lady Jane* go down. They'll think she's on her way – that Caleb's been got rid of. That gives us a bit of time to work out how we're going to get away from here. We don't want to be facing Sir Robert before we're good and ready for him."

No one asked what she meant by that. Amongst the convicts the hope that Sir Robert might be punished for his wrongdoing had died with Joseph Chappell.

In the end Caleb did light a fire, but only after dark

when the smoke would not be seen rising in the clear air. He chose a place on the beach where the cliffs curved around in an almost perfect semi-circle and it could not been seen from the mainland.

Roasted rabbit. Mussels. Whelks. They ate. They talked. And as they talked the plot that concerned the *Linnet* was stripped bare.

It was Richard Brendon who explained that it was not just the convicts who had been unloaded onto the island. The *Linnet*'s cargo had also been taken to shore and stowed in the cave. "It took one hell of a time. Every last barrel had to be lowered down into a little boat then rowed ashore."

"I should have known," Letty said. She turned to Caleb. "Didn't I say the *Linnet* was too low in the water, that it was a miracle she got so far before she sank? But why take the cargo off? Why sail an empty ship halfway across the ocean?"

Caleb considered her question. An aged, worthless vessel sinking, as everybody who knew anything about shipping had thought she might. It had been a lucky chance that the *Celandine* had been passing close enough to rescue the crew. Or had it? In front of Narcissus Puddleby the *Linnet*'s men had spoken of a terrible storm, but he'd endured a hellish tempest the night before and Letty's little boat had overturned. How could a ship the size of the *Linnet* be overwhelmed by waves when the rowing boat carrying the crew had survived? It occurred to him for the first time that the magistrate hadn't called upon the captain of the

Celandine to verify the story. Was it possible that this violent tempest had not, in fact, ever occurred?

He said slowly, "I saw papers in Sir Robert's study. I don't understand the business, but I did discover that he was paid a large sum of money when the *Linnet* sank. There were men in Torcester – what did they call themselves? – underwriters ... that was it. They covered the cost of the ship. Oh – and the cargo too. Could it be that her sinking was deliberate?"

The convicts shrugged. Shook their heads. Said nothing. Clearly the concept of compensation for a lost ship was as alien to them as it had been to Caleb.

Letty frowned as she thought the matter over. "You think she might have been scuttled? Yes ... that would make sense of things. Their tale of hitting rocks in the middle of the ocean didn't hang together at all."

"Would it be difficult to sink a ship?"

"No, not with timbers half rotten. They'd have driven a hook through the hull."

"And timed it for when there was another ship in sight to pick them up."

Henry Meddon spoke. "So your Sir Robert got paid for a lost ship. Got paid for a lost cargo too when it was sitting here safe the whole time."

"Is it still here?" asked Caleb.

"No. They sent little fishing boats to pick it up, bit by bit."

"He'll have sold the whole lot on," Jack Lancey said.

"Made twice as much money as he would on any honest deal." There was a pause and then he looked around the company and said, "You know what I was condemned for? Stealing a pie."

"I took a loaf," said Thomas Sinnett.

"Piece of bacon," said Mark Andrews.

"And why did we do it? Because our families were starving. This man – what d'you call him? – Sir Robert? He makes us look like mere beginners. I'll tell you this, boys: if you want to get away with a crime make it a big enough one, and make sure your name begins with 'Sir'. Can't no one touch you then."

He'd spoken no more than the truth. There was bitter laughter and after it had subsided, Caleb asked Letty, "Would no one notice the cargo coming into port?"

"Not if it was unloaded in Fishpool. The customs men wouldn't come out of Tawpuddle on account of a little fishing boat."

"Of course!" He'd seen it himself, hadn't he? That very first day he arrived: a cart coming up the road loaded with bales of linen making him climb into the hedge. And William Benson had been supervising the unloading of a fishing vessel the day they'd argued about parliament and the loss of eleven days in September. What had Benson's words been? "Keep your head down and mouth shut ... same as everyone else." Caleb had thought the words were meant for him and him alone, but perhaps they were also a warning to every man present on the jetty, indeed to every soul in Fishpool! Caleb had been too much of an innocent to understand their significance back then. "But why were you all marooned here?" he said, looking at Henry Meddon. "What was the purpose of that?"

"They said we got to build them a wall," replied Jack Lancey. "One that sticks out into the water from this beach. See over there? That's the beginnings of it."

"You're making a harbour?" The idea seemed preposterous to Caleb. "Why do that on a barren island?"

Before any of the men could answer, Letty spoke. "I reckon the *Linnet* was just the start. Sir Robert's an ambitious man, he's got big plans. Smuggling. Takes too long unloading a whole ship with just a rowboat. You anchor offshore by this island too long and folks are bound to notice sooner or later, start asking questions. But with a harbour in a hidden bay? One built by men who can't go telling anyone about it? A good solid wall a ship can moor alongside? That makes it all so much faster. Easy to do it from here. And no customs officers hanging around, like there are in Tawpuddle."

Caleb remembered the coins, slid between the sheets of the ship's records. "They can be bribed."

Letty shrugged. "True. Expensive, though. Say a big ship comes from the Americas. Sir Robert gets it unloaded here then takes the cargo on through Fishpool. Use the island as a base and he doesn't need to pay any bribes and he doesn't need to pay taxes either. All the profit goes straight into his pocket."

"And would there be much money to be made from such a scheme?"

"Once the harbour's up and running … yes, I'd say he could make a fortune."

"But the wall isn't yet finished."

"It ain't been easy," said Henry Meddon. "Us can only work between the tides, see? They was bringing gunpowder to blast more rock. Two or three times now we been well along with the work, but then a storm comes and smashes it back down."

"Perhaps that's just as well," Caleb said, for a chilling thought had occurred to him.

"What do you mean?"

Caleb looked from one man to the next, his eyes falling on each of the convicts in turn as he talked. "When the work is complete, what further use will you be? You're dead men – that's what the records say. Once you've done the job, he'll want to be rid of you. The same way he wants to be rid of Letty and me."

3.

They couldn't build a raft that would safely carry eleven men, together with Letty and Caleb, across such an expanse of water. If they were ever to get off the island they needed to find another way.

Letty's knowledge of the sea and of the shipping trade was vastly superior to any of the men's. When she spoke, they listened. "A signal fire. That's the way to do it. If we catch the attention of a passing ship – the right one, mind, not one of Sir Robert's – why then they'll row a boat over to pick us up, take us to the mainland, set us down."

"And what do we do then?"

"Time enough to decide that when we're back on the shore."

The lighting of a fire would take time, and couldn't be easily controlled. A beacon would be a blunt instrument – seen by too many ships. Yet as well as Pa's tinderbox Caleb had the hellfire pipe. A puff of breath – a single ball of flame, come and gone in an instant – it was a risky business, but it had more chance of being seen by only those whose attention they wished to attract. They must be prepared when the moment came. It was just a matter of waiting for the right vessel.

And so Letty and Caleb kept a lookout, daily climbing to the top of the island, pushing through briar and bracken to the northern side. They watched and waited, waited and watched. One day passed, then two, then three, and they were days of surprising contentment. There was a beauty to the place, a calm that Caleb found soothing. While the weather remained fine he thought there could be nothing more pleasant than to keep company with Letty, watching seals bobbing their heads above the water's surface, seeing dolphins leap and spin in pursuit of mackerel, and seabirds wheel and soar across the waves.

Removed from the village, removed from the silences and secrets that thickened the air, Letty and Caleb began to talk more freely than he would have dreamed possible.

She was grieving bitterly for her father and, like Caleb, she also feared for the future and for Anne and for Dorcas. Without the money Edward brought in how could Anne keep a roof over their heads? Dark thoughts indeed, and yet speaking them aloud seemed to lighten her load a little.

Letty talked of her father, and Caleb talked of his. He told her of the country house where they'd spent a winter. How Pa had scared the life out of him, waking Caleb one morning with a screech after he'd been up all night carving his new Punch. Pa had stood there with a grin on his face, his right hand raised in the air, the carved wooden head fixed to his first two fingers, a pair of puppet hands to the second two and his thumb. The puppet was as yet ungloved, unclothed.

Sitting there on the cliff, Caleb began to laugh at the memory. He told Letty, "There was no costume. The puppet was naked, you see? And when I said so Punch looked down and saw Pa's bare palm. He clamped his hands together as if he was covering his privates. It sounds absurd, but oh, it did make us both laugh. It made us laugh so much that Pa was doubled over and Punch's head came flying off."

Laughter, Pa always said, is like a contagion. Once one person begins, it spreads to all who breathe it in. It infected Letty then and she lay on the grass, chuckling.

"I do like the sound of him. I wish I'd known him. He was a good man, your pa," she said at last.

"As was your father. I am glad to have known him." He paused and looked at her. "It must have been strange for you when he married Anne."

"It was. But I was grateful for it, to tell you the truth. He was always away at sea – I got passed from pillar to post around the village until she came along."

"You never felt any resentment then?"

"Oh, there was a little at first, I suppose. Father was so wrapped up in her! He always treated her like she was a piece of porcelain. Me and her – we're so different. She's so delicate – makes me feel like a clumping great carthorse. But I like her well enough. I just can't be like her, that's all."

Caleb, thinking of what his own fate would have been without Letty said, "I thank God for that."

There was a pause while they both looked out to sea. And then she turned to him and said, "Did your Pa never speak of your mother?"

There was something in the way she asked, something in the frankness of those green eyes staring into his that made Caleb's heart contract. "No, he didn't. Why?"

She glanced down as if deciding something. Then she said, "Before you came … well, Father was at sea. One of the lads in the village started paying attention to me."

At once Caleb bristled. "Who was he?"

Surprised by his tone, Letty asked, "Is this jealousy, Caleb?"

"Yes. No! Perhaps. What of it?"

"I never thought to see you mind what I did."

"I do not! It is your own affair."

"Is that so?" Her eyebrows arched teasingly.

"Yes. No. I do … mind, I mean. There! Does that satisfy you?"

She smiled but carried on. "It was nothing – a bit of foolishness, was all. But Anne warned me off him. We had something of a set-to. I said how I'd do what I damned well pleased, that I was plenty old enough to have a sweetheart, that she couldn't stop me. So she told me of the trouble she'd had back years ago, around about the time her father lost all his money."

Goosebumps prickled along Caleb's arms despite the day's warmth. "Trouble? Of what sort?"

Letty was deadly earnest. "The worst kind. For a lady."

"Go on."

"You know how some well-to-do folk buy themselves a page boy? A pretty little African slave lad, dressed up in fine clothes, treated like a lapdog?"

"Yes," Caleb said grimly. He'd seen several during his travels with Pa. The sight had always sickened him.

"It's all well and good until they grow up," Letty sighed. "What happens to them then? I wonder. Anyway, Anne and your Pa were given one of them when they were small, name of Pompey, same age as her. He was supposed to be their playmate, only he was so sick for his home, so sad, it fair broke her heart. They became friends, all three of them, she said: true friends. And then your Pa was sent away to school and she and Pompey was alone. They'd grown up together. She loved him. Then her father's ship went down and all hell broke loose. The estate was broken up, everything taken by creditors, Pompey included. He got sold to the Indies and Anne had to go into service. Can you imagine? Only she was with child by then." Letty suddenly flushed.

Caleb looked at her narrowly. "I don't understand…"

She met his eyes full square and said bluntly, "Anne isn't your aunt. She's your mother. Pompey was your father."

For a moment he thought Letty had made it up. It was so ridiculous! And yet … no … it was like a broken plate being put back together, piece by piece, the pattern finally coming clear. Anne, looking for his father in Caleb's face. Anne in a fever, looking almost ready to kiss him; pained with disappointment, demanding, *Where's your father?*

"Why did you not tell me this before?"

"She made me promise to keep it quiet. She regretted telling me the moment the words were out of her mouth. Terrible state she was in. Made me swear on Father's life never to say anything to anybody." There was a catch in her throat. "On Father's life… No point keeping that promise now, is there? But I couldn't say anything before, Caleb. I just couldn't."

"And so she gave me away? As if I was nothing!"

Letty took his hand in hers. "What else could she do? Joseph promised he'd look after you, raise you as his own. He was glad to do it, Caleb. Pompey was his friend too."

"But to give away her own child!"

"Oh, Caleb! She had no choice. An unwed mother? A gentlewoman lying with a slave? Bearing his child? She was lucky not to fetch up in the workhouse or worse. She got a place as a lady's maid at Norton Manor. She had to behave like nothing had ever happened: like she never even had a brother, let alone a child. It tore her apart, but what else could she do? She said not a single day had gone by when she didn't think of you."

Once more the world had shifted in its orbit. Everything had changed. Pa was not his father, but his uncle? It was a bitter blow to bear. Caleb *wanted* to be Joseph's son, and yet he felt more powerfully than ever how good a man Pa had been, for he was not obliged to love Caleb but had done so. To find he had a mother after all these years was actually a great blessing. And Dorcas – not his cousin, but his half-sister.

Yet it was such a weighty secret to have lain so long in the dark! "Why didn't Anne tell me?"

A foolish question – he knew the answer before the words had left his mouth. Hadn't he seen enough women in the city streets reduced to beggary, dying in gutters, or condemned to the life of a whore? Women did not have children out of wedlock and remain in respectable employment. Not even the charity of the parish would support a fallen woman. If the village gossips heard of it now, Anne would be ruined. No one must ever know.

"Did you never wonder why she fainted when she saw you? You look like your pa, she said. Your real pa. She thought you were a ghost."

"Poor Anne! I didn't mean to shock her."

"It was quite an entrance." Letty laughed suddenly. "Stew all over the floor. The place full of street urchins."

"And then you appeared. Towering in the doorway, staring at me! You hated me from the moment I arrived."

"I never hated you!" She looked at him with tender

surprise. "How could you think that? The first time I laid eyes on you, I thought you were the most handsome man I'd ever seen."

Caleb felt himself to be teetering on the brink of something. He didn't answer. He couldn't. He was too scared to move.

It was Letty who leaned forward, took his face in her hands, and kissed him.

4.

Caleb knew that whatever lay ahead would be dangerous and difficult, but he and Letty would face it together, side by side, and there was great comfort in that.

By night they sat with the convicts by the fire to eat and talk over what should be done if they found a rescuer to carry them to shore. Caleb and Letty were determined that Sir Robert's crimes should be revealed. But to whom? Narcissus Puddleby was in his pocket. Of course there were other magistrates, other men of law, but having seen how a judge condemned Pa when he was perfectly innocent Caleb had little faith in any of them. Were there no honest men to whom they could appeal?

Nightly, they discussed the matter. Nightly, the matter lay unresolved.

There was, besides, the question of what they would tell the captain of any ship that picked up the felons.

"We tell the truth, do we not?" Caleb said.

"No. We do not." Jack Lancey was firm. "'Twas you who

251

said we're dead men. If we get off this place, well then, it's a chance to start afresh. We can take new names, every one of us."

"But won't you give our story your backing?" asked Caleb.

"Who'd believe the likes of us?"

"We have evidence." He turned to Letty. "You still have Pa's ring, do you not?"

Letty patted her pocket. "I've got it safe."

Jack Lancey still shook his head. "There isn't a man here who'll trust the law."

Caleb persisted. "If the case is made against Sir Robert, if it comes to a trial, you'd be needed as witnesses."

"Lord love you! You think I'd walk into court, tell them who I am?" Jack Lancey laughed. "And what would happen next? You think they'd let me go free? They'd have me in irons again soon as look at me."

"But don't you wish to see Sir Robert punished? He enslaved you all! Abandoned you here. A judge would surely make allowances..."

"Maybe he would. Maybe he wouldn't. Ain't no way of knowing, is there? Sir Robert might have all the judges and all the magistrates in the whole damned county in his pay. 'Tisn't worth the risk."

Henry Meddon intervened. "Look, lad, we all been sitting in that stinking gaol for months before we was put on board ship. Doesn't a man of us ever want to go back.

Ain't nothing you can say will change our minds."

Disappointed though he was, Caleb could hardly blame them. Pa had never had a good word to say about anyone in authority either. They were all out for themselves: whether in parliament or palace or church. An honest man was rarer than hen's teeth!

And then a thought snagged in Caleb's head.

"Letty!" he said. "The Bishop of Torcester! He spoke up for Pa. He knew him to be an honest man. A bishop's word would carry weight, wouldn't it? If we can convince him of the truth, surely we'll have a chance of justice?"

Letty and Caleb were decided. If they escaped from the island, if they safely reached the shore, if they could make the journey to the city without Sir Robert or his men catching up with them, it was to the bishop they would go.

Time was now running against them.

The same current that had carried Pa's body to the beach would take the *Lady Jane*'s sailors there too, Letty said, in time. Even if they were bloated, their faces distorted – a crew of eleven: one at least was sure to be recognized if not by a ring, then by an item of clothing, a birthmark, a tattoo. And if Caleb was not amongst the dead? It would not take long for Sir Robert to send men in search of him.

And so Letty and Caleb kept watch, come rain, come shine, come high and low water.

Ships passed the island daily, but selecting the right one

to hail was no easy task. One afternoon a vessel that Letty identified as Bristol-bound came into sight. Caleb readied himself and the pipe, but Letty stayed his hand.

"Might be slavers." She didn't say more. She didn't need to.

A day later another ship passed, this one from Ireland. It would have served, but a fishing boat was spreading its nets near by. If the fishermen saw a signal word would pass from them to the village and on to Norton Manor. They dared not risk it.

And then at last a Dutch vessel came sailing close to the island's northern shore and there were no others in sight.

Pulse racing, Caleb blew on the pipe. A plume of hellfire and smoke billowed out but the ship sailed on.

"Do it again!" cried Letty. She pulled off her apron and waved it over her head.

Caleb filled his lungs and blew harder. Flames singed his eyebrows, sending the stink of burning hair up along with the smoke.

There was a movement on deck. A small flash of light as the sun caught the glass of the telescope pointed in their direction. A command must have been given, for slowly the ship changed its course, tacking around the eastern edge of the island. It would come to anchor in the bay.

They must hurry, but Caleb couldn't leave the snares set – to trap a rabbit which would slowly die was a thing he'd not endure. Once he'd taken them up they ran down the cliff path to meet the ship, tearing clothes and skin on the brambles. By the time they reached the beach the eleven convicts were standing on the shingle and a rowboat was on its way to rescue them.

They were taken off the beach and before long were climbing the ladder and standing on the deck of the ship that had come to save them. Being on the water, Caleb's sickness returned and he was utterly unable to speak. It was Thomas Sinnett who told the captain a tale of a shipwreck, for what other excuse could any of them give for being stranded on a deserted island?

The captain had little English, so he did not question their story although he did not entirely believe it. But whatever had happened to this motley crew was hardly his concern. Best to be rid of them as soon as possible. Once the anchor was raised he turned his ship towards the shore. For a while Caleb dreaded that he would make for Tawpuddle, but it seemed the tide wasn't high enough to carry them over the bar. Instead they came to rest near a small fishing village some ten miles west. After climbing back down into the rowboat, they were landed without incident in a small cove. There Caleb and Letty took their leave of the convicts, each man giving them a solemn farewell, each man wishing them the best that good fortune could bring. And then they melted away, leaving Letty and Caleb free to pursue their own path.

5.

It was ten miles of walking. Ten miles along the coast on a path that climbed from cove to clifftop and back like a series of gigantic waves. On level ground it would have taken three, perhaps four hours. On this terrain it took twice as long and by the time they were in sight of Fishpool the light was starting to fade.

They had approached from the west, agreeing to wait until nightfall before going on. While Fishpool slept they'd creep to Anne's house, for they couldn't leave her without a word. Caleb had disappeared and then Letty: she must be in an agony of uncertainty about what had become of both of them. And – oh dear God! – they must break the dreadful news of the *Lady Jane*'s sinking and of her husband's death.

They made their way first to the barn in which they'd rehearsed Pa's show. Before they went to Anne they would collect both theatre and puppets. If, as seemed possible, they were destined for a life on the road they must have some means of supporting themselves. To retrieve the show made sense. Besides, neither could bear to leave the puppets behind: they meant life, a future, the hope that all would one day be well.

The sun was sinking into the sea as they approached the barn, both of them keeping low to the ground, staying on the far side of the hedge lest anyone should see them. Such caution seemed excessive until they came within ten yards of the barn door and heard from within a sudden cough followed by a curse.

"Damn you! *Keep quiet*, he said. We got to be silent as the grave."

"A man can't help coughing!"

"Want me to tell him that?"

"Don't you go squealing on me!"

"Well, shut your mouth, then."

"'Twas you started cussing."

A few more grumbles and then the men resumed their watch.

Letty and Caleb had frozen behind the hedge, but now, slowly, slowly, inched away to a distance where they could talk unheard.

Though the voices were familiar Caleb couldn't put faces to them. Letty, however, knew in an instant who they were. "Stanley and George. The men who took your Pa's body from the beach? They've been set on to keep an eye out for us, I reckon."

"What do we do?" The idea of leaving Pa's puppets – of

abandoning the show – appalled Caleb. But as far as he could see they had no choice.

He was surprised to see a smile on Letty's face. "I reckon our luck's in," she said.

"Luck? How so?"

"Didn't I say they're not the sharpest of men? I'll lead them off. Once I've got them running after me, you go in, fetch the show out. But be quick."

"I can't let you take such a risk!"

"You can't stop me."

"I'll do it."

"You will not. I know the land, I know the men, and you don't know either. I'll meet you down on the beach, right? Where you found your Pa. Wait for me there until I come. I shan't be any longer than I need to."

Hitching her skirts right up, tying them about her waist so she could run unencumbered, Letty – in a display of great theatricality that Stanley and George could not fail to miss – started towards the barn as if attempting stealth, pushing noisily through the hedge. She walked along its side, stumbling in the gathering dark so they'd hear her approach. Reaching its door, getting so close Caleb was sure they'd strike her over the head and knock her senseless, she then gave a cry of alarm as if she had seen something – or someone – in the barn. "Run!" she cried, as if to a companion standing just behind her. "Caleb, they're onto us! Run for your life!" Then she turned tail and fled inland, making plenty enough noise for two, running towards Fishpool and Norton Manor crashing through scrub and reed.

Her act would not have convinced more sensible men, but it was pitched perfectly for Stanley and George. They pursued, and when all three had disappeared into the night Caleb walked silently and swiftly to the barn. Hefting the theatre upon his shoulder, taking the sack of puppets in his hand, he walked, as quickly as he could, over the marshes and dunes to the beach.

Caleb waited alone on the sand, his back to the sea, squinting through the dark, straining for any sound that might herald Letty's return.

She, meanwhile, was leading her pursuers on a desperate dance through mud and mire, through ditch and field and then through the woods that surrounded Norton Manor. Whether by pure luck or divine providence she couldn't say, but, narrowly missing it herself, she led Stanley straight into a man-trap. The iron teeth clamped about his leg, biting deep through flesh and into bone, and his anguished shouts stopped George in his tracks. He abandoned the chase to assist his injured friend, yelling aloud for someone, anyone, to come to their aid.

Hard though it was to hear those screams, Letty did not stop running. How long it would take to free Stanley, how long it would take George to carry him to Norton Manor she did not know. But of one thing she was certain: as soon as the story of her flight and their pursuit was known to Sir Robert there would be more men on their trail and these would not be so easily eluded.

She ran from the woods straight across the manor lawns and from Sir Robert's own jetty took a boat and sailed it downriver. Going against the incoming tide, having to tack from one side of the river to the other, her progress was slow. But finally she was over the bar and sailing towards the beach.

Caleb waited in agonised suspense, hoping for her success, dreading her failure, fearing above all that he might lose her.

He was still looking inland, eyes straining to catch sight of her coming through the dunes, when she beached the little dinghy on the beach behind him. At the scrape of its hull on the sand Caleb jumped almost clean out of his skin. William Benson was here to kill him. Dear God, he'd give the man a fight for his money. His hands were up in front of his chest when he saw Letty's bunched skirts, her legs showing white in the darkness, and heard her cursing, "What the hell are you doing? Get a move on, Caleb."

Letty had picked the boat carefully. It was small but seaworthy and chosen to mislead Sir Robert.

"If he sees it gone he'll think we've sailed on up the coast to Bristol maybe. But if we take it back over the bar and head upriver, why then his men will be looking in the wrong place."

Caleb loaded the show on board but the minute they put to sea his stomach began to churn.

"Look at me," Letty said. "Watch what I'm doing. Take your mind off your belly."

He fixed his eyes on Letty's hands holding rope and tiller, guiding the boat with confident ease, and it helped a little. The wind was with them now, and the tide.

"When we're over the bar the water will be calmer. I'll let the current carry us then."

They were almost on it when something bumped against the hull.

It set the boat rocking, swaying from side to side. Letty cursed, pulling at the tiller to steady it while Caleb looked into the water. It was a mass of seaweed, he thought. But how could seaweed be so solid? As he and Letty watched, the shape rotated – slowly, slowly turning in the current. And then – for the briefest of moments – the moon emerged from behind a cloud and they saw the white face of the captain, Luke Slater, and smelled the stench of death.

One by one, the *Lady Jane*'s drowned crew were finally coming home.

6.

There could be no question now of going to Anne. If the barn had been watched then her house, too, would have its guard, whether she knew it or not. All they could hope was that her innocence and her ignorance would give her protection. Once they reached Torcester, once they had talked to the bishop, once the wheels of justice had been set in motion – only then could they send her word that they were alive and well.

Meanwhile they must go upriver, carried by the tide, using neither sail nor oar in case the slap of canvas, the splashing of wood in water was heard by any who watched for them. Letty, hand on the tiller, steered the boat to the side furthest from Fishpool, not letting it stray onto the mudflats where they might become stranded. Caleb said not a word, letting her concentrate on this most difficult of tasks.

Going past Norton Manor, all was quiet. The house slept. But then they heard shouting. Pinpricks of light punctured the dark, as if torches had been lit.

Stanley and George must have reached the big house, Letty guessed. The alarm had been raised. Benson was no doubt calling for men.

But they were sliding past the manor now, heading for Tawpuddle. No pursuit came by water. And Letty's ruse had worked. For when a voice did come from the jetty it was to declare that a boat was missing: the miscreants must have set out to sea.

Reaching Tawpuddle, they passed beneath the bridge, and now Letty deemed it safe to add manpower to tide. The river began to narrow here so sail was of less use than oars.

For the remainder of that night she rowed, and it was hard, hard labour. After an hour the tide turned and the river began to empty itself, threatening to push them back towards Tawpuddle and on to Fishpool. Letty didn't know the river south of the bridge – once or twice she ran aground on the mud and it was a slow, messy task to free themselves.

As dawn approached, they neared the point where the river ceased to be tidal. It would eventually become much shallower, Caleb told Letty, and she said it would be wise to abandon the boat and proceed on foot. They'd better sink it so it couldn't be found by any of Sir Robert's men.

After unloading theatre and puppets onto the shore they stripped to their undergarments. Letty fixed a rope to the mast top and, holding it between them, they capsized it

in the deepest part of the channel. And then they swam –
Caleb towing Letty – and from there waded through
stinking river mud and squelching marsh to retrieve their
livelihood. Dressing once more, they turned their faces
towards the city.

7.

⁓⋇⋇⋇⋇⋇⋇⋇⋇⋇⋇⋇⋇⋇⋇⋇⋇⋇⋇⋇

They did not follow every bend and curve of the river as Caleb had on his journey north. Instead they cut through fields and woods to make better time, yet the need for stealth meant it was still more than a week before they neared Torcester; more than a week in which they resorted to poaching and thieving to eat. A trout from a stream. Eggs from a barn. A rabbit or hare snared in the woods. Both knew that if they were caught they would likely be transported for it and yet they could not make that entire journey on empty bellies.

As they proceeded the landscape changed. Trees grew tall and straight, the sky stretched between them, the hills curved gently, the colour of earth transformed from dull brown to vibrant red, the colour of Letty's hair. To Caleb the scene was soft and familiar. The birdsong was sweet, the scent of grass and wild flowers rich and heady but now there seemed something excessive, almost overindulgent in all this bounty. He found himself missing the starkness of cliffs, the expanse of sea. Letty – who had lived all her life beside the water – was struck by the lush growth and the softly rolling hills, but she did not especially like them. She was a creature of cliff and crag, of storm and surge, Caleb realised: vital and elemental, and now as necessary to him as breathing.

On reaching the city, they went straight to the bishop's palace, only pausing to stop and wash faces and hands in the river that ran through the water meadows just below it, and to pull grass and seeds from each other's hair. Their attempts to look respectable were futile. After weeks of rough sleeping they were both dishevelled and filthy, their clothes tattered and torn. Letty remarked sadly, "We look like a pair of vagrants. Are you sure this man will see us?"

Caleb was far from certain, but said, "He is a man of God. And didn't Jesus choose to live among the poor and lowly?"

"Poor and lowly," she replied with a smile. "Well, that's us, right enough."

They walked to the palace, going to the front of the building rather than the kitchen, where they would more likely be taken for beggars.

The facade was not so opulent as Norton Manor's, but it was equally intimidating. Red brick. Narrow, leaded windows. A door of oak, dark with age, studded with iron bolts – a great slab of a thing, heavy as a tombstone. There was no knocker, but a rope that led to a bell hanging overhead. Caleb pulled it and a clanging announced their presence. In response there were footsteps on slate, taking an age but coming nearer. And then a great creaking as the door slowly swung open.

Whether the bishop would have seen them or not, they never found out. The door had been opened by a servant clad in a plum-coloured coat. The moment he saw what was standing before him he exclaimed in horror and recoiled, as if their poverty was a disease that he might catch. "Get away! Be off with you!"

"We wish to see the bishop!"

"Dirty black tramp!"

"My father was Joseph Chappell, the showman. Tell him. I'm sure he'll see me!"

"I'll set the dogs on you!"

He tried to close the door but Letty stuck her foot in the gap. "It's important," she pleaded.

The servant pulled the door wide open and for a moment Caleb thought they would be admitted, that in a few minutes' time they would find themselves in the bishop's study, that this whole sad tale could at last be given the right ending. But the man had pulled the door back only to give it more force when he slammed it in their faces. His whole weight was behind that great oaken slab and Caleb, dreading that Letty's foot would be crushed or her ankle broken, tugged her away.

The door banged, the noise echoing so loudly along the

corridor that the whole building seemed to be yelling, "Be off!" along with the servant.

Caleb and Letty stood for a few moments staring at the closed door. They looked at each other.

"That's that then," Letty said flatly.

Caleb opened his mouth to speak but then, from the back of the house, there were barks and howls. The servant's threat to set the dogs on them was not an empty one. Snatching up theatre and puppets, they fled from the palace before they could be torn to pieces.

"What do we do now?" asked Letty.

Caleb was shocked to see her so beaten, so lost. But the city was not Letty's territory; it was his. He knew the streets, knew the ways of its inhabitants and she did not. He'd relied on her for so much. Now it was his turn: he must make their plans. "We have to see the bishop," he told her. "He is the only man who can help."

"But how?"

"If not in his palace, why then, we must try the cathedral."

And so to the cathedral they went, where they received much the same welcome as before. The minute they stepped inside an elderly curate bustled over in a great show of outrage that such creatures should dare to enter so hallowed a building.

When Caleb stated their business the curate pursed

his lips and said sourly that the bishop was not there, that he was away dealing with church business and besides, an eminent man such as he could not be expected to have any dealings with the common folk.

"It is a matter of the utmost urgency," Caleb persisted. "When will he return to Torcester?"

"I'll not tell you just so you can go bothering him. Be off with you."

"He will wish to hear my tale, sir! My father looked upon him as a friend..." Caleb's voice rose to the rafters like a prayer. Which went unheard.

The curate did not threaten them with dogs but said he could call men to forcibly remove them if they did not leave at once. And so they did, walking aimlessly over the cobbles, across the green and then through the city streets until at last they found themselves sitting on the wall outside the prison.

Letty said nothing the whole time, but Caleb's mind worked frantically, trying to think of something, some way of getting to the bishop without first having to go through the people who protected him.

It was late in the day. His stomach rumbled noisily. They had not eaten and did not know where they would sleep that night. Justice for Pa, he thought, might have to wait a while.

It was not market day and yet the city was still busy enough to attract a crowd, albeit a small one.

"We need money, Letty. Have you the strength to perform?"

Letty's eyes – which had been filled with dark despair a moment before – lit up with excitement. "You try stopping me."

They set up the show not by the cathedral, where they feared the curate might send men to drive them off, but in the small square near Porlock's Coffee House. The smell of roasting beans and hot chocolate, mutton pies and gravy drifted from the door, making both their bellies grumble.

Caleb introduced the show as he had done at Norton Manor but this time he had no fear before he stepped out. This time he felt he wasn't donning Pa's personality like a coat, but wearing his own.

Once he had whipped the small crowd into a state of excited anticipation, Caleb stood by the side of the theatre. Letty began. As the show progressed and the small crowd began to swell, Caleb found himself being directly addressed by Mr Punch or the jester. The banter that began to pass between him and the puppets was as hilarious as it was spontaneous. More people stopped to watch, drawn by the laughter of the audience. Mrs Porlock herself stepped from the coffee shop to see what had attracted so many people. For the first time not only did Caleb feel comfortable in the middle of the city, he thrilled with the challenge of amusing a company of strangers. Yes, he thought, this was something he could grow used to.

Punch was given the baby by his wife. He set it on one corner of the stage and returned to the other, sitting with his legs dangling over the playboard. The baby looked around. And then Letty mimicked the babble of Dorcas. The baby was making the chuckling, gurgling noises of a small child and every parent in the crowd smiled, their hearts melting with affection for the grotesque puppet baby.

And then – oh the miracle of it! – the baby spoke its first words.

"Papa?"

"Aaaah!" Punch – the proud father – was delighted. He stopped ignoring his child, got to his feet and drew nearer to the infant.

"Papa?" The baby's voice was softer this time.

"What?" Punch drew still nearer to hear it.

"Papa?" Even softer, even sweeter.

"What?" His head was down, ear cocked right by the baby's mouth.

A pause. And then, *Waaaaaaaah!* The baby bawled into Punch's ear.

The shock of the sudden noise made the audience jump almost out of their skins and then burst into explosive laughter.

Punch picked up his child and rocked the baby – none too gently – and its cries finally ceased. He set it back in the corner of the stage and retreated as far as he could.

But the baby spoke again with the same meltingly endearing tones. "Papa?"

Letty repeated the trick once, then twice. And then, rocking the baby to silence a fourth time, Punch set the baby down and it emitted a loud fart. Punch's reaction told the audience that the baby had soiled itself.

Then – to Caleb's surprise – Punch picked up the baby and threw it straight at him. "You have him," he screamed.

Caleb caught the infant puppet, sniffed it, pulled a face and threw it back. "I don't want him."

"Neither do I." The baby was tossed between them, the crowd shrieking at the outrageousness of playing catch with a baby, until Judy appeared onstage with a large stick, threatening to beat Punch for his wickedness.

Tears were running down Mrs Porlock's cheeks. Now would be a good time to collect, Caleb thought. Letty had hooked them and moment by moment more people joined the throng, delighted smiles creasing their faces.

The show went on. After Punch had beaten the Devil, Caleb went around once more.

The crowd had numbered barely a quarter of those who would watch Pa's show on a market day so Caleb might have expected to only collect a quarter of the sum Pa would have made. Yet the bottle felt heavy. And when the crowd at last dispersed and they had time to count the coins, they discovered they had made more money than either would have believed possible in so short a space of time.

"All those months of rowing after ships!" exclaimed Letty. "All those months of washing stinking shirts and you and Anne sewing and patching and us all scrimping and worrying and you and me could have been doing this all along! We are made, Caleb! Lord, I can hardly believe it."

They were further astonished when – after they had packed down the show – Mrs Porlock came from the coffee house once more and pressed a pie each into their hands. Though Caleb tried to pay, she would take nothing.

"All I ask is that you don't come back," she said with a nod and a wink. "You're too entertaining by half. If people are watching you they're not eating and drinking in my place."

And so that night – for the first time in weeks – they were able to sleep under a roof. Not knowing what the future had in store, they dared not spend too freely, taking only the cheapest of lodgings. They found themselves sleeping squeezed together in a bed that they shared with five strangers who grumbled about being in a chamber with a man of Caleb's complexion until Letty silenced them with a look.

While men snored and women belched either side of them, Caleb and Letty whispered about what they would do the next day. They could perform again, and do more than one show, trying different locations to see which earned them the most. They could, perhaps, even afford to buy new garments so they didn't look quite so destitute. And then, in three days' time when it was market day once again, they would set up the theatre by the cathedral and hope not only that the bishop had returned, but that he would come and watch the show.

8.

On market day they set the theatre by the cathedral green in exactly the place where Pa had performed for the last time. Though the curate scowled at them, he did not send them away. They looked more respectable now having bought a dress for Letty – a second- or third-hand garment found in a back-street trader's that was worn but which fitted her well enough. Caleb had bought britches and a coat, threadbare but clean, from the same seller. The crowds who gathered were large and welcoming. Many remarked that they had missed the show when Pa was gone and were delighted to see Punch back and up to his old tricks.

The pieman was there, and the big-bosomed flower seller, but the bishop did not come. Not for the first nor the second, not for the third nor the fourth show.

Despite this disappointment Letty's energy and exuberance remained undimmed. Indeed her skill seemed to exceed even Pa's that day and the crowd's response drove her to yet greater heights. The people gave generously and the bottle grew heavy with coins.

They came to the fifth and final show of the day and it went as well as the first four had done. Punch killed the ghost and knocked down the magistrate. He hanged Jack Ketch and now the Devil had come looking for the old sinner. Yet there was still no sign of the bishop. Whatever business had taken him away obviously continued to keep him.

No matter, thought Caleb. They had plenty of money now to keep them fed and housed until next market day and beyond. He and Letty were managing much better than he could ever have imagined. He would have been happy for the situation to continue indefinitely if only he wasn't so worried about Anne. She must know of Edward's death by now – the poor lady would be running mad with grief. Fear for her and Dorcas was keeping him awake at night.

His mind full of musings, Caleb heard the Devil say, "I am B-B-Beelzebub. I am L-L-Lucifer. I am S-S-S-S-Satan." Dimly he registered that the puppet had developed a stutter. Had something happened? Was Letty all right? It had been a long day. Oh hell, had she exhausted herself?

He looked at the stage. The puppets looked as lively as ever. Punch was mimicking the Devil, "L-L-Lucifer? S-S-S-*Sir* Satan? Oooooooh! *Sir* Satan. My very humble respects." Punch bowed low, but when the Devil did the same Punch whacked him over the head with his stick. "Take that, Sir bleeding-high-and-mighty Satan!"

Letty's newly improvised joke made Caleb snort with laughter. He was almost bent double when underneath the crowd's noise he heard a low, rumbling chuckle – warm and familiar.

Swinging around, he scanned the crowd. And yes – there at last was the bishop! Oh, thank God! But for him, Pa would have hanged. Caleb's heart went out in gratitude.

The bishop, Caleb knew, did not like to have his entertainment interrupted. The man had only just arrived and yet he could not miss this opportunity. He pushed his way through the throng. "May I speak with you, sir?"

The bishop looked at him. "You are the puppeteer's lad?"

"I am."

"By God, you've grown! I'm happy to see you, boy. It was a most unfortunate tragedy! He was transported, was he not?"

"He was, sir. I am thankful that you spoke for him."

The bishop nodded his head in acknowledgement. "Mr Chappell was a good man. Who does the show now?"

"My..." Caleb was stumped for a moment. How was he to describe Letty's relationship to himself? He could scarcely admit to a churchman that they shared a bed – albeit with five others – and yet were not wed! "My cousin," he lied.

If the bishop noticed his hesitation he did not remark on it. "He does it well."

"Ah ... sir, my cousin is a woman."

"Indeed? You surprise me." The bishop seemed a little perplexed by the notion but he did not intend for it to spoil his enjoyment. He turned back to the show, indicating that the conversation was over.

But Caleb was not ready to be dismissed. "Sir, there is something I want to tell you."

"Talk away, boy."

He lowered his voice. "Not here, in the street."

The bishop's eyebrows were raised. "A private matter? Very well. Come to the palace."

"We tried, sir. We were turned away."

The bishop laughed and the flesh on his belly seemed to roll in waves from chest to groin. "Threatened you with dogs, no doubt? My servants are, alas, inclined to be a little overzealous. I will tell them I'm expecting you. Come in the morning. Eleven o'clock. I will await you then."

9.

They received a warm welcome at the bishop's palace the following morning. Caleb felt nothing but gratitude and a strange kind of lightness, for they had left the puppets and the theatre in their lodgings and it was odd to walk without that weight on his shoulder.

The man who opened the door with exaggerated courtesy showed them to a study lined with books. A second servant in the same plum-coloured livery as the first brought a silver platter of victuals. When the bishop arrived he himself poured them tankards of rich mead and pressed fresh-baked cakes into their hands.

Though the bishop urged Letty and Caleb to eat and drink neither did so. Both were desperate to tell him the entire history of what they had discovered.

Caleb began to speak of Pa's transportation and how he had been delivered not to Maryland, but to a barren island three or four miles off the county's northern coast. "He was set to work there, he and the other convicts. They were to build a harbour wall – a quayside, if you like – somewhere that ships might tie up to. They were enslaved, but my father escaped. You met him, sir – you know he would not have endured such ill-treatment. He made a raft, but it didn't survive the crossing to land. He drowned. I found him on the beach and knew him by his ring and yet everyone denied that it was him. His finger was hacked off so that he couldn't be identified."

Caleb expected a reaction. Consternation. Disbelief. Amazement. Anything would have sufficed. His was a tale that would have gripped any listener, but he was surprised to find himself being interrupted once then twice more by the bishop – not asking for more details or more information, but simply insisting that Caleb should eat and drink what was on offer.

"Come, lad, are you not hungry? Take something, do. It will make the telling of your tale easier."

It was the bishop's pressing insistence that began to make Caleb uneasy, for his host ate nothing.

A well-fed man with a belly as round as the Virgin Mary's on Christmas Eve…? Caleb would have wagered that the bishop was the kind who could not pass a tray of food without consuming every last scrap. And yet not one crumb passed his lips. Why, he might almost think it was contaminated!

Frustrated by the bishop's interruption, Letty took over the telling of the tale. "They all said he was Thomas

Smith, see? That he was a sailor who'd gone in the water up Tawpuddle way. Only I've lived in Fishpool my whole life and I know that folk who go in the river off the bridge or the quay wash up on the other side, not there on the beach, so I knew Caleb was telling the truth and they weren't. But we had ourselves a look at the body, just to make sure."

Gravedigging. Surely the bishop would react to this revelation? But no, his face remained impassive. While Letty continued speaking Caleb's eyes darted about the room. He took in what he had not seen before: several decanters of spirits assembled in a neat row on a sideboard. The bishop clearly had a taste for fine living and while Caleb knew little of such things, he could guess that one or two at least would be full of Jamaican rum or fine French brandy. The kind of cargo sometimes brought in by smugglers...

Caleb's palms had already begun to prickle when he glanced out of the window. In the courtyard at the rear of the palace Caleb saw a ginger-haired youth. He was neatly dressed in the same plum-coloured coat that the other servants wore. The bishop's man then. Walking, not running. And yet...

It couldn't be! He was surely mistaken? But no... As the lad turned and crossed the courtyard towards the house Caleb realized with a sickening jolt that this was the very same youth who'd punched Pa in the belly and dropped the stolen purse at his feet.

Caleb looked at the bishop. He opened his mouth to

point out the lad, to say he was a thief, but something stopped his speech. Letty was still talking but it was Caleb the bishop watched. The man was corpulent, the flesh of his face puffed out, inflated with fat, like a pig's bladder will inflate with air. Yet beneath – wasn't the curve of his cheekbones, the line of his nose somewhat familiar? And the bishop's eyes, boring into him, fixing him to the spot, like a weasel with a rabbit. No … not a weasel.

A wolf!

Caleb snatched up the bottle of coins and swung it at the bishop's head.

To knock a man senseless is a ghastly thing. To split flesh, to break bone, to see him fold and fall, taking the table, the food and drink, a pair of chairs to the ground with him – it was enough to leave Caleb trembling. Hell! He'd struck a bishop! A man of God lay at his feet still, unmoving, save for a trickle of blood seeping across the slate floor. He'd just committed a hanging offence!

Letty looked at him as though he had taken leave of his senses. Her mouth dropped wide open and she croaked like a frog. It would have amused Caleb if their situation hadn't been so perilous.

A man so large couldn't fall without making a noise. There had been a crack and a thump and a clatter of plate and glass so loud that every servant in the palace must have heard it.

The ginger-haired youth had. He was coming at a run

through the courtyard, entering the house, shouting, raising the alarm. If he came here to the study they'd have no chance of escape.

Already there were footsteps in the passage, coming from both the front and the back of the house, a way off yet but rapidly getting closer. Caleb ran to the study door, closed it and turned the great iron key protruding from the lock. Their only means of escape was through the window to the rear.

Picking up a chair and swinging it at the glass, he managed to say to Letty, "The bishop is part of this!" before it shattered, throwing shards across the cobbles.

Without a word, Letty was up on her feet and across the room, seizing a rug from the floor and laying it on the fractured glass in the window's frame before climbing through. Caleb was a moment behind her and together they ran across the courtyard, out of the gates and over the water meadows towards the river.

It was not long before they were pursued. Letty and Caleb could move fast, but they could not outrun a horse. The ginger-haired lad was mounted and after them in a matter of minutes. If they could only reach the water and the woods beyond they might lose him but he was gaining on them with each step. The ground pounded with hoofbeats. Yet there were two of them and he was alone – was it possible they could overpower him? Caleb glanced back and with horror saw the lad wielded a knife and was pointing it directly at Letty as though this was a cavalry charge, and she the enemy.

They couldn't avoid him. And yet they could, Caleb thought suddenly, take him by surprise.

Thrusting the bottle of coins at Letty, he kept running but as he ran he unbuttoned his coat, his stride breaking as he slipped it off one arm, then the other. The horse neared. It was almost on top of them when Caleb stopped, turned and flicked his coat towards its face.

The youth had not expected resistance, that much was clear. Startled by the coat's movement, the horse reared, its hooves thrashing the air, clipping Caleb on the side of the head, knocking him back, before it fell, pulled over by its rider's weight.

Dazed, Caleb was on his knees, pressing his hand to his cheek, feeling the blood run between his fingers. His sight had momentarily blurred and it was a few moments before he could look about him. The horse was on its feet, unharmed, untroubled by its fall, but the lad lay on the grass, not moving, his leg twisted at an impossible angle to his body. He had fallen on his own knife. It was embedded up to the hilt in his throat.

Letty was white with shock. "We've killed him! We've killed him."

Horror hit Caleb like a fist but there was no time for regret. Cries came from the palace. They needed to get away.

Caleb had rarely ridden a horse and never something as fine as this. He put his left foot in the stirrup and hauled himself into the saddle. Reaching a hand out to Letty, he pulled her up behind him. Her arms about his waist, they set off towards the river, fording it, and coming out into the woods beyond. They could not move fast here but amongst the thick vegetation it was more difficult for them to be seen. They wove their way between trees, splashing through another stream, riding in silence, straining to hear the men that followed and then – oh Lord! – came the baying cries of dogs. Caleb's heart sank, but the horse, clearly used to running with hounds, pricked its ears. It was hard for him to hold it in, for it fought the bit, dancing, sidestepping in its eagerness to be off.

They came to the edge of the wood. Beyond was a stretch of heathland. Caleb didn't ride well enough to go at full gallop across it but close by was an ancient oak – a great lofty tree with a branch low enough for him to reach from the saddle of the horse. He reined the animal in beneath it and urged Letty to climb. Once she was safely up, he grasped the branch himself, and then, with all his might, kicked the horse in the rump so it went galloping across the heath, bucking in its excitement. Praying that it would not return to its fallen master like a dog, he swung his legs over the branch and began to climb.

The ruse worked. While Letty and Caleb clung to the oak's rough bark, six men clad in plum-coloured coats passed beneath them, their dogs' noses to the ground, not looking up. And the horse – bless its foolish, highly-bred hide! – disappeared over the horizon and carried on running in wild glee, thinking itself the leader of the hunt.

10.

Their reprieve couldn't last long. As soon as the riderless horse was discovered they would be pursued once more. Clambering down from the tree, they splashed along from stream to river so that the hounds would find it harder to pick up their scent. Where the city buildings crowded closely together they emerged from the water and returned swiftly to their lodgings.

Caleb had wounded a bishop, perhaps killed him. The ginger-haired youth was certainly dead. They'd be accused of stealing the horse. If they were caught there would be no saving either of them from the gallows.

What were they to do now? Where in the world were they to go?

Without a word they gathered together theatre and puppets and, leaving a few coins as payment, slipped from the building.

They kept to the back lanes and to the alleyways, moving quickly, Caleb leading the way, thinking only that they must leave Torcester, that they must move on somewhere, anywhere, that they must get beyond the reach of those who would do Letty harm. But where? Think, think! Where had he been with Pa that he and Letty could be safe? Where in the wide world could they hide that Sir Robert would not find them? The man was like a spider; the threads of his silken web reached everywhere.

Caleb paused for a moment to catch his breath, crouching in a doorway at the rear of a tavern with Letty beside him. He didn't know the back roads, the narrow paths as well as he'd hoped. He'd thought he was leading Letty out of the city, but now feared he was simply heading into the heart of the labyrinth. He was desperately trying to fathom which direction to go next when she asked him, "Why'd you hit him, Caleb?"

"The bishop?"

"Who else?"

"He's related to Sir Robert, I believe. Brothers, maybe. Or cousins."

"Never!"

"He has the same nose, the same high cheekbones. And the same eyes, that wolfish look. When I first saw Sir Robert at church he seemed familiar. That was why."

"But Caleb, even if they're related … it doesn't make the bishop a villain."

"Do you doubt me?"

"No! I just want to know what made you hit him."

The crunch of bone. Split skin. Blood. Caleb's flesh

crawled recalling it. It was instinct that had led him. Had he been mistaken? He struggled to explain. "I thought what happened to Pa was bad luck – a terrible accident. That the thief was running scared, dropped the purse, lashed out in panic. But he was there at the palace – he was the lad that rode after us. Pa wasn't taken by mistake – they chose him."

"But you said the bishop liked your Pa."

"And so he did! Only yesterday he said he was a good man. *Was* a good man, Letty. As though he already knew Pa was dead." Caleb cast his mind back to the previous summer. "His regard was a sham. Pa was flattered by him. The bishop admired Pa's new theatre, he spent an age asking about the frame: wanting to know how Pa had got the idea, how he'd managed to build it, whether he'd done it all himself or employed a craftsman…"

Caleb stopped. What did any of it amount to?

Yet Letty was nodding thoughtfully. "Sir Robert would have needed a clever man, someone who could take charge: supervise the building on the island. Your Pa would have been perfect for them."

"The bishop saved his life and Pa was so grateful, as was I. They played us for fools. Transportation was their intention all along."

They could talk no more. There were dogs. Barking. Yelping. Distant, but getting louder. The manhunt had turned back towards the city.

Caleb and Letty ran first down one alley, then another.

Paths twisted and turned and Caleb became ever more confused. They sloshed through filth, mud, waste – both animal and human. Speed seemed of more importance than discretion and yet with every step the hounds came nearer.

They could hear the shouts of men now too. The cries of women, the excited shrieks of children. People were turning out of their houses, leaving their shops to see what was the cause of so much noise and fuss. Slamming doors. Questions. Word spreading from mouth to mouth.

"Bishop's been attacked."

"The bishop?"

"Who by?"

"Darkie."

"Redhead whore."

"Did they come this way?"

"No. But if I see them I'll yell."

The cause did not matter. Innocence or guilt was immaterial. A chase was afoot and who could resist the thrill of the hunt? With every second that passed, more people joined the pack.

Turning another corner, Caleb at last knew where he was. He'd brought them to the edge of the city. Ahead lay the street that would take them to open fields but the way was blocked. At the end of the alley stood a man, a large stick in his hands. His face was turned away so they ducked into the shadows, pressing themselves flat against a wall, edging back. But before they were quite out of sight he saw them.

"Down here!" he yelled. "I see them!" He lumbered in pursuit, shouting all the while.

They were running flat out now, every remaining scrap of caution thrown to the winds, shoving aside the elderly man in their path, emerging into a broad street. Pursuers were behind them, a hostile crowd ahead.

"Them! That's them!"

Ducking sideways into the back yard of a large house, they sent chickens flying. There was but one entrance. One exit. Oh God, they were trapped! But no – there was a gate! Yanking it open, Letty tried to run through but instead Caleb seized her by the hand, pulling her the other way towards the coach house, where an empty carriage had been parked, its horses released from the shafts so they could be fed and watered. Squeezing in, crouching on the floor, their pursuers ran on through the gate. For a moment they were safe, but this respite could not last long.

"Where now?" asked Letty.

Caleb had no answer to give her. He hung his head while his mind raced. *Think, think, think.*

And then the smell of coffee drifted in on the breeze.

They were not far from Porlock's. Indeed it was just around the corner. Porlock's. Where the whole damned business had begun.

All Caleb's fevered, panicked thoughts were gone. He knew with perfect clarity where he and Letty must go next.

11.

Once more Letty looked at him as if he had taken leave of his senses. "We need to get the hell out of here, Caleb, not sit about sipping coffee!"

"I don't want to go there for a drink! Letty ... a man of business – what does he care about most?"

She laughed bitterly. "Making money."

"Exactly! And those men – those underwriters – they have been tricked. Made fools of. Do you not think they'll wish to know it?"

"They're gentlemen. Would they listen to the likes of us?"

"Their purses have been touched. Where money is involved I think they might make an exception..."

They were agreed. It was a wild, desperate measure, but – if only they could get there without being caught – to Porlock's they would go.

Yet he and Letty were so easy to identify! Her red hair. His skin. With such a hue and cry in the city there was not a soul who wouldn't raise the alarm the very second they were seen. It seemed impossible, but the attempt must be made.

For a time they were blessed by providence, for they managed to leave the carriage and cross the courtyard without being observed. Keeping their heads down, walking slowly and steadily as if merely going about their daily work, they passed into the street and along it, rounding the corner without anyone giving them a second glance. Across the square was Porlock's. Gentlemen were coming and going from there, but their minds seemed only on their own business, not on the pursuit of a pair of vagabonds. Letty and Caleb were within a few yards of the front door when a a man's yell stopped them.

"Stand still!" He wore a plum-coloured coat. A mastiff on a length of chain was barely restrained at his side. "Stay where you are or you'll feel his teeth. Don't move." He turned his head a little, calling over his shoulder, "They're here, lads. Come get them."

Two more of the bishop's men entered the square carrying sticks. If they'd been constables, Letty and he would have been taken straight to gaol. By the look in these men's eyes, Caleb doubted they would ever reach there alive.

"Run! Get inside!" he shouted. Letty darted towards Porlock's but she had not reached the door and Caleb had not gone more than two steps when he heard the sound of a chain being dropped and the scrape of claws on stone. With an eager yelp, the dog bounded towards him.

Caleb turned to face it. As it took a great leap, jaws agape, aiming for his throat he swung the theatre from his shoulder. As he fell backwards with the force of impact the dog's teeth sank into sack and wood. It did not at first realize its mistake for its jaw was locked, its instinct telling it to hold on hard to its prey. It growled and shook its head from side to side, smashing the theatre against the cobbles, reducing Pa's masterpiece to firewood and rags.

Caleb had rolled sideways and tried to stand but the bishop's men were on them now, laying hands upon Letty, pawing at her, swinging a stick against Caleb to knock him back down. He cried aloud, in pain and desperation, "The *Linnet*!"

Letty followed his lead. As her arm was forced behind her back she screamed, "The *Linnet* was scuttled."

"There was no storm!" Caleb yelled. "You have been robbed!"

The men's shouts and the commotion all around them were so loud Caleb thought they had not been heard. A great mob of people rained blows upon him with fists and sticks. His arms were over his head so he did not see the gentleman who stepped through the door of Porlock's.

But he did hear a voice cutting through the chaos, "Desist! Leave the man alone. Let him speak."

It was with great reluctance that the bishop's men ceased their attack. But in time they and the dog were brought under control. Whoever had spoken carried enough authority to quell them. As they drew back, he stepped forward and Caleb, getting to his feet, saw before him a gentleman smartly but not gaudily dressed. A gentleman who regarded him with keen interest.

"The *Linnet*, did you say?"

"I did, sir."

"And who might you be?"

"Caleb Chappell, sir. And this is Letty Avery." She stepped forward and slid her hand through Caleb's arm.

"What do you know of it?" asked the gentleman.

Letty said, "My father was one of the crew."

"And he spoke to you of the shipwreck?"

"No, he didn't. But we found out some things. It didn't happen the way they said in that affidavit."

The gentleman studied them for some moments. At last he said, "Mr Brimming is my name. I am a magistrate, but I am a man of business too. I was one of the ship's underwriters."

"Then you have been deceived, sir, and your money stolen," Caleb told him. "Do you wish to hear more?"

"I do, but not here in the street. Will you step inside?" He addressed the bishop's men: "You will wait here. You may yet be needed."

Picking up the remains of the theatre, Caleb and Letty followed the gentleman into Porlock's Coffee House.

"Mr Johnson, Mr Bowers?" Mr Brimming nodded

towards two other men, who stood as he spoke their names. "Will you come with me?" Addressing Caleb and Letty, he said, "These gentlemen too are underwriters. We are three of those who paid out a considerable amount of money when the *Linnet* was lost. There is someone else upstairs I believe would be most interested to hear what you have to say. Come, follow me."

They did as they were bid, Letty and Caleb walking behind Mr Brimming up the stairs and into a large room. Mr Johnson and Mr Bowers were close behind, along with a clerk. The door was shut, puppets and mangled theatre set down upon the polished floor. It took a moment for Caleb's eyes to adjust from the brightness of the street to the gloom within. When they did his heart almost stopped.

Standing in one corner was William Benson. Sitting in a chair by the fire was Sir Robert Fairbrother.

12.

"I do believe these are the vagrants who assaulted my brother," were Sir Robert's first words. "The Bishop of Torcester lies bleeding. Will you not arrest them at once?"

"In time, in time," replied Mr Brimming blandly. "I have enquiries of my own to attend to first." To Caleb and Letty he said, "Sir Robert is here on business." Caleb then heard him whisper an aside to the clerk who had accompanied them up the stairs, "Send for the constables, would you?" To the room in general he said, "Sir Robert is here to make a second claim for a ship. The *Lady Jane*, I believe. He has indeed been most unfortunate to lose two vessels in such rapid succession. Let us hope his other ventures fare better."

"I pray so daily," Sir Robert replied smoothly.

"These people say they have information regarding the *Linnet*," Mr Brimming told him.

"The *Lady Jane* too," Caleb said. "We saw her go down."

"Indeed?"

"Come now, this is absurd!" Sir Robert scoffed. "It is

impossible either of them saw what happened to the *Lady Jane*! She was lost far out at sea."

In a steady voice Caleb declared, "We were on board."

There was a stunned silence.

Sir Robert broke it. "On board? How could that be possible, even if they were stowaways? What? All hands lost and yet these two survived?" His tone was scathing. "It is not credible! Mr Brimming, this black-skinned wretch is troubled in his mind. He should by rights be confined to an asylum. His father was a convicted felon, transported to the colonies. God alone knows who or what his mother was. There is bad blood in his veins. Since he arrived at his aunt's he has been full of the most fantastical imaginings. Pay him no heed."

"My wits are perfectly intact, sir." Caleb looked directly at the magistrate. "Mr Brimming, will you hear us out? Then you may judge who is telling the truth here."

"You would listen to a pair of vagabonds?" Sir Robert was behaving as though this was a mild irritation, something faintly comic that he would later regale his friends with over a fine dinner. His calm contempt, his overweening confidence, unnerved the businessmen. Mr Brimming exchanged an uncertain glance with Mr Johnson and Mr Bowers. Caleb could see that none of them wished to offend a man of Sir Robert's standing.

He thought at any moment they would be bundled out of the coffee house and so he said, "The *Linnet* was sunk – scuttled deliberately. As for the *Lady Jane* – she was struck by lightning."

"Lightning?" Mr Brimming echoed. "I believe that would not normally down a vessel."

"She was carrying gunpowder."

"Gunpowder?" Mr Johnson's eyebrows shot towards the ceiling. "That was not listed as part of the cargo…"

"Because it was not on board!" Sir Robert sighed wearily. "This is all nonsense." Turning to Benson, he commanded, "Take them. Really, gentlemen, they must go to the city gaol without delay."

Obediently, Benson took a step towards them but Letty now found her voice. "He's stealing from you. Can't you see it? He's taken your money and gone laughing all the way back to Norton Manor. Are you going to let him get away with it?"

Benson laid a hand upon Caleb's arm but Mr Brimming said, "Leave him be. I do apologize, Sir Robert, but I wish to hear what these young people have to say."

"It is fantastical. Absurd!"

"That's as may be. Let us, the underwriters, judge whether their tale is fact or fiction before they are removed."

He sat himself down at the table and the two other gentlemen did the same. "What is it you have to tell us?"

The essentials of the plot were laid before them. Caleb spoke of Pa's arrest, of his sentence and the bishop's intervention, of how cargo and convicts had been landed on the island, the former being sold on from there, the latter being set to work. Letty described how a harbour wall was to be constructed to enable a smuggling operation. "You can see where they started the work," she said earnestly. "Go take a look at the island."

"Smuggling?" said Sir Robert. "They'll be accusing me of piracy next!" He laughed as though genuinely amused by the notion. "Will you have me hanged? Here, I offer you my wrists. Go on, clap me in irons."

They did not do so. Smiling reassuringly at Sir Robert, Mr Brimming told Caleb to continue, but his tone had grown cold.

Right was on their side but with Sir Robert's eyes on them Letty and Caleb became increasingly awkward and tongue-tied. Put baldly, fact after fact, their story did indeed sound fanciful. Brave, bold Letty stumbled over words, as did Caleb. And the more they stumbled, the more flustered each of them became, the less convincing they were. They tried to sound sincere but every sentence, every phrase seemed to ring false. The underwriters sat in silence, listening, but Caleb was aware that word by halting word their incredulity was growing.

When he explained how he had found Pa's body, how he and Letty had opened the grave and discovered that the corpse's finger had been cut off the underwriters pressed handkerchiefs to their mouths as if trying to stem a rising tide of nausea. Yet still Caleb pressed on, telling of his uncle's return and what had followed after that. Of entering the manor on gala day and what he had discovered in the desk drawer. Of his abduction on the *Lady Jane* and Letty's rescue; the convicts' escape. He spoke, too, of the bishop's involvement and what had occurred at the palace that very morning.

In desperation Letty at last pulled the silken package from her pocket and laid it on the table.

"This is Sir Robert's handkerchief," Caleb said, pushing it towards Mr Brimming. "See the initials there? I found it in the drawer of his desk. And look inside, gentlemen." Unwrapping it, he added, "See here? This is Pa's finger, cut from his dead body so he wouldn't be identified. If you look at the ring you'll see why. It was his father's. Those are his initials – this is my grandfather's seal."

The underwriters were reluctant to look closely.

Sir Robert – who had done nothing but peer down his nose for the duration of Caleb and Letty's tale – now burst into howls of derisive laughter. He raised his hands and applauded loudly, as though Caleb had just completed the most extraordinary theatrical performance.

"Bravo! I congratulate you. This has indeed been most entertaining." He turned to the round-bellied underwriter. "And now I tire of this farce. Will you send them both to gaol? I believe it can accommodate yet more villains."

The gentlemen shuffled uncomfortably in their seats

but did not give the order. Caleb had not convinced them his tale was true, but their money was involved. The fear that they had been tricked still stayed their hands.

"They did not want my father identified. The proof is there," Caleb said, pointing at Pa's ring.

"Proof?" Once more Sir Robert scoffed. "A ring on a withered finger with nothing to say who it came from or how it was got. How do you know he did not cut it from its owner himself?"

"But the handkerchief is yours!"

"Oh, that I do not deny. This lad is a thief. He entered my house without permission – which he freely admits – and stole my handkerchief. But I assure you, gentlemen, he did not take the ring from there." Sir Robert suddenly leaned forward and jabbed Caleb with his forefinger. "You will be hanged for stealing, boy. And I will make sure the sentence is not commuted to transportation."

There was a moment's silence.

"The ring is very distinctive," Mr Brimming ventured. "Could we not—?"

Sir Robert interrupted him noisily, his show of amusement gone. He was angry now but no less withering. "Indeed. You think a lad like this would have such a thing in his possession by any honest means? This whole tale is mere fancy! It is a fable, I tell you, a fiction constructed from nothing. Gentlemen, you have had the affidavits of eleven men, sworn before the magistrate, which state that the *Linnet* sank with all her cargo in a storm in the middle of the ocean."

"She was unseaworthy!" Letty protested. "She should never have sailed."

Sir Robert was on his feet, seizing Letty's arm. "Here we have a girl who ran away from home with the bastard son of a blackamoor whore. She is a slattern. Can you take anything she says as truth? Regard this pair carefully. Would you really take their word against mine?"

In that instant Caleb knew that they were beaten. Hell and damnation! What had he led Letty into?

"You are right, Sir Robert," Mr Brimming conceded. He tapped his fingers delicately against the table. "Indeed, we cannot give credence to the word of vagabonds."

"Then take them," Sir Robert commanded. He turned to Caleb. "I shall see you and your pretty whore dance the hangman's jig."

Blind terror squeezed Caleb's chest. He gasped for breath. He was sinking, drowning, desperate for something, anything to save him. *Come on, Caleb! You have a brain in that head. Use it!* He looked to Mr Brimming. The man had been about to say something. What? Sir Robert had interrupted him. Why? The magistrate had mentioned the ring's distinctiveness. He'd asked – "Could we not?" Could we not *what*? What had he meant to say? *Could we not find out to whom it belonged?*

Yes! That was it! The ring was the answer! Caleb said,

"You will not give credence to us. Would you listen to an earl's daughter?"

"An earl's daughter?" Mr Brimming looked to Mr Johnson and Mr Bowers. They all nodded. "To whom do you refer?"

"My aunt – Anne Chappell, as was. Her father was the Earl of Gravesham."

Sir Robert frowned, looking momentarily perplexed. *"Anne Chappell, as was?"* Then he threw back his head and laughed. "You mean Anne Avery? She was my wife's maid! She is nobody. A servant!"

Caleb persisted. "Her father lost his fortune, sirs, it is true, but she was born a lady. Lady Anne Chappell, the Earl of Gravesham's daughter. She will recognize the ring. Will her word not carry weight?"

"She knows what happened to the *Linnet*?"

"She does not. She was married to one of the crew but I'm sure her husband didn't speak of it. And neither Letty nor I told her anything."

"Why not?"

"She is a lady, sir, of a delicate constitution. We wished to protect her."

Mr Brimming was silent for a while. The thump of feet on the staircase announced the coming of the constables. He sighed and, throwing an apologetic look at Caleb and Letty, said, "Take these two to the gaol."

In a sudden panic, Letty threw her arms about Caleb's

chest. Triumph lit Sir Robert's face and Caleb longed to pound the expression off it with his fists but to his surprise Mr Brimming's next words did the task for him.

"Take this gentleman's servant too."

Caleb and Letty looked at each other, startled. Benson arrested? There was a chink of hope here. Mr Brimming could not, without firm and certain proof, detain a man of Sir Robert's standing, but taking his servant was surely a form of security to ensure the master did not leave the city?

Sir Robert was rendered speechless. He reddened, opened his mouth, but could produce no words.

Mr Brimming continued, "I apologize most sincerely, Sir Robert, but my colleagues and I will have the truth of this. Your man must be detained, and I would ask most humbly that you remain in Torcester while we send for the lady."

"She! You think to have the truth from a maid? Anne Avery would say anything to save their skins!"

"Never fear, I will make sure she is given no information relating to this matter. She will know only that a Torcester magistrate wishes to see her on a matter of grave importance."

"She won't get here safe!" Letty was in tears. "Sir Robert will see her dead before she is allowed to speak! He already threatened her daughter. A little girl, not yet two!"

Mr Brimming looked from Caleb and Letty to Sir Robert and Benson. "Let me say this. If Anne Avery and her child do not arrive in Torcester alive and well we will assume that these two are telling the truth, vagabonds or not, and act accordingly." To the room in general he said, "Let us discover if she knows the ring when she sees it. If she is indeed who this lad says there will be others who can confirm her identity. We will make all the necessary enquiries. Meantime," he said to Caleb and Letty, "you two must abide in the city gaol." Turning to Sir Robert, he said, "Will you be staying with your brother? Very well. We will send word to the bishop's palace the moment we have news."

13.

The week that followed was the stuff of nightmares.

The ginger-haired youth lay dead and the bishop had been assaulted. Even if their tale concerning the *Linnet* could be proved true, such things must weigh heavily against them.

Sir Robert had bought his manservant privileges from the gaoler – good food, a private room – so they did not have to face Benson. But they were incarcerated with thirty others in the barn-like cell where Pa had been imprisoned. Caleb did not grieve for himself, but that he should have brought Letty so low! To see her – not in her rowboat, not tugging its oars, chasing the tide – but sleeping on soiled straw, pissing in the corner, eating stale bread crawling with weevils… To have her next to him but so quiet she barely spoke, to see her so pale, so anxious was a horror he could barely endure. And the fear that he would have to stand beside her and see her swing! The days of waiting seemed to stretch into eternity.

* * *

While they waited, Anne – sick with grieving for her dead husband and brother, riddled with fear for Caleb and Letty – was travelling to Torcester in the coach of Mr Brimming.

The messenger who'd knocked on her door had not told her anything and she did not ask, so befuddled was she with pain and anxiety. She simply did as she was requested, wrapping Dorcas tightly in a shawl, leaving the house empty-handed save for the few coins she had in her possession.

She passed the journey in a numbed daze and was scarcely aware of how long it took, of how many stops they made to change the horses, to rest, to eat, to sleep. When at last the coach stopped outside the coffee house and she was told to go inside, she did so, too weary and sad to have even an ounce of curiosity about what was happening.

Mr Brimming pressed a cup of coffee into her hands and her fingers closed around it, but she did not drink. He talked, but she heard not a word. Only when he laid the bundle upon the table and unfolded the silk handkerchief to reveal what lay within did she give a sharp intake of breath and look around with confusion.

"I am heartily sorry to show you something so unpleasant, but this is a matter of utmost importance. The ring," he said gently, "do you know it?"

Anne stared into Mr Brimming's face. How was she to answer?

Long, long ago, when she had given her baby into her brother's keeping, Joseph had told her to say nothing of what had happened. He had urged her to deny that she had a brother. To say to one and all that she was plain Anne Chappell, a lady's maid, not the daughter of the Earl of Gravesham. Conceal the past, he had said, so she might have a future.

She opened her mouth to say she had no knowledge of the ring.

But her lips would not frame another lie. The words would not come out. For what had so many untruths brought her these many years? She had given away her own child! And now he was gone once more and she knew not where. Letty had vanished. Her husband had been washed up dead. She'd had to bury him. But he at least had a grave. Her brother, poor Joseph, lay chained at the bottom of the ocean in the *Linnet*'s broken belly. Save for Dorcas, everyone she cared for was gone. What future now was there for her and her child? Alone, she could not pay the rent. There was only the workhouse. Death on the streets would be preferable. What could she possibly lose by telling the truth?

"It was my father's ring." She trembled as though seized with a violent chill, but continued, "My brother had it on his death."

"And who was your father?"

"The Earl of Gravesham."

The men in the room looked at each other. Even in her numbed state Anne could feel their excitement. One muttered into the ear of a clerk – something concerning the bishop's palace – and he at once left the room. When the door was shut, Mr Brimming asked, "Lady Anne, are there others who could verify this was his?"

"It was his seal. Anyone he ever corresponded with would recognize it. His friends, his lawyers, his creditors."

"We will make enquiries."

"How came you by it?" Anne fought to control her agitation. "Joseph is dead. He drowned at sea. As did my poor husband!"

"Is it possible your brother sold the ring? Or that it was stolen from him?"

"No. The ring was too small for him. Once there on his finger, he could not take it off. Dear God, can you not see that for yourselves? I ask again, how came you by it? Who cut his finger from him? Caleb swore he had seen the ring, but he was mistaken. The parson himself said the drowned man was not Joseph, and a man of God cannot lie! Can he? Tell me, I beg you. Did the parson lie, gentlemen?"

"Alas! It seems he did."

It was Anne's habit, when suffering an excess of emotion, to faint away. Her heart was already full to bursting when Caleb and Letty – who had been brought from the gaol in anticipation of her arrival – were led into the room. The sight of the two she had thought were lost for ever so filled her with joy that she collapsed into Caleb's arms before he could utter a word.

* * *

Anne had been almost destroyed with grieving. But now her son was restored to her. And Letty, dear Letty! When she was at last recovered from her swoon she clung to them and they to her. She did not intend to ever lose sight of them again.

When Anne had calmed herself a little Mr Brimming informed them that the family were free to go. They must remain in Torcester while enquiries were carried out, he said, but a return to gaol was not necessary. The assault on the bishop, the death of his servant: if Caleb and Letty's story proved true, as appeared likely, these things would not count against them. They were preparing to leave Porlock's Coffee House when one of the clerks brought news from the bishop's palace.

It seemed that when the constables were sent to detain Sir Robert they found the palace deserted. When they at last discovered a maid hiding in the scullery she informed them that he and his brother had long since fled.

14.

Enquiries were carried out as the law required and statements taken, but in the minds of those concerned with the case nothing confirmed Sir Robert's guilt as clearly as his flight. Summer turned into autumn and though he and his brother were sought the length and breadth of the country it was to no avail.

Mr Brimming remained confident that Sir Robert would, in time, be apprehended. In his absence his land and property were impounded by the court and without income, the magistrate assured Caleb, Sir Robert's power and influence were reduced to nothing. The villain could not keep running for ever. One day the law would find him and then justice would be done.

Caleb did not share Mr Brimming's confidence. Sir Robert had fingers in every pie: he was sure to have means of support that remained as yet undiscovered. For all they knew he had fled abroad and if that was the case there was no one to bring him back.

As for justice – hadn't Pa told Caleb often enough that the law was something designed by the gentry to serve their own ends? "Better to be rich and guilty than poor and innocent, my boy. So many rotting in gaol! Poverty, not guilt, keeps them there. Yet a wealthy man with a clever lawyer will seldom swing, though his sins be black as pitch."

Despite Sir Robert's flight, Caleb and Letty were not overly downhearted. They had, after all, achieved what they wanted. They were believed. Sir Robert's villainy and the bishop's complicity had been revealed and the wrong done to both their fathers exposed.

Pa's name had been restored to him.

On their release from gaol Caleb had written to the parson with instructions. A month later he received a lengthy, humbly apologetic reply telling him a headstone had been erected and a service belatedly carried out at Pa's graveside. Every member of Fishpool's congregation had attended. The parson assured Caleb that Joseph Chappell had joined Edward Avery on the long litany of drowned souls prayed for by his flock.

Soon after receiving the letter Caleb and Letty were drinking coffee in Porlock's when two learned men of the university came in. Caleb recognized them at once – Pa had often sat with them debating matters of philosophy and politics – but he did not expect them to acknowledge him. Yet word of Pa's fate had evidently spread, for on seeing Caleb the men came at once to his table to express their sincere condolences. He had the satisfaction of hearing them speak of Joseph Chappell with honour and respect. Pa's passing was at last marked with the tributes and words of praise that were his due.

Redeeming the underwriters' money through the courts had taken months, but in expectation of their fortunes being restored to full health they had rewarded Caleb and Letty with a sum sufficient to pay the rent on a small house in the city, where they lived with Anne and Dorcas comfortably throughout the winter. There, Caleb and Letty built themselves a new theatre.

When the weather began to turn warmer they were at last permitted to leave Torcester and set forth, touring from town to town and village to village throughout the county, pulled ever northwards by the call of the sea.

Whether he'd asked her, or she him, or whether the question had ever been uttered aloud Caleb couldn't afterwards remember. It had happened as naturally as waking and sleeping, eating and breathing. One fine spring morning Caleb found himself standing in church beside Letty, holding her hand in his and promising to love her until death.

15.

Tawpuddle quay.

A bright spring morning.

Low tide.

Ships sitting at half-tilt on the mud. Sailors and fisherman, merchants and shopkeepers, housewives, maids, seamstresses, whores, all crowded together on the cobbles in anticipation of a spectacle.

Caleb and Letty breathed in the crowd's scent, seeing their own intoxication reflected in the other's eyes. And then, sunlight glinting off the ring he now wore on his third finger, Caleb stepped out to introduce the Punch and Judy show.

Anne stood near the back, holding Dorcas by the hand, watching Caleb with a gentle smile on her face. It could never be said in public – she remained his aunt in name – but privately and in their hearts they knew themselves to be mother and son and that was enough for both.

Letty and Caleb had taken Pa's show and turned it into

their own, making new puppets and devising whole new routines. One involved a landlord and his lapdog, Punch refusing to pay the rent and beating both roundly over the head until they fled. Another involved a horse that Caleb had made for Punch to ride. At first the beast refused to go, digging its heels in stubbornly. When Punch dismounted to see what ailed it, the creature lifted its tail and deposited a heap of dung upon his head. He made the horse sit down like a dog, then ordered it to stand on its head. Next it lay on its back, legs waving in the air while he tickled its belly. Finally ordering the beast to stand and remounting he tried to ride again, and once, twice, thrice the horse did not move. Then – without warning – it ran away with him, bolting around the stage, setting the whole theatre rocking from side to side so badly that the crowd screamed, thinking it would collapse. Punch was hurled into the air and turned a somersault before Letty caught him again neatly on her right hand. He then lay there on the playboard, noisily claiming, "I'm dead! I'm dead!"

Coming to his aid was a surgeon who, attempting to bleed Punch, lacerated his own arm by mistake. Caleb had devised an ingenious contraption using a pig's bladder filled with watered-down wine, and it spouted from the puppet in great fountains over the front rows of the crowd.

The show went on, Punch laying waste to every figure of authority he came across, knocking the teeth from the mouth of the parson, pulling the wig from the judge. He did what every man and woman in the crowd longed to do and they were in raptures of anarchic delight. Caleb knew his family would eat well that night, and indeed for the week to come. They'd stay at the inn on the outskirts of town. And in the morning, they'd pay another visit to the churchyard where Joseph Chappell and Edward Avery rested in peace.

He and Letty were revelling in the wild nonsense of the performance but, on this particular day, when they reached the hangman scene Letty perhaps did not give it so much energy as usual. For this particular day was one of great significance.

William Benson – complicit though he was in all Sir Robert's villainy – had been given the chance to turn King's evidence. If he had testified against his employer, if he had verified the bishop's involvement in every nefarious scheme, if he had revealed the gentlemen's present whereabouts – he might, perhaps, have saved his own skin.

But he did not.

He – who had carried out every command with such zealous relish – had an unshakeable faith in the might of his master. He had firmly believed – through his trial and conviction, through his imprisonment and right until the very moment of his execution – that Sir Robert would somehow save him.

While Letty's Jack Ketch explained to Punch the process of death by hanging, while Punch wilfully misunderstood and ducked first to the left and then to the right, while Caleb stood by the side of the show and the crowd's eyes streamed with mirthful tears – William Benson was driven, hands bound, in an open-topped cart through the city of Torcester.

And Jack Ketch was not his hangman: he did not bungle the execution. William Benson was not Punch; he did not outwit Death or the Devil.

At Gallows Hill he hanged, loyal to his very last breath.

AUTHOR'S NOTE

Two or three years ago I was on board the *Oldenburg*, sailing out of Bideford, bound for Lundy – a small island twelve miles off the coast of North Devon.

As the ship moved downriver we passed Knapp House.

Tucked in a valley that leads down to the water, the house is now a campsite and activity centre, but back in the eighteenth century it was home to Thomas Benson, landowner, merchant trader, High Sheriff of Devon, Member of Parliament and, in his spare time, smuggler, fraudster and notorious villain.

I'd read about Benson some years before, but seeing the house from the water and making that crossing over the sea made me think about how things might have been for the ordinary people living in the area back then.

Hell and High Water is a work of fiction inspired by the sinking of Benson's ship the *Nightingale* in 1752 and the extraordinary scandal that followed. I've taken liberties with North Devon's geography to make the story work, so all the place names are invented ones, but the novel's heart and soul are rooted in the West Country.